Felicity Radcliffe

# THE DARK SIDE OF
# THE BOOK CLUB

*A tale of friendship and revenge
in Middle England*

*This book is dedicated to Chris G, with love*

# CONTENTS

## Author's Note

'Dark Side' is a work of fiction, as are all the characters in it. However, some of the characters were inspired by real people - in particular, the wonderful group of women in a certain real-life book club of which I am privileged to be a member.

If you have inspired one of the fictional characters, I have already spoken to you in person to check that you're OK with it. If we haven't spoken, any resemblance to you is purely coincidental.

## Acknowledgments

First of all, I would like to thank everyone in the real book club – you know who you are! You had the original idea of writing the book and listened patiently whilst each chapter was read aloud in our monthly book club meetings. You all offered invaluable advice and encouragement, weirdly seeming to sense when I was flagging and invariably reviving me with a cheery and supportive message on our book club WhatsApp group.

I hope that this project has entertained and amused each one of you. As we have often said, we really do have the best book club in the world; but I hope there are lots of other book club members out there who think the same thing about their own unique group of readers.

They say that it takes a village to raise a child – well, it certainly took a village to raise this novel! I am immensely grateful to Sip S. de Vries for designing the cover – we all think it's amazing. It's so handy to have a genuine Dutch artist living just down the road! Thanks also to Régine Riviere and Pam Watson, two of Sip's pupils, who both live in the village and whose work features on the cover.

A huge thank you as well to Helen Findley, Penny Simmonds, Helen Chalkley, Dorothy Bennett, Rebecca Pearson, Kim Sewell, Joanne Lewis and Val Newman – and to Kate - for reading the manuscript and providing such insightful help and guidance. You are all incredibly busy women and I really appreciate you giving the book your time and attention.

Another massive thank you goes to Keren Pope of CES Photography* for taking my author photo. You did a fantastic job, especially given the raw material you had to work with!

Thanks also to Julia Pearson for casually suggesting the idea for the title. It was fitting, I think, that it was decided over a long, lazy Sunday lunch.

None of the people mentioned above took a penny in fees, which has enabled me to donate all the proceeds from this novel to Cancer Research. Thanks so much all of you – I am very grateful. Let's hope we raise lots of money for this great cause which is close to all our hearts.

Finally, I would like to thank you personally for reading this book. I am delighted that you have chosen to give it your time when I'm sure you have lots of other priorities. I hope you enjoy it and I would love to hear what you think. Contact me via social media – just search 'Felicity Radcliffe Books' on Facebook, Twitter and Instagram.

**Felicity Radcliffe**

**February 2019**

* Search @CESphotography.co.uk on Facebook

PS: Mary Berry – we don't mean it. We love you – and your canapés!

# List of Characters

**The Oak Welby Book Club** (*and families*)

**Peggy**
Sassy and strong.  The centre of everything. Emily's mother. Married to...
*Stan*
The original farming guru. Lorelei's brother

**Emily**
Feisty and fun.  Peggy's daughter. Runs a successful farming business with her husband...
*Josh*
Another farming guru - an agricultural innovator
*Billie*
Emily and Josh's daughter. Cake-making genius
*Dan*
Emily and Josh's son – Outstanding young cricketer

**Lucy**
Intelligent and cute.  Successful psychologist, married to...
*Edward*
Captain of industry and self-confessed Star Wars geek
*Henry*
Edward and Lucy's cool and self-assured elder son
*Harley*
Edward and Lucy's younger son – a charmer

**Anna**
Classy and kind.  Well loved teacher, married to...
*Kit*
Financial genius and fitness fanatic
*Alexandra*

Anna and Kit's beautiful eldest daughter and bride-to-be
*Tom*
The tall, dark and handsome groom
*Elise*
Anna and Kit's beautiful, assertive middle daughter
*Caitlyn*
Anna and Kit's beautiful, laid-back youngest daughter

**Gemma**
Organised and vivacious. Well loved teacher, married to...
*Robert*
International businessman
*Tabitha*
Gemma and Robert's witty and spirited daughter

**Nicky**
Glamorous and riotous. Talented hairdresser. Married to...
*Bill*
Property tycoon
*Riley*
Nicky and Bill's attractive and stylish daughter

**Verity**
Clumsy but friendly. Itinerant project manager. Married to...
*Aidan*
Tough law enforcement expert
**Jocelyn (Jos)**
Elegant and artistic. Hard-working GP. Married to...
*Mack (the Knife)*
Leading orthopaedic surgeon
*Esme*
Jos and Mack's younger daughter. Talented thespian and

mum-to-be

**Alice**
Witty and insightful. Homemaker par excellence. Married to...
*Sandy*
Successful venture capitalist
*Beatrice*
Alice and Sandy's mature and academically gifted youngest daughter
*Alf*
Alice and Sandy's only son – the youngest of their four children. Emotionally intelligent and kind

**Lorelei**
Warm and hilarious – a free spirit. Stan's sister, Emily's aunt and Peggy's sister-in-law. Married to...
*Lenny*
Highly skilled workshop manager

**Irene**
Charismatic and grounded. Runs a successful business with her husband...
*Judd*
Experienced property developer

**Arabella**
Stylish and confident. Works in education and travels the world with her husband...
*George*
International insurance expert

**Everyone Else**
**Jane**
Embittered woman with a past

*Rick*
Pub regular, village stalwart, farm worker and gardener
*Rory*
A very handsome bagpipe player
*Tim and Toby*
The landlords of The Mallard
*Bridget*
Toby's mystery business partner
*Jan*
The no-nonsense but warm-hearted barmaid at The Mallard
*Dave*
Pub regular and retired civil servant
Ron and Wesley
Pub regulars - father and son farming team
*Melvin*
Pub regular and retired RAF officer
*Pat*
Reserved, knowledgeable local historian
*Claudine*
Warm and attractive Belgian yoga teacher
*Sim*
Charismatic Dutch painter and art teacher
*Sean*
Barman at The Partridge
*Xanthe*
Very glamorous Pilates teacher
*Andy*
Manager of The Mill at South Napton

**The Dogs**
*Deefer*
Emily's and Josh's dog – the noisy one
*Butch*
Emily's and Josh's dog – the quiet one

*Roxy*
Melvin's beer-loving dog
*Clipper*
Lorelei's dog – a top performer in the dog agility class
*Dolly*
Pat's sweet and obedient dog

# PROLOGUE

The Partridge was the cosiest place to be at Christmas time. Golden light spilled from its long, low windows, welcoming hungry guests in from the dark December night, from the damp and the cold. Into the Ark they went, stamping their feet as they walked through the door and pulling off their coats and gloves.

Inside, every inch of exposed wooden beam was twined with holly and twinkling fairy lights. Decorations were suspended artfully from the antique farm machinery hanging from the ceiling, a respectful nod to the local farming heritage. Tinsel adorned the framed prints, a temporary crowning glory for the horses and hounds in the pictures.

Early arrivals relaxed, glasses in hand, on the overstuffed sofas around the roaring, crackling fire. Others lounged in wing-backed armchairs or perched on bar stools. The clamour at the bar grew noisier and more frenetic as more people arrived and the drinking tempo quickened. Menus appeared, orders were placed, restaurant tables swiftly filled.

By mid-evening, the inn was full of happy noise and Christmas sparkle. Smells of game, spices, wine and chocolate filled the air. The decibel level peaked at a large table on the far side of the restaurant, tucked away in a corner to provide other diners with a modicum of sound-proofing from its occupants. This ploy was wholly unsuccessful.

The women at the corner table drew frequent glances from the other guests for their exuberance and apparent self-assurance as much as for their recurring, prosecco-fuelled shrieks of laughter. A glorious mixture of glossy blondes and brunettes, they sparkled from head to toe in the shiny, sequinned and glittery clothes that were de rigeur at this time of year. The absence of men was noted by the men at the other tables. Women wanted to be them and men – well, no prizes for guessing...

On the other side of the restaurant, the kitchen door flew open. A skinny, harried waitress shouldered through, plates ranged skilfully up her arms. Strands of dark hair, streaked through with grey, clung damply to her forehead. Her face shone pink from the kitchen heat and her uniform hung limply from her spare and bony frame. Dodging her way neatly between the tables and through the throng at the bar, she made for a table of four on the far side of the restaurant. Spotting the women at the corner table nearby, she felt a familiar flush of envy for their camaraderie, their light-hearted ease and the fun they were so obviously having. Turning away with a scowl, she morosely delivered game terrines and smoked salmon to table twelve.

On the way back she stole another glance at the women. She knew it would darken her mood still further to look again, but somehow she couldn't help herself. That was when she saw her. Head thrown back with laughter, glass in hand, looking remarkably unchanged, though so many years had passed. The waitress stood frozen, her nimble movements halted, until another of the women at the table called out to her, waggling an empty prosecco bottle in the air.

"Hey! What's wrong with this picture?" she cried.

The waitress approached the table, struggling to appear normal. "Excuse me?" she replied. She waited, heart in mouth, to be recognised. Braced herself for the tentative enquiry: "Don't I know you from somewhere?" But nothing. Her old enemy did not even glance in her direction.

"I'm sorry for my friend" said another of the women. "What she means is – please could you take this empty bottle of prosecco away and replace it with a full one, if you would be so kind? And she apologises for stealing Sigourney Weaver's line from Avatar".

"Oh bugger off - you're too bloody polite for your own good! Also, you watch far too many films" her friend retorted amiably. Turning to the waitress, she smiled and whispered theatrically: "Better make that two bottles. I'm going to need it, with this lot".

The waitress slammed the empty bottle on the bar. "Two bottles of prosecco for the raucous office party on table ten". Sean, the barman, eased the corks out of the bottles. "Not an office party" he corrected. "That's the Oak Welby Book Club. They always come here for their Christmas dinner, but most of them are regulars as well. They eat here all year round, with their husbands, kids, you know. They're good tippers too, so it pays to play nice".

Husbands, kids. Of course. An idea began to form. "Oak Welby. That's just a few miles down the road, isn't it?" she enquired. "Yes" replied Sean, moving away to serve another customer. "Nice little village. Not much there though – no real reason to visit".

On the contrary, mused the waitress. She had every reason to pay Oak Welby a visit. Finally, after all these years, she was going to make that woman pay for the pain she had inflicted long ago. At last, with some careful preparation and planning, she was going to get her revenge.

\* \* \*

# CHAPTER 1

*January Book Club*

"**B**ollocks to Mary Berry!" yelled Emily. The baking tray frisbee'd across the farmhouse kitchen, launching canapés in all directions. Pastry shattered on the tiled floor and sundried tomatoes slithered in leisurely fashion down the walls, leaving snail trails of olive oil in their wake.

Right on cue, Deefer and Butch bounded into the kitchen and began happily wolfing pastry from the floor. "Dogs, leave!" shouted Emily, to no avail. "Christ, they'll be shitting everywhere later" she muttered glumly to herself.

Josh wandered in from the living room. "What on earth is going on here?" he enquired affably.

"I was trying to make some Mary Berry canapés for the book club meeting tomorrow" explained Emily. "Sodding things were a disaster – wouldn't rise, all soggy – and I lost my rag and chucked the whole lot across the room. So now Deefer and Butch are having a little impromptu picnic, as you can see."

"You never learn, do you?" smiled Josh. "You should know by now that there is a tried and trusted formula for book club success. Number One – at least six bottles of lovely fizzy lady petrol. Number Two – a shedload of Waitrose canapés – aisle ten, as I recall. Number Three – cheese – from the cheese counter if you can be bothered - plus biscuits and grapes. Number Four – anything with chocolate in it. There you go – job done. No Mary Berry business, no puking dogs".

"You're right", sighed Emily. "I just occasionally get these delusions of domesticity".

"Don't worry Em – I can take your mind off it" said Josh, raising his eyes suggestively towards the ceiling and the bedroom upstairs.

"I thought you were watching the rugby" said Emily.

"I was planning to" replied Josh "but it has been cancelled – the pitch is frozen. What can I say? Northampton Saints' loss can be your gain – if you play your cards right..."

"Tempting, smarmy git" retorted Emily with a smile "but now that I have failed the Mary Berry domesticity test, I have to go to Waitrose before I pick up the kids from Sasha's birthday party – so there's no time, I'm afraid".

"How about I go to Waitrose while you pick up the kids?" suggested Josh. "I promise to get the cheese from the counter – no vacuum-packed stuff".

"Now you're talking!" cried Emily happily. "Sold!" She grabbed Josh's hand and dragged him towards the stairs, leaving the dogs to hoover up the last of the pastry crumbs.

* * *

"I love these little pastry things!" said Lucy. "Did you make them yourself? "

"You're kidding aren't you?" replied Emily. "Waitrose - aisle ten as I recall".

"Who cares – they are delicious!" Anna reached for the plate and grabbed a few more. "I'll never get into my mother of the bride dress at this rate..."

Supportive cries along the lines of "course you will!" and "shut up you skinny old moo!" arose from around the table.

The January meeting of the book club had been in session for an hour or more. True to form, no mention had yet been made of the book that the group – or at least some of them – had read. First there was the important matter of village gossip to be shared, dissected and enjoyed.

Most of the group had attended the usual New Year's Eve bash at the pub – after which Rick, one of the more colourful pub regulars, had apparently woken up on the playground swings at four in the morning with three sausage rolls in each of his pockets and a pink beanie on his head, the provenance of which was unknown. This was the cause of much merriment.

Anna had been whisked away on a supposedly 'romantic New Year's trip' to Palma by Kit, only to find that he was scoping the location, hotel and nearby golf courses for the partners' Spring Strategy Conference. Once rumbled, he was suitably contrite, and Anna took maximum advantage in Desigual and El Corte Inglés. Her new leather jacket and charm bracelet were admired by all.

The next topic of conversation was the new yoga class that had recently started at the Village Hall. Several of the book club members had attended the first few sessions and enjoyed them hugely. True to form, however, the book club discussion focused less on the physical and spiritual benefits of the yoga classes and more on how to avoid farting whilst performing the various asanas. The general conclusion was that farting was an occupational hazard whilst doing yoga, but that excessive giggling at the farting of others could make it difficult to keep your balance.

Finally Gemma called the group to order – it was time to discuss the book. This month's offering was a lengthy bonk-buster crammed with sexy and badly behaved aristocrats, impossibly glamorous women, stately homes, fast cars, thoroughbred horses and wayward pets. Some of the group had happily devoured all 800 pages, others had ploughed through doggedly to the end whilst a few had simply shared the page numbers of the best sex scenes on the book club WhatsApp group and skipped the rest.

Everybody exchanged views on what they had read. Many people outside the group would have been surprised at the spirited and insightful discussion of plot and characterisation that took place every month – far superior to that of the more serious, self-consciously learned book club in the next village. Lucy was the last to comment. She summed up her remarks by saying that, although she had enjoyed the book, she felt that it could easily have been condensed into 200 pages.

"I agree" said Emily, "but where's the fun in that? Especially as we would miss out on the bit that happens on page 683."

"Which bit was that?" enquired Anna.

"The bit where they all get it on in the horsebox" smiled Emily.

The group immediately erupted into shrieks of helpless laughter. "I had forgotten all about the horsebox!" laughed Peggy, with tears rolling down her face.

"I spent ages trying to work it out" giggled Gemma. "I

mean, is it even possible to adopt that particular position in a horsebox? Is there enough room? It doesn't strike me as very comfortable..."

"It's not supposed to be comfortable!" laughed Emily. "And anyway, some horseboxes are bigger than others. Plus she did have two men in there with her, so I guess that would have made it easier..."

More shrieks of laughter followed, along with comments such as: "so that's where I have been going wrong all these years!" and "I'm not sure I could summon up the energy!"

Eventually the group calmed down sufficiently to score the book. Following the club's agreed protocol, each person gave the book a score out of twenty, after which Gemma calculated the average and recorded it in the book club log. Reading out the result, Gemma noted with amusement that the total for the bonk-buster was exactly twice that of the Booker prize-winning novel that the group had reviewed the previous month.

"Well, at least no-one can call us pretentious culture vultures" observed Lucy. "Not like some others I could mention..." everyone else smiled knowingly, thinking of the rather snobbish, but much less popular book club in the neighbouring village.

By now it was getting late and the group reluctantly began making moves to leave, pushing back their chairs from the table with its empty prosecco bottles, ravaged cheese board and decimated canapés. Then Peggy remembered something. "Hang on a minute – sorry I forgot. I need to ask you all a question before we leave." Everyone sat back down, intrigued as to what Peggy might be planning.

"Stan and I were in the pub on Friday night, and we met this nice woman who has just rented Bob's old cottage. We got talking, and she mentioned that she had heard about our book club. She said she is really keen on books and wondered if she might be able to join. To be honest, I think she is a bit lonely and wants to make friends. She's been single since she split up with her partner last year. That's why she moved to the area – to make a fresh start. Do you think we can fit her in?"

"If she's really keen on books, we might not be the best club for her" laughed Gemma. "Seriously though, I'm a bit worried that we will end up with too many people."

"She has only rented the cottage for the rest of this year, though" replied Peggy "so it would be a temporary thing. She's on a fixed term contract as front of house manager at The Mill in South Napton, then she's off to work in a ski resort in France."

"That would work out quite well, then," remarked Arabella. "Don't forget I'm going to Dubai next week on secondment for nine months, so she could replace me for most of the year. On one condition – that you lot arrange mates' rates at whatever ski resort she's going to".

"Oh of course – doh. I'm trying to block out the fact that you're going away, Bella – we're going to miss you so much. OK then - that should be alright" conceded Gemma, who had started the book club so had the final say on who got to join. "What's her name?"

"Jane" said Peggy. "I didn't catch her surname but I made a note of her mobile number. If everyone's happy, I'll give her a ring, ask her to the February meeting and add her to the WhatsApp group".

"What does she look like?" asked Lucy. "Just in case we run into her in the pub..."

"Well, she's got short, red hair" began Peggy. "She's probably in her forties, quite pretty, but looks a bit worn out – as though she has been through a hard time. Oh and she's very slim – on the skinny side, I'd say. I'll double up on the chocolate brownies next month". Peggy had agreed to host the February book club meeting.

Finally the various members of the Oak Welby Book Club exchanged hugs and dispersed into the cold, dark night.

\* \* \*

"Thanks so much, Peggy – see you soon". Smiling to herself, Jane hung up the phone. Part One of her plan was falling nicely into place. The cottage was old-fashioned, damp and gloomy, but she had been lucky to find it – smaller rental properties were hard to come by in Oak Welby, which consisted mainly of spacious family homes. The new job in South Napton, with a promotion and a slightly higher salary, would pay the rent and had removed the risk of working just a few miles down the road with Sean and the team at The Partridge.

Jane stared at her face in the bathroom mirror, confident that her old enemy would not recognise her after all these years. The new haircut and colour had transformed her appearance – not to mention the fact that she was nearly 20 years older, and two stone lighter, than when they had last met. Her regional accent was long gone and the scars on her face had faded. These days they could simply be concealed with make-up - unlike the psychological scars, which took a bit more effort to hide.

Time for a drink to ease the pain. Stumbling slightly on the rickety staircase, she made her way down to the tiny kitchen, where she grabbed a bottle of wine from the fridge and poured herself a generous glass. Downing half of it in a single gulp, she spotted over the rim of the glass the calendar on the kitchen wall. Grabbing a pen, she circled Wednesday February 12$^{th}$ – the date of her first book club meeting. There was a lot to do before then; she would need to focus her efforts to ensure she was well prepared. It was time to find out a lot more about her old enemy – her friends, her job, her lifestyle, her children – and her husband. The time had come for Jane to execute Part Two of her plan.

\* \* \*

# CHAPTER 2

*February Book Club*

The low-slung winter sun was cloaked in early morning mist. The frosted lawn behind the house glittered in its pale, muted glow. From the kitchen window, Peggy gazed serenely upon the scene. Mornings were her favourite time of the day – a time of stolen moments and blessed peace. Most of the time.

Through the haze, she could just make out the nearest of the alpacas in the field beyond the garden. Like woolly periscopes, their heads turned this way and that, gazing vacantly into the middle distance. Buffoons, every last one of them, thought Peggy – not like cows, who were quite intelligent. Still, she had come to like the alpacas in the six months since she and Stan had acquired the herd. There was something rather endearing about them…

An insistent beeping interrupted Peggy's reverie. Turning from the window, she picked up her oven gloves, crossed the kitchen and pulled open the oven door. Instantly, the kitchen was filled with the delicious smell of chocolate. Smiling to herself, Peggy removed a tray of perfectly square, perfectly cooked chocolate brownies and arranged them neatly on a large cooling tray. A similar tray nearby was an orderly parade ground of vol-auvents and mini quiches, each one a symmetrical, golden brown culinary triumph, ready to be enjoyed at tomorrow's book club.

Peggy reflected for a moment on the subject of baking. Did these things skip a generation, she wondered, thinking of Emily's canapé debacle before last month's book club. Maybe so – her granddaughter Billie was a superb cake maker, whose skills were celebrated on social media every time one of the family had a birthday. She definitely got her baking talents from me, not from her Mum, thought Peggy as she reset the timer, slid the second batch of brownies into the oven and carefully closed the door. She poured herself a mug of coffee from the pot, then returned to the window to enjoy once again the peaceful scene outside.

At first, she could not quite work out what had changed since she last looked. Then she realised that the barbed wire fence separating the garden from the field appeared to be shaking and bending, almost as if someone were trying to climb over. As her eyes adjusted to the light, Peggy could just make out, through the mist, two bare legs gingerly straddling the barbed wire. Then, as the person hopped over and sprinted away, Peggy was treated to the sight of a pair of naked male buttocks receding into the distance. Peggy had no trouble identifying the bum in question...

"Stan!" yelled Peggy, even though she realised he couldn't possibly hear her. "Stan, you silly man, what on earth are you playing at?" Pulling her dressing gown tightly around her, Peggy rushed into the hallway, grabbed Stan's Barbour and ran out of the door, heading for the field.

A few minutes later, a breathless Peggy pushed open the gate into the field and clanged it shut behind her. Stumbling on tussocks of grass, huffing, puffing and cursing her husband, she bustled across the field as fast as she could in her dressing gown and slippers. Suddenly a disembodied voice cried out through the mist:

"Shush, Peggy! Keep the noise down and approach slowly..."

Peggy slowed down and walked silently towards the scene that gradually revealed itself. Stan was gently stroking the neck of a white alpaca. The animal's snowy hindquarters were streaked with blood and the frost on the ground below was clotted pink. The alpaca's head was bent towards the ground, moving rhythmically as it gently but firmly licked a small, steaming bundle of wool and bones to life.

Stan took hold of Peggy's hand. "After you got up to do your baking, I dozed for a bit, then I took a look out of the bedroom window at the herd" he explained quietly. "This one seemed as if she was about to give birth but she was having real problems, so I ran down here to look after her".

"In February. In the nude...over the barbed wire fence" observed Peggy.

"I didn't have time to worry about clothes and it was quicker to climb over the fence than go through the gate" retorted Stan. "Now I know she's OK, though, I do feel a bit cold."

"Good job I brought your Barbour, then" smiled Peggy. "Put this on, and well done for delivering our very first baby alpaca".

"It's called a cria" corrected Stan. "A baby alpaca is called a cria."

Peggy gazed at the newborn woolly bundle and pulled Stan in for a hug. "You'll never stop caring about all this, will you, love?"

"Never" agreed Stan, gazing over Peggy's shoulder towards their house. "Peggy" he said, suddenly sounding alarmed.

"What is it, Stan?" asked Peggy.

"What's all that smoke coming from the kitchen?"

"Oh Christ!" shouted Peggy "it's the second batch of brownies!"

The two of them sprinted chaotically towards the house, Stan's Barbour flapping around his bare legs. The alpaca, its new baby and the rest of the herd gazed after them in puzzlement.

* * *

"So if any of the food tastes a little bit smoky, that's the reason why!" laughed Peggy, as she finished sharing the alpaca story with the assembled book club.

"The food's fine" giggled Nicky. "I'm more worried about Stan's crown jewels on that barbed wire! I hope they weren't damaged as he was climbing over, Pegs!"

"You're a fine one to talk about crown jewels after Burns Night" teased Emily.

Immediately the book club erupted into a chorus of "yeah, Nicky" and "what's this about you and that bagpipe player?"

At that moment the doorbell rang, saving Nicky from having to explain herself. Peggy went to answer it and returned swiftly, accompanied by the book club's newest member.

"OK you noisy rabble – can I introduce Jane?"

"I'm so sorry I'm late" said Jane. "I had a bit of trouble finding your house".

"Not a problem, we are quite relaxed around here, as you can see" replied Emily. "You've missed a bit of gossip but we can fill you in".

"I wasn't sure if I was meant to bring something to eat" ventured Jane shyly, pulling a Tupperware out of her bag "so I made these peanut butter cookies. They're kind of my speciality".

The book club fell silent and all eyes turned towards Gemma.

"Oh God I'm really sorry – we should have told you" Gemma began. "You see, I have a really serious nut allergy – I can't even be in the same room as nuts. I have a terrible allergic reaction, but I always carry my kit with me just in case" – she lifted up her bag – "otherwise I'd end up in hospital".

"Oh no - I'm so sorry – I'll put them straight back in the car" cried Jane.

"It's OK - you weren't to know" Gemma reassured her.

"It was a nice thought, though, to bring the cookies" said Peggy kindly "but the person who hosts the book club provides the refreshments. I should have mentioned it when we spoke on the phone".

Jane turned and headed out to the car. As she closed the door behind her, the members of the book club fell silent and looked at one another in consternation.

"Good start" remarked Emily drily.

Outside, in the dark, Jane carelessly threw the Tupperware onto the back seat of her car. As she turned back towards Peggy's house to rejoin the book club meeting, she smiled to herself. So far, this was going unexpectedly well.

Opening the door to the house, Jane heard the sound of

laughter and clinking glasses. The members of the book club had clearly put the peanut incident behind them and quickly reverted to normal. When she returned to the sitting room, she was greeted warmly by Peggy.

"Good timing, Jane!" cried Peggy. "Nicky is just about to tell us what she got up to at Burns Night last Saturday…"

The annual Burns Supper was one of the highlights of the village social calendar, providing a welcome opportunity for villagers to forget New Year's resolutions, dry January and bad weather and let their hair down. Everyone took full advantage, drinking copious amounts of whisky, reciting Burns' poetry with drunken gusto and playing a special game called Toss My Caber, invented by Lucy's husband Edward who was always the MC on Burns Night.

This year's event had been enhanced by the addition of Rory, a very handsome young bagpipe player from the local RAF base. As he piped in the haggis, his charms did not escape Nicky's attention.

"So I said to Emily" began Nicky "Wow! Look at him – I wouldn't kick him out of bed for eating haggis. Em said 'yeah I agree, but the burning question is – is he a real Scotsman?' I didn't know what she meant, so she explained that a real Scotsman wears nothing under his kilt. So I said to her – right, I am going to make it my mission to find out!"

Emily took up the story.

"So I bet her a bottle of prosecco that she wouldn't be brave enough to tackle this question head on, so to speak. Of course I forgot how our Nicky likes a challenge, especially when she has got a bit of Dutch courage inside her…"

"So I had a few more wines and wee drams during the

meal, then I went up to him afterwards and said I needed to check what was under his kilt" laughed Nicky. "He was a bit reluctant at first, but as you all know, I can be very persuasive…especially when I'm pissed!"

"Anyway, just when Nicky thought there was nothing doing and she was going to lose the bet, Rory suddenly lifted up his kilt and flashed her!" smiled Emily.

"So what did he have on underneath?" enquired Jos. The whole book club leaned forward as one, eager to hear the answer.

"A very fetching pair of boxer shorts, emblazoned with the Scottish flag!" laughed Nicky. "Probably just as well…"

"He was incredibly obliging, though" continued Emily. "He was quite happy to flash us a few times more, so I could get some pictures on my phone…"

At this point the members of the book club jumped up from their chairs and clustered around Emily, desperate for a glimpse of Rory and his boxers. Amid cries of "oh I see what you mean, Nicky!" and "nice pair of legs!" Nicky proudly brandished her winnings.

"I thought we could all share my bottle of – what does Josh call it – lady petrol!" cried Nicky triumphantly.

The bottle was passed round the table and the book club members all happily sloshed some into their glasses, until it came to Verity.

"Not for me, thanks" said Verity apologetically. "I've given up booze".

"What's brought this on?" enquired Lucy. "You normally love a bit of fizz – and pretty much anything else alcoholic".

"I know" admitted Verity "but that was before the skiing

incident".

"What skiing incident?" the group chorused. Quite a few of the book club were keen skiers, so skiing stories were often swapped at book club meetings during winter and spring.

"Well, it happened after lunch" began Verity. "I had already drunk quite a lot of vin chaud, and then they brought round free shots of Génépi after the meal, so I necked a few of those. Then we went off skiing again afterwards but the piste was quite icy at the top – and as you know I hate the ice.

Anyway, it looked nice and fluffy off-piste and I was feeling brave after all those drinks, so I said to Aidan that I was going to give it a go. He was a bit surprised and said it looked steeper than I was normally comfortable with, but I just ignored him and launched myself into the powder.

To cut a long story short – I ended up on a very steep bit with my bum in the air, my arms around a small, conveniently located sapling and my skis and poles scattered all over the place" finished Verity. "It seems funny now, but at the time I was bloody terrified. It was a wake-up call that I need to lay off the drink for a while".

"Where was Aidan while all this was going on?" asked Lucy.

"Well, you know he has just decided to enter the 21$^{st}$ century and get himself an i-Phone?" replied Verity. "So that's where he was, snapping away on his new phone and having a right laugh. I'm sure he's got a wide-angled lens on that thing – he made my bum look enormous! I've got some of the shots here – I'll put them on WhatsApp..."

The group immediately grabbed their phones to look at the book club WhatsApp group. Much laughter followed, along with various comments along the lines of "you don't see that on Ski Sunday!" and "I'll be interested to see how long you stay off the booze – I give it a week!"

Eventually Gemma called the group to order. "I'm sorry, ladies, but it's really time to discuss the book. Jane will be thinking that all we do is share drinking stories and gossip".

"Just one last bit of news" begged Jos. "It's not even a drinking story – although it is drink-related – and I'll be really quick. It's a biggie, though".

The group leaned forward expectantly. Jos was not normally one for sharing gossip, so she must have something interesting to reveal.

"The pub is up for sale" announced Jos.

For many years the village pub, called The Mallard, had been run by Tim and Toby, former work colleagues who had purchased it together when Tim retired. There had been talk of a possible sale for some time, as Tim was getting on and needed to put his feet up – but it was still a shock now that it was finally happening.

Villagers liked to complain about the pub and speculate on how they would run it differently if they were in charge, but in truth the pub was treasured by all of them. Above all, they did not want to see it close.

"Do we know if anyone has put an offer in?" asked Peggy.

"I don't know anything more" replied Jos. "Tim just mentioned it to Mack when he dropped in for a pint the other evening, but Mack didn't ask for any more details – typical! Anyway, keep it under your hats for the moment".

"Right – now it's really time to discuss the book" said Gemma, in a tone that made it clear she would accept no further diversions. Obediently, the group settled down to business.

This month's book was a thriller centred upon a sexy but enigmatic leading man who led a double life. To his neighbours in his apartment block, located in an upmarket and genteel part of town, he was a mild mannered accountant who spent his spare time in the gym and kept himself to himself.

In reality, he was a ruthless, trained killer who took revenge on behalf of people who had been wronged but were unable to fight back - a sort of Robin Hood crossed with James Bond. Along the way, he managed to sleep with a variety of beautiful women, most of whom got caught in the crossfire during the various revenge-taking episodes, thus conveniently creating a vacancy for a glamorous successor.

The general opinion was that the book was gripping and entertaining, and that its leading man would certainly provide a decent night's fun – although he was deemed to be firmly in the 'shag not marry' category. However, some of the more literal-minded among the group questioned the plausibility of some of the scenes in the book. At times like this, it was useful that the book club included among its members both a doctor and a psychologist.

"Jos, give us your professional opinion" declared Gemma. "Would it really have been possible for him to strangle that gangster with a bra?"

In one scene, the hero had been caught 'in flagrante' by his arch enemy and a fight had ensued. Conveniently, the undergarments of the hero's current paramour were within reach, and the enemy had been despatched with a lacy number from Victoria's Secret. Needless to say, the woman had also met her end during the same scene.

"In theory, yes" replied Jos after a moment's thought. "It sort of depends on how robust the bra is. If it was underwired it could help, I think. But if it was too flimsy, it could give way under the pressure. All in all, it depends on style and brand, I would say".

The group then debated whether a scanty Victoria's Secret bra was really the ideal tool for the job. The general conclusion was that the hero would have been much better off with a strong, sensible number from Marks and Spencer.

On a more serious note, the group then discussed whether it was possible for the leading man to keep up his double life indefinitely, and what effect it would have on him in the long term. Lucy's expertise as a psychology PhD was invaluable at times like these.

"It would inevitably take its toll" concluded Lucy. "The longer the double life went on, the greater the potential for damage. I'd say he could only keep it up for two sequels, max" she observed wryly.

"Oh I don't know" countered Jane.

All eyes turned towards Jane, who had been silent up until that point, although she had looked with interest at Emily and Verity's photos earlier.

"What do you think, Jane?" asked Peggy, keen to get the new girl involved in the discussion.

"I can only speak from experience" said Jane "but I know people who have managed to keep up a double life for years, with no apparent ill-effects. One person in particular..." she broke off suddenly.

"Is this person a woman?" asked Nicky.

"Yes" replied Jane, looking uncomfortable.

"Well that explains it!" laughed Nicky. "We're much better at maintaining a double life than men – it goes with our ability to multi-task!"

Everyone laughed – Nicky never failed to bring a smile to everyone's face at book club. Jane's momentary awkwardness was immediately forgotten.

The rest of the book club proceeded without incident and the thriller got a decent score, although not quite as high as last month's bonk-buster. At the end of the evening, Lucy volunteered to host the March book club.

"Your mission, Lucy, is to deliver the book club refreshments next month without any baking-related incidents!" quipped Anna.

"There's an easy solution to that" replied Lucy "which is to avoid baking altogether! I'll stick to that approach I think..."

"You're far too modest, Lucy" remarked Jos. "You always put on an amazing spread".

As the group made its way out, Peggy collared Nicky with a question.

"Sorry Nicky I forgot to ask earlier - could you fit me in for an appointment next week? Stan and I are going away for a few days and I could do with a cut and blow dry before we head off for our mini-break..."

As Nicky pulled out her phone to check her appointments, Jane shyly approached the two women.

"I don't mean to interrupt" she ventured politely "but did I hear you say you were a hairdresser, Nicky?"

"That's me" smiled Nicky. "Hairdresser to the stars – and this motley crew as well. How about Wednesday at ten, Peggy?"

Peggy gave Nicky the thumbs up as she hugged Gemma goodbye.

"Do you think you could fit me in for an appointment, too?" asked Jane. "I really need my roots doing, and I wasn't too happy with the hairdresser in Hanningford who did it last time".

Nicky cast a professional, appraising eye over Jane's hair.

"I suggest we do your roots and put a toner on as well, to brighten your colour up a bit. I can give you a trim too if you like, to sharpen up your cut."

"Sounds great" said Jane, and they fixed an appointment. "I work from home" explained Nicky "I have a salon in my house. Give me your mobile number and I'll text you the postcode".

Finally the last of the book club stragglers filed out into the dark, bitter cold winter night. Peggy shut the door behind them, poured the last of the remaining wine into two glasses and went to look for Stan. Her husband had wisely retreated to his study while the book club was in progress, to watch a repeat of the Rugby World Cup highlights with his headphones firmly on.

* * *

Jane closed the cottage door firmly behind her and dropped her bag on the floor. Heading straight to the kitchen, she pulled open the fridge door and poured herself a large glass of white wine. As she had been driving, she had restricted herself to a single glass of prosecco, which really hadn't been enough to help her cope with her first book club meeting. Still, next month would be easier. Lucy's house was just down the road, so no need to drive.

She wandered into the sitting room, glass in hand, settled herself with difficulty on the lumpy sofa and reflected on the night's events. It hadn't gone perfectly – she had been too unguarded at times and, although she hadn't given herself away, some of the book club women undoubtedly thought her a bit odd. Who cares, though, she told herself defiantly, taking a large gulp of wine. She wasn't there to make friends, after all.

On a more positive note, she had acquired some very interesting and potentially useful information about the various members of the book club – way more than she had expected from the first meeting. It was handy that they were all so open and willing to share the details of their lives. Jane could not imagine being so frank and honest with other people – that was a luxury reserved for those who were luckier than she was.

It was on her second glass of wine that her plan began to crystallise further. It's a long shot, but it could work, she thought. True, having a doctor in the book club could be an obstacle – she would need to work out how to get around that problem. Also, some innocent people would suffer, but on balance that was a price worth paying…

First things first, Jane scolded herself. If you rush things, you will make mistakes – and you have got all year. She sternly reminded herself to focus on her immediate priorities – the first of which was her hair appointment with Nicky. How fortunate that Nicky worked from home. Jane hoped that it was just her – no other hairdressers or juniors to get in the way.

Second priority was the pub. Jane planned on becoming a regular there – and a loyal customer in Nicky's salon. These two simple steps would help her build up her plan of action for the coming months.

As she finished the last of her wine, Jane smiled to herself. She was on her way.

✳ ✳ ✳

A few days later, Emily's car screeched to a halt in front of Verity's home and its driver sounded the horn urgently to summon her friend. As usual, the Pilates posse was running late. A flustered Verity appeared at the front door, fumbling for her keys and hoisting her battered rucksack onto her shoulders. Hastily she locked up and scrambled breathlessly into the passenger seat.

"Sorry I'm late" Emily began. "It was all going so well this morning, then halfway to school Dan realised that he had forgotten his rugby kit so we had to head back home to pick it up, and it all went downhill from there. When I eventually got back from school, I found that Butch had taken a dump on a copy of Fabulous Farmer magazine so I had to clean that up, then the insurance people called with all sorts of stupid queries about the diesel that was stolen from our tank last week. Total nightmare".

"I can relate" Verity replied. "I was happily working through my to-do list and everything was going according to plan, until one of my clients rang up requesting a whole bunch of changes to my final report, when he had said only last night that he was ready to sign it off! I just got it on the wires a few minutes ago so my phone will probably start ringing in a minute – sorry".

Emily swerved abruptly off the road onto a gravel driveway where Alice, swathed in copious layers of winter clothing, stood shivering disconsolately in front of her house.

"Oh look, it's Nanook of the North!" laughed Emily as Alice climbed into the back seat. "Sorry I kept you waiting – everything went tits up this morning – but I've switched your heated seat on for you as I thought you would need warming up".

"Thanks Em" said Alice gratefully. "I know I'm such a wimp about the cold, but even you've got to admit that it's freezing this morning! I don't know how Lucy and Gemma can bear to go out running in this weather. I suppose they have got to keep up their efforts all year round – it seems like they're always in training for some race or other".

As Emily sped out of the village in a bid to make up for lost time, Verity's phone lit up as predicted and her friends kept silent for a few minutes whilst she established that her client was happy with the changes to the report. As soon as she hung up, the conversation turned to the newcomer at book club.

"Well I think she's a bit of a weirdo. I mean, what was all that business about people keeping up a double life? She doesn't seem to have much of a sense of humour. I'm not sure she's going to fit in very well with us lot, to be frank". Emily slowed down as they entered the next village and performed a neat chicane around the traffic calmers.

"Well I felt a bit sorry for her – I mean, it was unfortunate that she brought those peanut butter cookies and had to put them back in her car. It wasn't an ideal way to begin. I think we should give her the benefit of the doubt until we get to know her better" said Alice gently.

"I know what you mean, Em – I did find her a bit odd – but I think Alice is right - we need to reserve judgement. After all, it can't be easy being a newcomer to a close-knit group like ours" Verity concluded.

"Well I think you are both too soft-hearted for your own good and that I will be saying 'I told you so' before the year is out, but let's see what happens. In the meantime, you can congratulate me for getting us here with a full two minutes to spare!" Emily brought her car to an emphatic halt next to Nicky's and the three friends hurried inside the hall for their Pilates class.

Xanthe, the alarmingly glamorous Pilates instructor,

waved at them whilst warming up with some stomach crunches and casually munching a protein bar at the same time. The three women took their places with Nicky and the rest of the class next to the orderly row of Pilates paraphernalia and waited smugly for the final two participants, whose mornings had clearly also failed to go according to plan.

To an outside observer, the Pilates class might have appeared gentle and relaxing. Indeed, at times the class hardly seemed to be moving at all – but appearances can be deceptive. Xanthe was a stickler for correct technique and the precise, measured movements she demanded from the women in her class exercised muscles they never knew they had – until the after effects were felt over the following few days. After an hour of controlled exertion, the three friends gratefully beat their customary retreat to Daisy's coffee shop for some caffeine, calories and a good gossip.

Like Verity and Alice, Nicky too was inclined to give Jane the benefit of the doubt.

"I did find her a bit serious during book club – and she didn't have much to say for herself when she came into the salon. Give her time and she'll probably relax. You wait until you see her new haircut, though. She might be quiet and serious but when it comes to her appearance, she's much less conservative than you lot!"

At that point the coffee and cake arrived and the friends settled down happily to undo the good work done in Pilates. Nicky brought out her phone to show pictures of her daughter Riley's new dog and handed out the various hair products that her friends had ordered from her. The conversation turned to half term skiing holidays and progress with the sale of Nicky's barn, expertly converted and renovated by Bill. The book club receded into the background for another month and Jane, the serious-minded newcomer, was forgotten.

\* \* \*

# CHAPTER 3

*March Book Club*

Lucy gazed with satisfaction upon the blank canvas of her large back garden. During the previous afternoon the lawn, shrubs and orchard had all received a comprehensive buzz-cut, courtesy of the shiny new Husqvarna garden tools that she and Edward had bought each other in the January sales.

Here and there intrepid daffodils were already starting to pierce through the broad expanse of green. Bluebells and hyacinths would soon follow. In another month, spring would be properly underway and the garden would be invaded by colour, thanks to Lucy and Edward's expert care. She was so looking forward to those first rays of warm sunshine after the relentless cold of a long, tenacious winter...

The doorbell jolted Lucy back to the present moment. Right on time, the Ocado delivery man was here with the week's groceries and the book club goodies. This month the group would be feasting on baked camembert, plus a smorgasbord of the finest delicacies Waitrose had to offer, before finishing off with Lucy's new speciality - 'melt in your mouth mindfulness truffles'.

Lucy's recent lecture on mindfulness had gone down a storm. Half the village had crammed into the Village Hall to learn more about this popular topic and practise mindfulness techniques under Lucy's direction. Lucy had discovered that people found it much easier to be mindful with a mouth full of chocolate, so the idea of the truffles was born.

Lucy had promised the book club a quick refresher course at the end of the evening, complete with her truffles. She suspected that sugar, rather than stress relief, was their prime motivation, but nevertheless she was a dedicated professional, committed to doing things properly. 'These truffles will be made mindfully, even if they are not eaten that way' she vowed to herself.

Focusing upon the here and now, Lucy broke the chocolate into squares and dropped them into a saucepan, relishing the delicious smell and the satisfying way that the chocolate broke evenly along the grooves with a firm but yielding snap. She then poured in the double cream and syrup, reflecting on the difference in texture and thickness and savouring the sweet aroma of the syrup. As the ingredients began to melt and flow together, she stirred them slowly with a wooden spoon, maintaining an even pace and keeping her attention totally in the present moment…

"Lucy!" A loud voice from Edward's study upstairs interrupted her blissful, mindful cooking. "Come up here – I've got something to show you!"

"Give me a minute – I'll be right with you!"

This had better be good, muttered Lucy grumpily to herself. Edward really had his moments. She turned off the cooker, put the truffle mixture to one side to cool and set, then stomped up the stairs to his study.

As she opened Edward's study door, she was startled to see that the furniture had been moved aside to make way for a large projection screen, with an orderly semi-circle of chairs arranged in front.

"I've set the room up for the inaugural investor group meeting" explained Edward. "I borrowed the screen and the chairs from work. I think it's very important that we impress them with the new Mallard pub concept from the word go, so I want it to look really professional".

Once he heard that the village pub, The Mallard, was up for sale, Edward had immediately begun work on a business plan to turn it into a community-run pub, managed and funded by the village. A number of villagers had shown an interest in investing, and an initial meeting of these potential venture capitalists was scheduled for the following Thursday.

"So what do you need from me?" asked Lucy, inwardly breathing a sigh of relief that she had her own office in a separate building in the garden.

"I just want to take you through the presentation and get your feedback" replied Edward.

"No problem; I've got a few minutes to spare while the truffle mix is setting" said Lucy. "In any case, I'm intrigued by the idea of a new concept for The Mallard. I thought you were going to tread carefully there – evolution rather than revolution, if you like".

"I take your point" agreed Edward "but reserve judgement until you have seen the presentation – and prepare to be amazed!"

Edward dimmed the lights and tapped the screen of his i-Pad. Immediately a familiar soundtrack filled the study and a photo-shopped picture of the pub's exterior filled the screen. Lucy's mouth dropped open in shock.

"What the…" she began, then gave up, lost for words.

"Say goodbye to The Mallard" announced Edward proudly "and hello to The Millennium Falcon – the very first Star Wars-themed pub in our area!"

Edward flicked on to the next slide and Lucy gaped in astonishment.

"As you can see" he continued "the bar, games room and restaurant area have been completely gutted and remodelled to create a replica of the Cantina bar in the Mos Eisley spaceport from Star Wars".

"Completely gutted is what the regulars are going to be when they see this" remarked Lucy drily.

"I don't think so" countered Edward. "Remember the quote about Mos Eisley from the film: 'you will never find a more wretched hive of scum and villainy' – I thought it was kind of appropriate for the Mallard regulars".

"I'll let you explain that to them" muttered Lucy grimly.

Undeterred, Edward ploughed on. "Anyway – let me show you the details before you pre-judge. On the bar, we have replaced the boring old snack dispensers with these two lovely replicas – R2D2 for the peanuts and BB8 for those little biscuits".

"So you've turned the pub into a film set from Star Wars, but you're keeping the same old snacks" observed Lucy.

"Of course – you have got to maintain some continuity" replied Edward, without a hint of irony. "Look at the bar staff, though – we have shaken things up in that department".

Lucy looked more closely at the slide and noticed that the barman, who looked remarkably like Toby, was sporting a Han Solo costume, whilst the barmaid was dressed as Princess Leia, complete with the white dress and the iconic Danish pastry-style hairdo.

Smiling suddenly, Lucy did her best Yoda voice. "Dress as Princess Leia Jan will not" she began. "Takes no crap from no-one, she does. Snap your lightsaber in two she will".

Edward reflected upon Jan, The Mallard's formidable and forthright barmaid.

"I guess you're right" he admitted. "It's just as well I thought to include a Star Wars dressing up box for the customers. If Jan won't dress up as Princess Leia, maybe you could do the honours, just for the opening night? You have got the right hair for the Danish pastries and with your figure, I think you could go for the gold bikini rather than the white dress..."

Lucy held up her hand. "Enough!" she cried "tell me this is a joke, right?"

"Guilty as charged" replied Edward, with a smile and a cheeky wink. "The investor group meeting is scheduled for April 1$^{st}$, so I thought I'd have a bit of fun with them at the beginning, to warm them up. Keep it to yourself, though – I don't want to spoil the surprise".

Edward then showed Lucy the real business plan for The Mallard, which was detailed and comprehensive, with cash flow projections and a provisional balance sheet and profit and loss account. Not a Droid or an Ewok in sight.

✻ ✻ ✻

Lucy had trouble keeping Edward's secret at the start of the book club meeting, as the early arrivals immediately started discussing the plans for the pub. Alice, whose husband Sandy was one of the investor group, asked Lucy: "Have you seen Edward's business plan, Lucy? Sandy is wondering how much he will be asked to invest and how radical Edward's ideas are, so he can evaluate the level of risk before he makes a decision".

"Tell Sandy not to worry" smiled Lucy. "I can't steal Edward's thunder by giving away the precise details, but let's just say that he has been – conservative - in his approach…"

At that moment the doorbell rang and all thoughts of the pub were soon forgotten, as Lucy came back into the room accompanied by Jane.

"Wow" exclaimed Anna "you look amazing, Jane!"

"You certainly do" agreed Peggy "your hair looks fantastic!"

Jane blushed and stared at her shoes. "It's all down to Nicky" she mumbled "she did a great job".

"Thanks, Jane, you're too kind" said Nicky. "Of course I am super-talented as you all know, but it's not everyone that could get away with that cut – you have to have the right face shape. Next time you come, maybe we could take a couple of photos of you for my website – would that be OK?"

Jane's eyes widened in horror and her face turned red. Luckily she was saved from having to reply, as at that moment Lucy brought in the last two book club members and the group was distracted by their arrival.

Emily waved hi to the assembled group, hugged those nearest to her, grabbed a glass of prosecco and sat down between Jane and Jos. The other woman, whom Jane did not recognise, came over to Jane and shook her hand.

"Hi, you must be Jane" she began. "I'm sorry we haven't met before – I couldn't make last month's book club. I'm Lorelei".

"You're – what?" Jane looked puzzled.

"That's her name" explained Jos gently. "Lorelei – named after the Rhine maiden – the mermaid who sits on the rock in the river Rhine. Her song is supposed to enchant sailors and lure them to their death. It's from German mythology".

"That's as may be" said Lorelei "but that's not why I was given the name".

Turning back to Jane, she smiled. "I should explain. I'm Stan's sister – you know, Peggy's husband? So I'm also Emily's aunt".

Jane nodded.

"Anyway, our parents were Laurel and Hardy fans" she continued. "So when their first child was born and he was a boy, they called him Stan, for obvious reasons. Then, when our Mum got pregnant again, they were hoping for a second boy, so they would have two sons to help run the farm. They were going to call him Oliver – as in Oliver Hardy - but then I came along instead and messed up their plans. They hadn't thought of a girl's name so they called me Lorelei as it sounds a bit like Laurel – you know, Stan Laurel?".

"Yeah I get it" said Jane. "But they could have just called you Olivia – or maybe Lauren".

Emily, Peggy and Lorelei burst out laughing. Emily put her arm around Jane, hugged her and gasped through her giggles "you know, in the whole history of our family, no-one has ever suggested that! Can you believe it? It takes a new face to point out the bleeding obvious…wait until I tell Dad!"

"Maybe our father was into German mythology – who knows?" laughed Lorelei. "You got one thing right, though, Jos. Anyone who hears me sing, they're going to want to kill themselves…"

"That's not quite how the story goes…" began Jos, then though better of it. "Anyway, I have got some more news…"

"More gossip, after last month's revelation about the pub? You are really spoiling us, Jos" said Gemma in her best Ferrero Rocher accent.

"I have had to keep this one quiet for a while, I'm afraid" continued Jos "but now she has said I can tell you – Esme is pregnant".

The group erupted into squeals of delight. They knew that Esme, Jos and Mack's younger daughter, had been trying for a baby for some time, so they were all delighted for her and her husband.

"Is she feeling OK?" asked Gemma.

"When is the baby due?" enquired Verity.

"She has got hyperemesis so she is feeling poorly, but otherwise the pregnancy is normal and she is due in October. She has asked me to stay with her for a while after the baby is born, so I'll probably miss the October book club" replied Jos.

"Looks like it's time to start knitting booties" remarked Verity.

"Or checking out the Mothercare website, in your case" quipped Emily.

Everyone laughed. Verity's complete lack of handicraft skills was well known to the group, some of whom regularly turned up at the Village Hall for the weekly Knit and Natter group, referred to by some villagers as Stitch and Bitch.

At that point Lucy brought in the baked camembert and everyone eagerly dived into the food, topped up their glasses and continued with the baby talk. Eventually, as usual, Gemma attempted to call the group to order and encourage them to begin discussing the book. This time, though, Nicky had other ideas.

"Give me a minute, Gemma" she pleaded. "I have one last piece of gossip to share – you're not going to believe this one".

Intrigued, the group fell silent.

"You'll never guess who came in this week for a haircut" she began. "Apart from the lovely Peggy and Jane, of course".

"Brad Pitt?" ventured Emily.

"Ryan Gosling, perhaps?" enquired Alice with a smile.

"That's never going to happen" said Irene, bringing them all back down to earth. "It's got to be someone closer to home. What about that bloke off East Enders, who lives in Acton Risbury..."

"No, not him" replied Nicky "he gets his hair done at Hair Apparent in Hanningford. You can tell – it's a right old mess. I really should try to poach him – note to self. No, we're talking even closer to home than that".

"We give up" cried Peggy "tell us!"

"Rick" announced Nicky.

Cries of disbelief and amazement filled the room. Rick, one of The Mallard's most faithful regulars, was well known for his wild, long and unkempt hair and beard, which normally did not see a pair of scissors or a razor from one year to the next.

"No, I'm not kidding" protested Nicky. "You wait until you see him in the pub. He asked for something modern – so I gave him a complete restyle and trimmed his beard right back. He's just got a hint of designer stubble now. OK we're not talking a Pitt or a Gosling, but you'll be surprised how well he scrubs up. What's more, he asked how often he needed to come back for a trim – and booked a follow-up appointment for six weeks' time!"

The group pondered what could have prompted Rick to seek a change of image, but no-one had a clue, so Gemma seized the opportunity to begin the book discussion.

Despite all the preamble and gossip every month, the book club members were normally keen to talk about the book. This month was different, though. No-one wanted to go first. The women looked at each other uneasily, until Irene caved in.

"OK I'll start" she began. "I began reading this and I just couldn't get my head around it at all, I have to admit. I struggled through the first few chapters and was about to give up. Anyway, as luck would have it I was in the dentist's waiting room last week trying to battle through a few more pages, when I happened to spot a copy of the Times Literary Supplement, with our book on the front cover! I was amazed to see that it had won the Booker Prize, so I thought I'd read the review and see what I was missing.

Anyway, they called the book, and I quote: 'a coruscating satire on race relations and contemporary social mores' whatever the hell that's supposed to mean. All the reviewers absolutely loved it. I'm really sorry if I sound thick, but I have to disagree with the lot of them. I honestly preferred the root canal work I had done that morning – and I'd rather have it done again, without anaesthetic, than read the rest of that book".

The relief in the room was palpable.

"God I'm so glad you said that, Irene" gasped Nicky. "I was afraid I'd be the only one who thought it was total crap."

"It made me think of The Emperor's New Clothes" remarked Lucy. "You know, where lots of very clever people are saying it's great, because they think that's what they should say, and no-one will admit that it's rubbish".

"Until Irene called it!" laughed Emily. "They could do with your honesty on the TLS, Irene – I'd apply for a job if I were you..."

The group then happily laid into the book, which was set in the crime-ridden suburb of West Adams in Los Angeles, a world away from areas like Beverly Hills and Santa Monica, which some of them had visited on holiday.

"To be fair, I think that's the problem" countered Jos, who was often the voice of reason in these types of book club debate.

"You see, I just think that the subject matter is completely outside our frame of reference" she continued. "We live in a leafy little rural village in middle England, so we just can't relate to life in a squalid, rough part of LA. I mean, Oak Welby is not exactly the crime capital of..."

She was interrupted by a loud shout from above and the sound of Edward's feet thudding down the stairs.

"Lucy – call 999 - now!" he yelled as he charged through the living room and out of the back door. "We're being burgled!"

Lucy grabbed her phone and dialled the police.

The group all began talking at once, unsure of how to help.

"Verity, shouldn't we ask Aidan to run down here?" enquired Anna. "It might be quicker than waiting for the police to arrive..."

"He's in London I'm afraid – on the late shift" replied Verity. "Anyway, he wouldn't be much help unless someone had been raped or murdered – and I suspect this is a shed burglary we're talking about. Still serious, of course, but not really Aidan's territory".

Jane had gone very pale. "I – I don't understand" she stammered.

"Aidan's a Police Officer", explained Verity "but he is based in London and does not cover this kind of crime. He deals more in the sort of thing you find in West Adams – or Peckham".

"Right, the Police will be here in a few minutes" announced Lucy, just as Edward walked back in through the back door.

"Too late" he said grimly. "Those bastards have already escaped over the back fence, with all our new Husqvarna garden tools. I thought I heard a strange noise when I was in the study upstairs, so I looked out of the window and there they were – breaking into our shed. As bold as brass, with some bolt croppers and a chainsaw".

"I can't believe they would break in while the house was full of people!" exclaimed Lucy. "So much for a crime-free, leafy little rural village…"

At that moment the doorbell rang – the Police had arrived.

"Lucy, I think we should leave you to it" said Gemma.

The group nodded in agreement. Now was not the time to score this month's book, and all of a sudden the subject matter seemed a little too close to home. The women filed quietly out of the house, hugging Lucy as they left and reminding her and Edward to call them if they needed anything.

Lucy's melt in your mouth mindfulness truffles sat untouched on the kitchen counter.

✳ ✳ ✳

Back at her cottage, Jane poured herself a cold glass of chardonnay from the fridge, settled herself on her well-worn sofa and tried to reflect dispassionately on the night's events and the unexpected drama of the burglary. She knew that she should be thinking about the interesting and helpful information she had acquired during the evening and how she could put it to good use in damaging her old enemy. Tonight, though, her brain was refusing to co-operate and her heart was firmly in charge.

Jane felt an unfamiliar warm glow as she thought about how the women had admired her new haircut. She smiled at the memory of Emily hugging her and laughing at her response to the story of Lorelei and her curious name. For the first time in more years than she could remember, she had felt accepted and valued. In this most unlikely place, quite unexpectedly, she was starting to feel as though she belonged...

Abruptly, Jane slammed her empty glass down on the coffee table. This would not do at all. She must not lose focus at this crucial point. The information she had acquired at tonight's book club meeting should enable her to deal her enemy a more devastating blow than she had originally anticipated, but only if she did not allow herself to be distracted. Perhaps the time had come to accelerate her plans and make a start. Delaying further, and potentially starting to feel part of this little community, was just too risky.

Jane walked slightly unsteadily back into the kitchen, refilled her wine glass and raised it in a silent toast to herself. Here's to remaining an outsider and a stranger, she thought. That way, she would avoid getting hurt again, and she would get her revenge. No more delays. It was time to begin.

* * *

One chilly afternoon the following week, Lucy stood shivering in the school car park waiting for her sons Henry and Harley to emerge from their after-school clubs. As usual, both of them were running late; being sociable and popular boys, they had stayed behind chatting with their friends and were in no hurry to leave. Their mother, on the other hand, was busily fielding emails and texts on her mobile and needed to get back home to her office as soon as possible to finish her day's work. Impatiently she pawed at the screen of her smartphone, glancing repeatedly towards the school gates as she searched anxiously for her boys.

As she drove into the car park, Alice spotted Lucy's diminutive figure, wrapped up in a cosy down jacket and with a funky bobble hat pulled down over her long, wavy hair. Alice had not bothered to bring a coat or hat as she had been planning to stay in her warm car whilst waiting for her youngest, Alf, to finish his Mathletics class. However, on spotting Lucy, she resolved to brave the chill in the interests of friendship, figuring that her friend could use some support after the trauma of the burglary.

"Hi Lucy!" Alice called as she trotted over, arms folded protectively across her chest in a futile attempt to keep out the cold.

"Oh hello Alice – sorry" said Lucy distractedly as she looked up from her phone. "Just answering a few pleading emails and texts. It seems that some of my students have yet to learn the meaning of the word deadline…"

"Much the same as our kids, then" replied Alice with a

wry smile. "Of course we're just their PAs, with nothing better to do than wait around for them in the freezing cold. Nothing new there. Anyway, how are you? Have the police managed to catch the people who burgled your shed?"

"No they haven't – and I'm not holding out much hope, to be honest" said Lucy glumly. "I've been assigned a crime number and that's about as far as it will proceed, I suspect; so I have made the decision just to let it go and claim on the insurance. I was pretty furious at the time, but I figured that holding on to my anger would only hurt me, not them. I'm sure that they will get their comeuppance in the end, one way or another – I'm a great believer in karma".

"Well who'd have thought it! A dedicated psychologist like yourself, indulging in mysticism?" Neither Alice nor Lucy had noticed Emily approaching. Like them, she was waiting for her children to finish their after-school activities and had abandoned her car near theirs.

"I'm allowed the odd indulgence, surely?" laughed Lucy.

"Of course you are – but make sure it comes out of a bottle like a normal person!" teased Emily. "Seriously, though, I'm glad I caught up with the two of you" she continued. "I ran into Gemma in the supermarket earlier, and she has offered to host the April book club. Obviously we didn't get a chance to choose the next host at our last meeting, as it all ended rather abruptly, so I'm glad she has agreed to take it on. Any news by the way, Lucy?"

Lucy shook her head.

"Oh bad luck mate, but I have to say I'm not surprised – it's always the same when we get stuff nicked from the farm. Just claim on the insurance and move on".

"That's just what I was saying to Alice" Lucy agreed. "So,

has Gemma chosen a book for us?"

"She has" replied Emily "and I'm just trying to remember the name of the sodding thing. 'Somebody or Other is Completely Something' – oh crap - it was along those lines; I can't quite remember. I'll check with her and post the title on our WhatsApp group. Oh look – here come the kids at long last. Oi you lot – what time do you call this?"

Henry, Harley, Billie, Dan and Alf sauntered casually across the car park, oblivious to their mothers' impatience. The three friends chivvied their children into their respective vehicles, waved each other goodbye and set off for home, glad that the April book club meeting was safely in Gemma's capable and efficient hands.

* * *

# CHAPTER 4

*April Book Club*

T he rain scythed relentlessly across Oak Welby, the trajectory of the raindrops distorted and strengthened by a fierce, icy north wind. Angling her umbrella against the deluge, Jane scuttled along the pavement, her chin tucked into a voluminous woollen scarf and her raincoat belted tightly around her.

As she approached The Mallard, her left foot was abruptly engulfed by a deep puddle in the unmade car park, obscured by the dark of the starless night. Swearing under her breath, Jane stumbled on towards the pub, shaking water and liquid mud from her shoe.

Just before she reached the sanctuary of the pub's porch, a rogue gust of wind seized her umbrella, turned it inside out and snapped one of its ribs with an emphatic crack. "Shit!" yelled Jane loudly. "This had better be worth it" she muttered to herself. So far, her regular visits to The Mallard had yielded precious little information, but she kept reassuring herself that it was early days yet.

All eyes turned towards Jane as she entered the pub. This was customary whenever a new arrival walked in the door. "Poor Jane, you're soaked!" cried Dave, a nightly fixture whose arrival and departure times could be used to set one's watch. "Let me take your coat and scarf" he offered chivalrously.

Jane settled herself on a barstool. "Your usual, Jane?" enquired Toby.

"Yes please, Toby" Jane replied, suppressing a smile of satisfaction. She had never had a 'usual' before in any pub. While she waited for Toby to bring her glass of chardonnay, she looked around to see who was in tonight. Melvin greeted her warmly, holding out his pint glass to his dog Roxy, who eagerly lapped the last few drops of beer from the bottom. Even after numerous visits to The Mallard, Jane still found this habit slightly alarming.

From across the bar, Verity raised an arm in a casual greeting. She and Aidan were seated in the corner, deep in conversation with a group of people whom Jane did not recognise. No other book club members were in evidence. In the snug, Jane could see Ron and his son Wesley laughing together, before Ron walked towards the front door, roll-up in hand, on his way for one of his frequent fag breaks. You had to hand it to the man – he liked a challenge. "You're going to struggle to light that, Ron, in this weather" Jane ventured. "I'm a patient man, gel" Ron replied with a suggestive wink "I'll get there in the end". Amen to that, thought Jane.

Dave, who had been chatting to Rick, now turned his attention to Jane, asking her all about her job at The Mill in South Napton – the clientele, the menu, her colleagues and her hours. Jane was happy to tell him all the details and to compare her work experiences with Dave's own career in the civil service. However, sometime during her second glass of wine the questions, although still innocuous, grew slightly more personal. Did she have family – brothers, sisters, parents maybe? Where was she from originally? How did she come to be in Oak Welby?

Jane responded with her usual, carefully curated mix of truth and falsehood. No, she had no brothers or sisters and her parents were both dead. She was from the West Country – a little village called Evercreech in Somerset - and yes, she had lost her accent over time. At this point, Melvin joined in – he had been based at RAF Boscombe Down for some years and loved the area where Jane had been brought up. Grateful for an opportunity to steer the conversation into less dangerous territory, Jane chatted away to Dave and Melvin about Somerset, waving goodbye to Verity and Aidan as they left with their friends.

"Is anyone going to be seeing Gemma?" asked Toby suddenly. "She left her jacket here on Saturday".

Jane looked at her watch. "I have to walk right past her house on the way home, so I'm happy to take it". She swallowed the last of her wine. "If I leave now, I can drop the jacket off before it gets too late. I was going to head off anyway".

"Thanks Jane" smiled Toby. "See you again soon".

Jane swathed herself in her long scarf, buckled up her raincoat and bid goodbye to the small group of regulars who remained in the bar. Once outside, she was grateful to discover that the rain had finally stopped. Ron's remaining fag breaks would be more comfortable, she reflected, dumping the remains of her wrecked umbrella in the wheelie bin outside the Village Hall. Like Ron, she was going to need to be patient, Jane concluded. So far, the clientele of The Mallard had found out a lot more about her than she had about them, which was precisely the opposite of what she intended.

\* \* \*

The lights in Gemma's house shone warm and welcoming as Jane approached and rang the doorbell. Gemma opened the door, gave Jane a friendly hug and ushered her into the house. Jane gazed in admiration at the spacious, tastefully furnished hallway and breathed in the delicious smell of spicy scented candles.

"Hi Jane – how lovely to see you! You have come at just the right time – I have a rather nice bottle of sauvignon blanc in the fridge and I was just about to crack it open. Fancy a glass?"

"If you're sure I'm not disturbing" ventured Jane politely. "It's just that - I was in the pub and Toby told me you left your jacket behind on Saturday, so I volunteered to return it – as I had to walk past your house anyway".

"Then you definitely deserve a glass of wine!" cried Gemma. "That jacket is one of my favourites and I have been looking for it everywhere. I remember now – I had it on under my overcoat when I went down to the pub, so I didn't notice it was missing when I walked home – and then I forgot where I had left it. I even accused my daughter Tabitha of borrowing it, but she just said – 'as if'!"

Gemma smiled, adopting a typical teenage pose and rolling her eyes in imitation of her daughter.

"Anyway, I could use the company. My husband Robert works in Prague during the week and Tabitha is staying with friends tonight, so I've got the house to myself. Come on into the kitchen. I'm sorry about the mess – I have just been marking my Year 4 creative writing assignments, which is why there is paper everywhere".

With her back to Jane, Gemma carrying on chatting as she moved around the kitchen, fetching wine glasses from the cupboard and removing the chilled wine from the fridge.

"You wouldn't believe what the children come up with when you ask them to be creative" she mused. "I'm constantly amazed at the ideas they have. Mind you, I think one of my class was getting a bit bored by the end. He finished his assignment off rather abruptly with this closing line…'and then they shot them and went home to tea!' I rather like it actually…"

Gemma handed Jane a glass of wine and continued chatting.

"I always say that teaching is the best job in the world – although it's hard work and long hours, as you can see. The marking can be a bit of a drag and the lesson prep is quite time-consuming, but I wouldn't do anything else - and I know Anna feels the same way. It sounds corny, but we love making a difference to children's lives. Do you have kids, Jane?"

Caught off guard by the unexpected question, Jane hesitated before replying. "No I don't. It's not that I didn't want them, but let's just say that – life didn't work out that way for me."

Gemma stared in surprise at the sudden bitterness in Jane's tone, before quickly recovering her poise.

"Well it's not always a bed of roses, particularly when they are small babies – or teenagers for that matter. Shall we go through to the living room? It's a bit more comfortable in there".

Jane thought that Gemma's stylish kitchen diner, with its large table and tasteful mood lighting, was actually very comfortable, but she said nothing as she followed Gemma into her beautifully appointed living room and settled down opposite her on one of the sofas.

Gemma asked Jane how she was enjoying book club and the two chatted about the recent meetings, the awful burglary at Lucy's house and the forthcoming April meeting, which Gemma was looking forward to hosting. "Hopefully it won't be as dramatic as last month's meeting at Lucy's" remarked Gemma. "And after that, of course, we have our weekend away in May to look forward to".

"What weekend away?" asked Jane in surprise.

"Oh – did no-one tell you? Sorry about that" apologised Gemma. "Well, let me fill you in. Peggy and Stan own a beautiful holiday home not far from here – about half an hour's drive away. It's called Waterside View as it overlooks a stunning lake that forms part of the grounds. We go there once a year for a special book club weekend, to give us some more time together. We still review a book as normal, but we also cook dinner, watch films, play games, have drinks – obviously – go walking in the grounds and take a trip to the nice pub down the road. For those who feel more energetic, there's also boating and paddle boarding on the lake – and a tennis court. We have such a laugh. I hope you'll be able to join us…"

"How can they fit us all in – I mean, where do we all sleep?" asked Jane. "The house must have lots of bedrooms if it can accommodate us all…"

"The house is pretty big – but there isn't a bedroom for everyone, so we all share rooms. It works out quite well – in fact it makes it even more fun. It's a bit like being a kid again – sharing a room with a friend".

Gemma smiled at the memory of bedtime chats and laughter lasting well into the night.

Jane looked alarmed. "Do we get to choose our roommate?" she enquired.

"Peggy sorts out the rooms" explained Gemma. "You can put in a request, though. We normally try to avoid Verity as she snores a bit – so Peggy pairs her up with Lorelei, who is a sound sleeper and doesn't seem to mind the noise. You're pretty safe with the rest of us".

Jane looked relieved. "That – should be OK. I'll save the date in my phone and book the weekend off work. I've never been on a group weekend away before. It should be an – interesting experience!"

"It'll be fun – I promise!" reassured Gemma. "One thing's for certain – you'll never have had a weekend quite like it…"

"Just one more thing" ventured Jane cautiously. "You mentioned that you play games over the weekend. What sort of games are we talking about?"

"Ah – now I think we should keep that as a surprise" smiled Gemma. "Don't worry – it's nothing weird. It's a game we invented ourselves – it has become a sort of book club tradition – our speciality, if you like. I don't want to spoil the surprise, but trust me – you'll love it".

"OK, fair enough". Jane looked at her watch and finished the last of her wine. "I had better be heading off – I'm on the early shift tomorrow" she said. "Thanks so much for the wine".

"You are most welcome" smiled Gemma. "Feel free to drop round any evening during the week, if you feel in need of some company. Robert is away most of the time, so I'm often home alone!"

"Thanks, that's very kind" replied Jane. "If I don't see you before, I'll see you at book club next week. Goodnight".

Jane's footsteps crunched on the gravel driveway as she headed off into the night. From the doorway, Gemma gazed thoughtfully after her as her diminutive figure was swallowed up by the darkness.

Back in her kitchen, Gemma put the half empty bottle of

wine away in the fridge, loaded the glasses into the dishwasher and made herself a mug of camomile tea. She then set the steaming mug down on the kitchen table, sat down and logged on to her laptop.

Ignoring the usual deluge of new emails exhorting her to buy something, provide feedback, download an app or sign an online petition, Gemma drafted an email to Lucy and Alice, asking them to pop over the following evening for a glass of wine and a quick chat, as she had something she needed to discuss with them privately before the next book club meeting.

Gemma hesitated slightly before pressing 'Send'. Then, with a few decisive clicks, she deleted the unread emails, shut down her laptop and headed upstairs to bed with her mug of tea. One by one, the lights in the house went out. Only the recently installed security lights remained on standby, primed and ready to burst into life at any sudden movement.

❊ ❊ ❊

Gemma poured the last of the sauvignon blanc into Alice and Lucy's glasses and opened a bottle of chardonnay in readiness for the inevitable refills.

"I just think there is something a bit odd about her" she continued. "I wanted to mention it to you both as, out of all the book club members, I think you two are the people most likely to pick up on any behaviour that might seem – a little strange".

"Well my training does help" remarked Lucy "but I can't say I have noticed anything in particular so far. She does seem a bit shy, but then who wouldn't be, when confronted by us lot?"

"I thought the same thing initially" replied Gemma "which is why alarm bells started ringing when I was on my own with her last night and she still behaved a bit weirdly, without the pressure of a big group of people".

"What did she do that was so strange?" asked Alice.

"Well, first of all, I asked her if she had children, and she sounded really bitter when she said she hadn't. She mentioned something about life not having turned out as she planned, and I got a sense of real pent-up anger there.

Then, later, I was telling her all about our weekend away at Waterside View next month, and I mentioned that she would have to share a room. Well, she looked really scared when I first mentioned it, then she suddenly seemed to change her mind and put the date in her diary. It just seemed odd that she would be so frightened and then suddenly have that change of heart…" Gemma tailed off and reached for the wine bottle.

"Well, for a start, lots of people are carrying around a burden of anger and resentment from their past" smiled Lucy. "It keeps psychotherapists in a job, after all!"

"Also, sharing a room with a stranger can be daunting if you aren't used to it or don't know the person well" reasoned Alice. "We are all so comfortable with each other, we tend to forget how difficult it must be for a person who hasn't known us for very long."

"That still doesn't explain why she suddenly changed her mind" Gemma pointed out.

"Maybe she just realised she was being a bit silly and told herself to go for it" suggested Alice. "I think she wants desperately to fit in – but she finds it a challenge at times".

"You're right – her behaviour can easily be explained away" conceded Gemma. "Also, I don't want to have a downer on her, as it is probably nothing. Please don't think I'm being mean, as I'm really not, but can we just all keep our eyes open? I still can't shake the feeling that there is something not quite right there".

"Let's keep our eyes and our minds open – then we can't go far wrong" said Lucy. "In the meantime, that bottle of chardonnay is not going to drink itself..."

The three friends refilled their glasses and the conversation turned to the latest village news and gossip. The awkward newcomer in their midst was temporarily forgotten.

* * *

The book club members settled themselves around Gemma's dining table, charged their glasses with prosecco and filled their plates with Gemma's delicious home-made canapés.

"Lucy, I hear that the investor group got more than it bargained for at the inaugural meeting the other week" began Jos.

"Yes, Edward certainly got his comeuppance!" laughed Lucy.

Several members of the book club looked puzzled.

"I don't know what you're talking about" said Irene.

Lucy proceeded to explain Edward's spoof, April Fool concept for turning The Mallard into the Millennium Falcon.

"I rather like the idea, actually" smiled Verity. "We'd attract geeks from miles around! Granted, it wouldn't be a target-rich environment for any girl who wanted to find a man, but then again, that's no different from The Mallard as it is now..."

"Well talking of geeks, let me tell you what happened next" continued Lucy, smiling at Alice.

"When Edward finished introducing his 'concept', Sandy stood up and gave an impassioned speech about how the Star Wars theme risked alienating the 'Trekkie' community – you know, people who prefer Star Trek to Star Wars. He said that hardly anyone likes both and that, as a Trekkie, he would personally struggle to drink in a Star Wars pub so he proposed adopting a broader sci-fi theme.

Anyway, Edward took the bait and started defending the 'integrity of the Millennium Falcon concept' until he realised that Sandy had twigged it was an April Fool and had come right back at him! At that point the whole group realised it was a joke and they all had a good laugh."

"Does it ever occur to you that we are married to two very twisted men?" asked Alice.

"All the time!" replied Lucy.

At this point the doorbell rang and Gemma ushered Anna into the room.

"Sorry I'm late, everyone" she began. "I've just been uploading a few hen party photos onto my phone – I thought you might want to see".

The hen party for Alexandra, Anna and Kit's eldest daughter, had taken place the previous weekend and the group gathered excitedly around Anna for a look.

"Of course I have only got a carefully edited selection here" admitted Anna "the ones that they think are suitable for Mum and her mates to see…"

"Any gossip to share, or is that embargoed too?" enquired Emily.

"Well it's mostly a case of what goes on tour stays on tour, as you would expect" replied Anna. "I have got one story I am allowed to tell, though".

"I should think so!" exclaimed Irene. "A group of gorgeous girls like that is bound to create a bit of a stir, and we want to hear at least a little bit about what went on!"

Anna's three daughters – Alexandra, the bride-to-be, and her two younger sisters Elise and Caitlyn, were well known for their looks and charm, much like their circle of equally attractive friends.

"OK - you know how most hen do's hire a male stripper?" began Anna. "Well, our girls got one free of charge - and quite unexpectedly! They were having dinner in a restaurant, before going onto a club, and the waiter serving them was apparently absolutely gorgeous. Anyway, the manageress noticed the girls admiring him and, unknown to them, suggested to him that he serve them a round of complimentary shots after dinner, wearing only his boxer shorts!

Anyway, he was more than happy to oblige – look, here he is posing with my girls and their friends. The rest of the night is off limits to me as mother of the bride, but I'm assured they all had a great time!"

The book club, huddled around Anna's phone, agreed that the waiter was incredibly fit and looked more than happy with his new career as an impromptu stripper.

At this point, as ever, Gemma attempted to call the book club to order so that they could begin discussing the book. As the women returned to their seats, Peggy suddenly remembered something.

"Before we start, could I just agree the arrangements for our weekend at Waterside View in May? First of all, can everyone make it?"

Everyone nodded.

"Gemma explained all about the weekend to me the

other night" said Jane. "If you don't mind including a newbie, I'd like to come".

"Of course, that goes without saying" replied Peggy. "Great – so everyone can come. All we need to agree, then, is who is willing to drive, who will go in which car and who is going to cook. I thought we would get a takeaway on the first night, so we only need to plan for dinner on the second night".

Normally it would take the group some time to agree arrangements like this. However, in stark contrast to the previous month, the members of the book club were eager to begin discussing this month's book and were conscious that it was getting late, so decisions were made with unusual speed. Before long, Peggy was happy that all the arrangements were in place for the May weekend and the book review could begin.

April's book was a heart-warming, beautifully rendered tale of a woman who initially appears to her colleagues, and to the reader, as a socially illiterate oddball. Out of step with contemporary life, she is ostracised by all who know her and maintains a solitary existence until a random accident on the street, and a parallel crisis in her personal life, cause the awful truth about her past to be revealed, gradually and with shocking power. The book's ending is hopeful and optimistic but skilfully saccharine-free.

Unusually, everyone in the book club agreed that they loved the book, although different parts of it resonated with different people. Nicky, unsurprisingly, appreciated the role played by the protagonist's new haircut in her recovery – how it transformed her image, made her feel so much better about herself and brought her closer to her colleagues.

"It's so rare to see hairdressing being portrayed positively in a book" she remarked. "Usually it is seen as just wall-paper, you know, not really part of the plot, and hair-dressers are dismissed as bimbos. It's good to see some-one recognising that changing your outside can help your inside, if that makes sense?"

Everyone agreed, although Anna noticed with amuse-ment that the manicure did not have the same impact. Alice then reminded everyone about the scene where the poor unsuspecting woman requests, and experiences, a 'Hollywood'. This episode struck a chord with some of the women around the table, causing a few winces amid the general merriment, with prosecco glasses being hastily drained and refilled.

Lucy, with her professional hat on, commented that, in her opinion, the book was completely convincing from a psychological point of view, and cleverly avoided any un-realistically rapid or pat solutions. "The book takes you on a journey with her, which has its ups and downs, as she makes progress and experiences setbacks. I found it very true to life in that respect".

Irene loved the description of the growing friendship be-tween the leading lady and her colleague on the IT help-desk at the firm where she worked. "At first you think that he is a complete loser, like you do with her, but then gradually you change your mind about him. For instance, it's quite clever the way he gets off with that glamorous hairdresser, so you realise he must actually be quite at-tractive on some level. Then, when the accident happens and later, when she has her crisis, you see what a star he really is. On the other hand, though, the author keeps it real – he doesn't miraculously give up smoking and the two of them don't walk off into the sunset at the end of the book."

"I have to disagree with you there, Irene" remarked Jane,

who had said little up to that point. All eyes immediately turned in her direction.

"I think it's pretty clear from the way the novel ends that the two of them are going to wind up together" she began. "After all, they do set a date to go to that concert. What I find really annoying about that – and about the endings of so many other novels – is the way that the heroine has to be rescued by a man!" Jane cried, gripping her glass tightly in her fist as she got into her stride. "I mean, for a start, in this day and age women should be able to rescue themselves and secondly, in real life, the man does not turn up on his white charger and save the damsel in distress. Does not happen, in my experience. Don't get me wrong – I liked the book – but I found the ending disappointing for that reason".

"I don't agree" said Lucy quietly. The group turned to look at her.

"I think that she does rescue herself. She saves her life, and turns it around, through an intense and challenging series of counselling sessions where she has to confront the truth about her past and deal with it. Sure, she gets some help from her IT colleague and others, but she has to find the courage to heal herself. Only when she has done that is she able to move on with her life. Whether she does that with or without a man is of secondary importance. The key point is – she has to help herself".

Lucy looked at Jane for a long moment, then looked away. As usual in this type of situation, Nicky came to the rescue and lightened the mood.

"Well I'm just glad that her mate got brownie points for getting it on with a hairdresser!" she laughed. I'll have to tell Bill that being with me is proof of his attractiveness..."

"Not that Bill requires any proof, of course" remarked

Alice and the group agreed, making various positive remarks about the looks and charm of Nicky's handsome husband and agreeing that he was, at the very least, an eight out of ten. At this point Gemma decided to call the group to order.

"Right, you lot – when you have finished scoring men, perhaps we could score the actual book?" she quipped with a smile.

Jos was the first to give her score. "I found it moving, absorbing and remarkably well written – in fact I read it in one evening!" she said. "I couldn't put it down. Luckily it was a Wednesday – Mack gave up on the idea of getting any supper at home and went down to The Mallard for fish and chips. I give it an 18".

A score of 18 out of 20 was remarkable from Jos, who was an insightful literary critic and not afraid to submit low scores for books that did not pass muster. The rest of the book club submitted similarly high scores, even Jane, despite her earlier comments. In the end, the book achieved one of the highest scores ever.

By this time it was getting really late. The members of the book club hurriedly finished the last of Gemma's delicious canapés, drained the final drops of prosecco and began putting on their coats.

"Don't forget – we must choose the next book before we go" Gemma reminded them. "It's going to be the one that we review during our weekend away, so let's make it one to remember!"

"I have a suggestion" said Peggy. "The book is called The Lavender Garden. One of the reasons I'm suggesting it is that it was turned into a film quite a few years ago and I was given the DVD by my cousin at Christmas. I haven't watched it yet – has anyone seen it?"

The book club members shook their heads. As luck would have it, none of them had seen the film or read the book, even though it was supposedly something of a classic.

"That's perfect, then" said Peggy. "We can read the book over the next four weeks, review it on the Saturday at Waterside View and then watch the film in the evening after dinner, with a few drinks".

Everyone agreed that this sounded like a perfect idea. They then grabbed their bags, finished putting on their coats and scarves and hugged Gemma one by one as they left the house, thanking her for a wonderful April book club.

Lucy was the last to leave. As she hugged her, Gemma whispered:

"So what do you think now? Am I just being paranoid?"

Lucy smiled and waved to the others as they disappeared down the drive.

"My diag-nonsense, following tonight, is 'harmless bunny boiler'. Keep your pets out of the way and you should be fine. Seriously, though, let's reserve judgement and see how she behaves next month at Waterside View, when we have a bit more time to observe her. That should give us a chance to find out what she's really like".

With that, Lucy took her leave and vanished rapidly into the dark.

* * *

Just a few hours later and several thousand miles away from Oak Welby, the sun blazed relentlessly down upon Jumeirah Beach where Arabella was relaxing on a sunbed, Kindle in hand, wearing a halter neck bikini and a large floppy sunhat. From under its brim, she glanced up from her screen and turned her gaze towards the cornflower blue sea, just in time to see her husband George whizzing by on water skis. Upon their arrival in Dubai, George had quickly been persuaded by the couple next door to join the water skiing club and he was now totally consumed by his new hobby. Arabella, on the other hand, was happy to remain on the beach and work on her tan during her time off work. Her job was proving to be quite demanding, so she was taking every possible opportunity to relax.

As the nimble water ski boat described a graceful arc in the clear blue water and headed back towards the other end of the beach, George veered outwards to cross the wake; a bold move for a novice water skier, given the slightly choppy conditions. It was all over in an instant – his skis were catapulted into the air and George hit the foaming waves with a resounding splash.

"Oops" murmured Arabella with a smile, reaching for her Virgin Mojito.

As she turned to pick up her drink, Arabella noticed two Emirati women walking arm in arm along the promenade behind her, past the large sign proclaiming 'no swimwear beyond this point'. Although they were dressed in the traditional Abaya and veil, both sported luxuriant false eyelashes and full-make up, in defiance of the scorching conditions. As they walked away from her, Arabella noticed that the taller of the two was wearing shoes with distinctive red soles. The Louboutins gave Arabella a touch of shoe envy – she was definitely overdue some retail therapy at the Dubai Mall. All she needed was a good friend to keep her company.

At that moment, the tall Emirati woman bent her head and whispered something in her companion's ear. The two of them instantly dissolved into giggles, bending forward and clutching each other as they shared their private joke. Watching them, Arabella was suddenly overcome with homesickness. In that instant, she would gladly have traded the hot weather, sandy beach and blue sea for a damp, chilly English afternoon and a cheeky glass of prosecco with her book club friends. With a deep sigh, she put her Kindle and her drink to one side and flipped down the brim of her hat, shutting out her sunlit world.

# CHAPTER 5

*May Book Club*

T he hazy spring sunshine bathed Nicky's stylish salon in a pale lemon glow. Inside, the air was liberally scented with the aroma of freshly ground coffee and fragrant shampoo. On the walls, cheerful framed prints jostled for position alongside posters advertising the latest miracle hair products - guaranteed to tame, colour, brighten and shine your wayward tresses. Power ballads from the 80's, emanating from the surround sound speakers, lent a hyper-emotional vibe to proceedings. Thankfully, the only poodle perms in the vicinity were on the rock stars.

Nicky's latest customer slumped in his seat, a towel wound turban-style around his head. As he waited for Nicky to bring him a coffee and cut his hair, he gazed vacantly at a poster of a beautiful girl on the wall opposite, confidently reassuring him that he was worth it. Let's hope so, he thought to himself. In the background, Foreigner repeatedly expressed their heartfelt desire to know what love is. Halfway through the song, Nicky strode purposefully into the room, cafetière in hand.

"Right, Rick, sit up straight", she commanded. "I'll never get your hair to look right if you slouch like that".

Obediently, Rick hauled himself upright as Nicky unwound the towel and paused just long enough for him to grab his coffee. She then set to with her scissors and clippers, quickly and expertly restyling Rick's hair to recapture the look that had so transformed him six weeks previously. Rick sat silently as she worked, meek and obliging as a lamb. Finally, Nicky applied a liberal dose of styling gel to Rick's hair, blasted it into shape with her hair dryer and trimmed a few stray hairs at the nape of his neck.

"There we go, Rick – all done!" Nicky proclaimed, brandishing a mirror behind Rick's head to show him the back.

"That's lovely, Nicky – thank you" muttered Rick, brushing a few stray hairs from his T-shirt as he walked towards the till and holding out a slightly grubby wad of cash with which to pay his bill.

As she took his money, Nicky enquired cautiously:

"If you don't mind me asking, Rick, why have you chosen to get your hair and beard cut now – after all these years? What has prompted this change of image?"

Rick stared at his feet in obvious discomfort.

"I don't want to go into too much detail at the moment, Nicky, in case things don't work out, but let's just say – I've decided it's time to turn my life around, if I can".

"Well I think that's brilliant!" cried Nicky with her usual enthusiasm. "I wish you the very best of luck – I hope everything goes according to plan and, if I may say so, a haircut is a great place to start, if you want to transform your life. Oh look, here's Jane – she's my next customer. Do you guys know each other?"

"Just a little – we've said hello a few times in the pub" replied Rick. "Hi Jane" he said hurriedly as they passed each other in the salon doorway.

"Oh hi, Rick – good to see you" replied Jane, looking slightly distracted.

"Right my lovely, come on in". Nicky ushered Jane in and seated her in front of the mirror. "Time to make you all beautiful, ready for your first ever weekend at Waterside View!"

"To tell you the truth, Nicky, I'm feeling a bit nervous about this coming weekend" confessed Jane. "There seems to be a bit of secrecy surrounding it, so I don't really know what to expect, and that makes me a bit apprehensive".

"Don't you worry" Nicky reassured her. "There are a few surprises in store, but they're all nice ones. We're just keeping some things secret to make sure you have as much fun as possible. Please don't fret – I can personally guarantee that you're going to love it…"

❊ ❊ ❊

Early that same evening, London's Buckingham Palace Road was pulsing with rush-hour traffic. Horns blared as frustrated drivers tried to negotiate the traffic jams whilst avoiding the have-a-go pedestrians who dodged and weaved their way between the near-stationary vehicles. On the pavements rucksack-toting commuters, heading for the train and tube stations, clashed repeatedly with slow-moving tourists dragging wheeled suitcases in the opposite direction towards the bus terminal.

Yet only a few yards away, down the side streets that fanned out from the main road towards Belgravia, the noise quickly faded into the background, to be replaced by an air of serene gentility. Town houses and flats, uniformly painted the colour of vanilla bean ice-cream, rubbed shoulders with tasteful, independent shops and restaurants. Not a Costa Coffee or a Pret à Manger in sight.

Inside Sposi, the upmarket wedding dress shop located discreetly in a quiet mews just off one of the side streets, Alexandra paced slowly back and forth across the mushroom-coloured carpet under the watchful eye of her mother, who was sitting bolt upright on the edge of her seat. On a nearby sofa Alexandra's two younger sisters, Elise and Caitlyn, slumped against each other with the unfocused gaze of two jaded viewers who have seen it all before.

"What do you think?" asked the bride-to-be a touch wearily. "Have they finally got it right this time?"

Anna looked up at her daughter, her eyes shining with tears.

"Oh Alex, I think it's just perfect. I know it has taken four fittings, but it was so worth the effort in my view. It looks absolutely amazing now – it fits you so well. Tom won't be able to believe his eyes when you walk down the aisle".

"Yeah it looks great, I agree" added Caitlyn, breaking a chunky Kit-Kat in two and handing half to Elise "but you had better lay off the pies until after the wedding – there's not much room for expansion in that dress..."

"She's right" teased Elise through a mouthful of chocolate. "No more Krispy Kreme doughnuts for you – no more pints and no more Jägerbombs..."

"That's quite enough from you two" scolded Anna. "You have both got bridesmaids' dresses to fit into, don't forget - and please put that chocolate away while you're in the shop. I can't afford to pay an extra bill for damages caused by your grubby hands! Also, it's me you should really be reminding to stay off the pies" she added with a smile. "After all, it's the annual book club trip to Water-side View this weekend. Based on past experience of what we eat and drink while we are there, I won't be able to get near my wedding outfit by next Monday!"

Alexandra laughed. "Yeah, Mum. It's hard to play the strict mother when you're really a debauched old bird – just like the rest of your book club mates!" Walking over to her mother, she pulled her in for an affectionate hug. "Seriously though, just have a great time this weekend and forget about the wedding for a while. You have worked so hard to give me a great wedding – you deserve a break. Then, if you want to lose weight afterwards, just do what I do when I've overdone it – don't eat for a week!"

"I'll pretend I didn't hear that" Anna replied. "I want no fad diets from you three in the run-up to the wedding – just sensible, healthy eating. Now, have we all said yes to the dress?"

"Yes - I believe we have". Alex smiled with relief as she high-fived her two sisters.

"In that case I will max out the credit card – then let's go to that nice wine bar round the corner and celebrate with a glass of champagne. Only ninety calories a glass, or so I believe…"

✳ ✳ ✳

Peggy relaxed in the cosy window seat at Waterside View. Located at the far end of the spacious living room, it commanded a spectacular view of the large, oval lake and the beautifully landscaped array of trees surrounding it. As Peggy watched, the mango-tinged setting sun dipped behind the willow trees, casting a benevolent light on a mother duck as she chivvied her brood of ducklings towards the water's edge. In a few weeks, the ducklings would be joined by Peggy's favourites – moorhen chicks, scooting around the lake like miniature, animated powder puffs.

These few moments of quiet contemplation were, as ever, soon interrupted. Peggy jumped when she heard the first blast of a car horn, then smiled in anticipation.

"And so it begins" she mused. "Another book club weekend at Waterside View. Here we go…"

Abandoning her window seat, Peggy hurried to the front door, just in time to see a small convoy of SUVs proceeding up the drive, each filled with its own excitable, animated driver and crew. The vehicles came to a halt and the book club posse was rapidly and noisily disgorged. Amid shouts of "Hi, Peggy!" and repeated hugs, Peggy helped them all into the house along with their innumerable bags – silent, squishy overnight bags and noisy, clinking bags full of prosecco, wine and gin bottles and a huge quantity of food.

Half an hour later, with the fridge, food cupboards and wine racks crammed full and the book club members making a racket in the kitchen, Peggy decided that it was time to impose some order.

"Right, you noisy rabble" she cried "let's get you organised into your bedrooms. Irene, you're with me as usual, if that's OK?"

Irene nodded happily in assent.

"Emily and Lucy, I've put the two of you together" continued Peggy. "Lucy, I have to warn you that there's a slight snoring risk with Emily – as I know from experience – but I find that, if you lob a pillow at her, she generally shuts up. Lorelei I have put you with Verity as usual, as I know you can cope with her snoring".

"Thanks, mate" said Verity warmly, giving Lorelei a friendly hug.

"Gemma, you're with Alice" announced Peggy "and Nicky, I've put you with Anna. Now, who does that leave? Ah yes – Jane and Jos – I've put the two of you together, if that's alright with you both".

"That's fine by me" replied Jos, smiling happily at Jane.

"Me too" breathed Jane, looking relieved.

"Great, that was easy" finished Peggy. "Let's get you all settled into your rooms – then I suggest we get started on the prosecco! I've got a few bottles chilling in the fridge…"

"Excellent – let's start as we mean to go on!" laughed Nicky.

"I hear oblivion calling!" yelled Emily.

"Don't forget, though – we need to pace ourselves for what's coming later" warned Lucy, winking at Emily.

"I think you'll find that prosecco will help, rather than hinder, given what we have got in store" retorted Emily.

Jane glanced nervously in Lucy's direction but Lucy, oblivious to Jane's discomfort, was already heading off to find her room.

Jos and Jane's bedroom was at the rear of the house, overlooking the lake. As Jane unpacked her clothes and hung them in the wardrobe, Jos relaxed in an armchair by the window.

"It's a shame that it's dark now, so you can't see the view" she remarked. "Make sure you take a look when you wake up tomorrow – it's guaranteed to take your breath away. This is such a special place" she added. "We're so lucky that Peggy and Stan let us take it over once a year".

"Um – yes" replied Jane, who was preoccupied and not

really listening.

"Jos?" she asked suddenly. "What did Lucy mean when she said – what's coming later? I know that we are having a Chinese takeaway, but what else is going to happen?"

"You'll find out in due course" Jos reassured her. "In the meantime, don't look so worried! You're going to have a great time".

By the time the Chinese takeaway was delivered, a sizeable dent had been made in the book club's stock of prosecco and Waterside View was filled with the sound of laughter and lively conversation. Over a starter of Peking Duck, accompanied by a delicious sauvignon blanc, the discussion turned to the investor group that had recently been formed and was putting together an offer package for The Mallard.

"So what's the final line-up, Lucy?" enquired Lorelei.

"Well, in addition to Edward and myself, we have got Verity and Aidan, Alice and Sandy, Anna and Kit and – this was a surprise, I have to say – Toby and a mystery business partner, Bridget, whom we have yet to meet. So that gives us ten people, which I think is a good number. We had a few drop-outs as they didn't feel they could raise the cash, but I think we've got a good solid set of compatible people and skills in the group" said Lucy, smiling warmly at Verity, Alice and Anna. "Toby is going to stay on as Manager in the first instance, but he ultimately wants to move on, so we're going to hire a full-time Manager once we have found the right person".

The group immediately began speculating excitedly about Toby's new business partner and the precise nature of their relationship.

"Well, you'll get a chance so meet her if our offer is successful, as she'll definitely be coming to the opening night, according to Toby" added Lucy. "By the way, if we do take ownership, we are going to open with a special sci-fi and superheroes theme night – in honour of our now famous April Fool's joke. So, if it's not tempting fate, you had better start getting your costumes ready!"

"Not everyone will need to dress up, of course" remarked Gemma. "I find that quite a few Wookies and Cyborgs get into The Mallard on a Saturday night as it is!"

Laughing in agreement, the book club hungrily tucked into their main courses and refilled their glasses.

Some time later, once the dishes had been cleared away and everyone's glasses had been charged once again, Lucy looked over enquiringly at Peggy, who gave her a discreet nod. Lucy got to her feet, tapping a spoon against her wine glass to call the assembled company to order.

"Ladies, if I could just have your attention for a minute" she began.

"We have now reached that point in the evening – our first night at Waterside View – when it is time to begin the initiation ceremony for our newest book club member – Jane!"

Jane's mouth dropped open in shock and she stared at Lucy in alarm.

"Let me start by telling you a story, Jane" continued Lucy smoothly.

"Once upon a time, the women seated around this table were young, lithe and – well – pert. If they had wished, some of them could have pursued careers on stage at the Moulin Rouge, twirling tassels on their assets…"

Lucy paused and gave a brief demonstration.

"You've still got it, Lucy!" shouted Emily, and everyone laughed – except Jane, whose eyes remained fixed on

Lucy.

"Suffice to say that none of us did, though" Lucy went on. "We all took different paths in life and had fun along the way. Dinners were eaten, wine and fizz were drunk, children were born to some of us, marathons were run…"

"You speak for yourself, Lucy!" laughed Anna.

"…diets were embarked upon and inevitably abandoned, and long hours were spent slumped over desks…"

"I can relate" muttered Verity gloomily.

"…what can I say?" asked Lucy rhetorically. "To cut a long story short – over the years, life took its toll on all of us and, gradually, those once perky assets headed south. As a result, tassel twirling is sadly no longer an option, so instead, we have devised an alternative. Alice and Anna – you're tonight's team captains. Please set up the toilet rolls".

Alice and Anna duly grabbed two large carrier bags from the corner of the room and emptied the contents onto the floor of the open plan kitchen adjoining the dining area where the women were seated. Jane stared, puzzled, at the two large piles of cardboard tubes taken from the centre of toilet rolls. As she watched, Alice and Anna arranged the toilet roll tubes in four orderly and symmetrical rows along the length of the kitchen floor.

"So tonight, Jane", announced Lucy proudly, "we have the pleasure of introducing you to our very own parlour game for the once, but no longer so perky. Tonight, the Oak Welby Book Club presents to you – Titswiping!"

As all the book club members, apart from Jane, clapped and cheered, Lucy produced with a flourish two capacious and sturdy bras, which she had hitherto kept hidden under the dining room table. Attached to the cups of each bra were two long strings from which dangled a weighty, glittering bauble. Jane gazed in astonishment.

"Our two captains will now demonstrate the Titswiping technique" proclaimed Lucy. "Alice and Anna – on with your bras!"

The two women quickly donned the bras over their clothing and took their places at the head of the four rolls of toilet roll tubes.

"The idea is" explained Lucy "that you swing your – ahem – assets and knock over your team's two rows of toilet roll tubes with the baubles hanging from your bra. The first person to knock over all the tubes in their two rows wins, then the bras are passed over to the next two players in the opposing teams. Next we set the tubes up again, replay the game with the new set of players, then move to the next pair – and so on. The team with the most victories is the overall winner. Is that clear, Jane?"

Jane could only nod in response.

"Good" said Lucy firmly. "Alice and Anna are both experienced Titswipers; they'll show you how it's done. Watch and learn. Right, Alice and Anna – you're up. On your marks, get set – Titswipe!"

Alice and Anna both bent over and made an energetic start, rhythmically swinging their bra-clad boobs from side to side and knocking over the cardboard tubes with their glittering baubles.

"They make it look easy, but it's actually trickier than it appears" whispered Jos to Jane, who could only gape at her silently, unable to form a reply.

Once the last toilet roll tube had hit the deck, the group quickly put them neatly back in place and the two captains removed their bras.

"Right, time to pick teams" instructed Lucy. "Captains, please take turns to choose your players – Alice, you start".

Taking pity on the new girl, who was clearly terrified by this point, Alice held out her hand.

"Jane, you come and join my team" she invited. "Don't worry – I'll look after you!"

In addition to Jane, Alice picked Jos, Emily, Lorelei and Gemma, whilst Anna chose Peggy, Irene, Lucy, Nicky and Verity. As usual, Verity was the last to be picked. Her well-known clumsiness and lack of co-ordination meant that she was not a talented Titswiper and was, frankly, a liability to any team.

Jos and Irene were the first pair to play. Jos gained an early lead, but Irene's consistent Titswiping rhythm meant that she caught up in the latter part of the game and eventually seized victory. The audience members clapped and yelled their appreciation and commiseration at an equally loud volume.

Emily and Lucy were next up. The two friends fought a close-run battle – both were skilful Titswipers and, as the creator of the Titswiping concept, Lucy was particularly keen to win. However, on this occasion, her baubles failed to hit a couple of their targets and Emily just pipped her to the post.

"Great contest, girls!" cried Peggy appreciatively.

Lorelei and Nicky went next. Both women were overcome by laughter, so much so that their baubles swung every which way, mostly failing to hit the toilet rolls and only doing so by accident. As a result, their game lasted quite a long time.

Jane, who was lined up to play next, was annoyed to find herself feeling nervous as she watched the two players. "Don't be ridiculous", she silently admonished herself "it's just a silly game". However, not for the first time since joining the book club, her body refused to obey the commands of her mind. With sweating palms and trembling hands, she waited for her turn to come.

In the meantime, despite their constant giggles and consequent erratic Titswiping technique, Nicky and Lorelei somehow finished their game, with Nicky managing to clinch a win, much to her delight. Alice then helped Jane put on her bra and she stepped up to her mark, standing alongside her opponent - Peggy.

"Go!" shouted Lucy and both women immediately began Titswiping, accompanied by lots of vocal encouragement from their respective captains.

"Oscillate those assets, Jane!" laughed Alice.

"Go on Peggy, swing your boobs!" countered Anna.

Jane made a shaky start. Annoyingly, her baubles seemed to circle the toilet rolls rather than hitting them, so Peggy took the lead and maintained it during most of the contest. However, Peggy was hampered by a dodgy knee, so Jane caught up as she gradually mastered the art of Titswiping. To her complete astonishment, she managed to fell her final toilet roll just ahead of Peggy and win the game.

Lucy did a quick tally at this point, and the book club members were excited to learn that it was all square, with just one game left to play – Gemma versus Verity. Anna, though, looked downcast. On past form, Gemma was a far better player than Verity, so it looked as though the contest was lost for her team.

Gemma and Verity, conscious of the pressure on them as players in the deciding game, flailed around energetically, and the number of toilet rolls diminished rapidly on both sides, despite their sometimes less than precise technique. Observing the close-run match, the captains voiced their surprise.

"Has Verity been practising, do you think?" Alice shouted to Anna over the general mayhem.

"I don't think so" replied Anna. "Maybe it's because she isn't drinking – her Titswiping skills might have improved as a result!"

"Could be" concluded Alice. "They say every cloud has a silver lining. Personally, I'd rather stay a rubbish Titswiper and enjoy a glass of prosecco here and there…"

The screaming and cheering reached a crescendo as the final game drew to a close. Eventually, each player had only one toilet roll tube left standing. Verity swiped crazily at hers, whilst Gemma coolly lined up her baubles, took aim, swung her appendages carefully and felled her final roll. Alice's team emerged the winners, but only by a whisker.

"That was an epic match!" concluded Lorelei.

Both teams hugged each other, then Peggy opened a couple of chilled bottles of white wine and the women settled down in the living room for a final glass before bedtime. Verity, secretly relieved not to have let the side down completely by playing badly, as she usually did, cracked open an alcohol-free beer to celebrate and went to join the group.

Once everyone was seated, Jos raised her glass.

"I propose a toast" she announced. "To my room-mate Jane – for an amazing debut performance!"

"To Jane!" chorused the members of the book club.

Embarrassed and thrilled at the same time, Jane blushed and stared at the floor as her book club friends lifted their glasses in her honour.

An hour later, everyone was in bed, tired after a long and

lively evening. Initially, conversation and laughter could be heard from every bedroom, but the giggles and gossip gradually subsided as, one by one, the women turned over and fell asleep.

Eventually, the only sound that could be heard was a gentle but persistent snoring emanating from one room. Surprisingly, however, the bedroom in question was not Lorelei and Verity's room on the ground floor, as Verity's alcohol-free evening had put paid to her snoring, ensuring Lorelei an unexpectedly silent night. Instead, the snoring was coming from Lucy and Emily's room on the floor above where Emily, oblivious to her friend's whispered requests to shut up, was sleeping peacefully.

After ten minutes or so Lucy, desperate for a solution and a restful night's sleep, suddenly recalled Peggy's earlier advice. The last sound to be heard in Waterside View that night was the resounding 'thunk' of a down-filled pillow. After that, the whole house was silent.

❋ ❋ ❋

Saturday morning dawned murky and wet, meaning that Jane's first view of the lake was not as stunning as Jos would have liked. Peggy and Irene were up first and busied themselves in the kitchen, brewing large pots of coffee and tea and making a start on breakfast. Gradually the other members of the book club shuffled in wearing pyjamas, slippers and dressing gowns. Blearily they helped themselves to tea and coffee, sat down at the dining table and peered disconsolately out of the window.

"This weather's pants!" grumbled Emily. "I was hoping to take a rowing boat out on the lake this morning, but in this rain – forget it".

"I was looking forward to doing a bit of paddle boarding sometime over the weekend, but it doesn't look too hopeful" added Alice gloomily.

"Don't worry, you lot" soothed Peggy "the weather is forecast to be much better tomorrow – warm and sunny. We'll be able to do some watersports tomorrow morning after breakfast, with any luck. In the meantime, Irene and I have been thinking - and we have a suggestion. How about we wander down to the pub at lunchtime and do our book review there, over a nice warming glass of their home-made mulled wine? Then we can come back afterwards, chill out for a bit, enjoy our cocktail hour followed by dinner, then watch the DVD of The Lavender Garden?"

"That all sounds wonderful!" exclaimed Anna. "Sounds like a plan! I only hope that I will still be able to focus on the DVD after all that drinking…"

"Of course you will, you lightweight" teased Emily. "Especially with the size of the breakfast that Mum and Irene appear to be cooking up – not to mention tonight's dinner. There'll be plenty of food on offer to soak up all the booze. And another thing – if I hear the word 'calorie' from you or anyone else, you're going straight in that lake – rain or no rain!"

"You haven't seen the dress I have to get into for the wedding" Anna responded "but this weekend is definitely a diet-free zone, I promise!"

The whole group agreed that Peggy and Irene's plan sounded perfect; guaranteed to dispel any gloom caused by the inclement weather. Towards lunchtime, therefore, after a leisurely breakfast followed by a lengthy period spent getting ready, the posse set out under a canopy of umbrellas. Their destination was the Blue Boar, the cosy village pub that was Peggy and Stan's local when staying at Waterside View.

The landlady was delighted to see Peggy and her group, helping them settle on the sofas in the comfortable snug and pouring them piping hot beakers of fragrant, spicy mulled wine from a large jug. Blowing the steam from her drink, Gemma suggested that, as lots of gossip had already been shared since their arrival the previous evening, they could jump straight to the book review. The group readily agreed, as everyone was keen to hear what the others thought about The Lavender Garden.

"Shall I start?" offered Lorelei.

Everyone nodded; they all looked forward to Lorelei's entertaining take on the books that they read each month.

"Right – I'll begin by telling you what I was expecting from The Lavender Garden" Lorelei began. "What I anticipated was a wistful, nostalgic and emotional story about youth abruptly brought to an end and innocence cruelly lost amidst the horrors of the Second World War. What I actually got was a…um…a"

Lorelei paused, lost for words.

"A shagfest?" suggested Emily helpfully.

"Yes – exactly!" cried her aunt. "It just seemed as though war came along and gave them all a happy excuse to let rip, drink heavily and leap into bed with friends and family in various different combinations. But what got me the most was the style in which it was written – that sort of jolly hockey sticks kind of tone…"

"I know just what you mean!" exclaimed Anna. "I thought it read a bit like Enid Blyton's Guide to Sex". Putting on an over the top, retro upper-class accent, Anna happily mimicked the novel's characters:

*"Oh what-ho, Biffy, shall we have it orf?"*

*"Oh rather, Celia, that would be spiffing…"*

Emily quickly took up the joke.

*"Oh bother – dashed air raid siren has gone orf, darn it – must get down to the shelter. Rumpy-pumpy will have to wait until next week, old girl..."*

The group dissolved into helpless laughter.

"What about that thing with the twins" giggled Nicky "how weird was that? And some of those old blokes didn't half give me the creeps..."

"There were some serious themes in it, though" countered Emma, attempting to rebalance the group's assessment of this classic novel. "For instance, there was that woman who didn't think that the Nazis were really all that bad. I think that a lot of people actually did feel like that at the time, because they didn't know the full horror of what was really happening. That came later".

The group agreed and calmed down a bit.

Verity, who fancied herself as a bit of a literary critic, remarked that she found the novel 'frothy and underwritten'. Jos agreed: "the characters are drawn so sketchily that you can't really care about them".

"I agree with all that" concluded Nicky "but to me it was still a shagfest, like Emily said".

The women laughingly agreed and commented that it was remarkable that an author in her 70s had written about sex with such abandonment and lack of inhibition.

"She must have been a game old bird!" concluded Irene.

"There's hope for us all yet!" added Peggy.

The group finished the book review by agreeing to score it after they had watched the DVD in the evening.

"I can't wait to see what it's like and how they manage to portray all that sex on screen" commented Irene, passing round the jug of mulled wine.

That evening, after a relatively peaceful afternoon spent reading, snoozing and playing cards and board games back at Waterside View, the various members of the book club felt refreshed and ready to embark upon cocktail hour. Lucy and Lorelei had each volunteered to create a gin-based signature cocktail for the group to try before dinner.

Lucy was up first. Her friends gathered enthusiastically around her as she carefully filled a row of martini glasses with an effervescent, pearly pink liquid, then topped each drink with a small spoonful of rhubarb puree. Handing a glass to each of them, she proudly introduced her bespoke pre-dinner libation:

"Ladies – I give you – The Titswipers' Tipple!" she announced. "A beguiling and zesty combination of rhubarb gin, Mediterranean tonic and a measure of Cointreau, with just a dash of Angostura Bitters. Enjoy!"

Alice was the first to comment. "It's lovely" she remarked. "A sophisticated little number – for a less than sophisticated group!"

"You speak for yourself" laughed Nicky. "I love it too, though".

Everyone agreed that the new cocktail was delicious and that Lucy had really excelled herself. The blender containing the translucent pink liquid was swiftly emptied.

Next it was Lorelei's turn. She lined up a row of highball glasses and slowly filled each one with a sparkling liquid that bore an uncomfortable resemblance to methylated spirits, before adorning each glass with a small purple sprig. Ignoring the worried glances passing between the members of her audience, she raised a glass of her purple potion and proclaimed:

"In honour of the extraordinary book we reviewed earlier today, I hereby invite you all to try my new creation – The Lavender Screwball! A no-holds barred fusion of gin, limoncello and lavender syrup, topped off with a sprig of lavender. I'm sure you will all love it, but be warned – after a couple of these, you might start to find your cousins dangerously attractive..."

The women eagerly polished off the second cocktail and requested that Lorelei prepare another batch, to be consumed whilst watching the DVD after dinner.

"After all" reasoned Irene "there are no cousins around this evening, so we should all be pretty safe!"

Following the successful cocktail hour, the kitchen quickly morphed into a hive of culinary activity. Despite, or perhaps assisted by, the alcohol consumed during the day, Peggy, Jos, Irene and Anna worked together like a well-oiled machine to produce a stunning Italian meal. The book club feasted on insalata caprese, followed by osso bucco and finishing with tiramisu, all washed down with a selection of wonderful Italian wines chosen to complement each course.

After the lengthy dinner at a convivial table filled with warmth and laughter, the women settled down in the living room where Verity, Lucy and Jane had arranged the various sofas, chairs and beanbags in a semicircle around the large flat-screen TV. It was finally time for the much-anticipated screening of The Lavender Garden. Clutching their second glasses of Lorelei's purple creation, the group eagerly leaned forward to take in the opening scene.

Ten minutes into the film, the ladies of the Oak Welby Book Club were beside themselves. Never had a group of unsuspecting viewers been assailed by such an unexpectedly graphic and frankly bizarre sequence of cinematic images. In one beach scene, for instance, they were treated to swooping, close-up crotch shots of the film's swimsuit-clad stars, complete with imperfectly groomed bikini lines.

"Bloody hell – they should have called it The Lady Garden rather than The Lavender Garden!" cried Lorelei.

"They all need a Hollywood – like that woman had in last month's book!" added Alice.

The twins' ménage a trois was rendered in its unexpurgated glory - prompting shrieks of merriment from all those watching - and the film continued in a similar vein for the next two hours. The all-star cast delivered performances that fell into the 'so bad they're good' category, whilst the cinematography was clearly delivered on a shoestring budget. The frenetic, tongue-in-cheek romp left everyone exhausted from laughing and yelling at the screen. It was just as well that there were no other houses in the vicinity of Waterside View.

Afterwards, the exhausted but happy group gave The Lavender Garden an average score of 16 out of 20, for providing them with an evening that they would never forget.

"How do we follow that?" remarked Peggy to Irene as they headed off to bed.

"I suspect tomorrow will be a little quieter than today" replied Irene.

"Well I for one hope so" whispered Peggy. "I think we could all use a little down time".

Just down the corridor, Gemma and Alice snuggled into their cosy twin beds. Turning towards her friend, Gemma admitted:

"You know, I guess I was wrong about Jane. I mean, she seems to be fitting in quite well here".

"She certainly appears to be enjoying herself" agreed

Alice "and she really got into the Titswiping in the end. Perhaps she just took a while to come out of her shell. However, I still think we should do as Lucy suggested and keep an eye on her".

"Will do, my lovely" murmured Gemma sleepily. "Goodnight; sleep well. It has been a truly memorable day!"

❋ ❋ ❋

The next morning, an early mist was quickly dispelled by warm golden sunshine, providing everyone with a welcome respite from the previous day's rain. Over breakfast, the pyjama-clad book club members were in high spirits as they looked out over the glittering lake and the surrounding trees with their newly minted, lustrous green leaves. Eager to take advantage of the benign weather, they wasted no time in planning their various activities.

"I'm going to take out a rowing boat, like I said yesterday" began Emily.

"Could I borrow a kayak please, Peggy?" asked Gemma.

"Of course" replied Peggy "all the equipment is there in the boathouse, just waiting to be used. Is anyone else up for some watersports? I think you mentioned yesterday that you would like to do some paddle boarding, Alice?"

"I certainly would" said Alice. "I really got into it when we were on holiday in Italy last year, so it would be great to see if I can still manage to stay upright!"

"I'm sure you will. You can borrow Billie's wetsuit. I'm just sorry that we don't have a dog on hand to accompany you, like Deefer does with Billie" remarked Emily.

"I don't understand" said Jane, looking puzzled.

"My daughter, Billie, is really good at paddle boarding" Emily explained. "Deefer, one of our dogs, loves standing on the board as she paddles round the lake. It's the only time we can get him to keep still! Look – here's a photo on my Instagram feed. They make a good team, don't you think?"

"They look brilliant" agreed Jane. "It's a bit too advanced for me, though. Could I by any chance take out a kayak, if there is a second one to spare? I haven't been kayaking since I was a teenager so I won't be very good – but it would be fun to have a go".

"Don't you worry" Emily reassured her "there's nothing to it. You'll pick it up again in no time. We have a selection of kayaks, so just take any one you like, after Gemma has chosen hers."

"Does anyone fancy a game of tennis?" enquired Lorelei.

"Great idea – I'd love to!" cried Jos enthusiastically.

"Me too – but I warn you now, I'm not very good" admitted Anna "I play the girls sometimes and we occasionally have a knock about on court at school, but I always lose".

"I'm even worse, I guarantee" laughed Verity breezily "but if you can bear it, I wouldn't mind making up a four-some for a doubles match".

"Excellent – doubles sounds like a great idea! I'm sure it will be suitably chaotic, with us lot on court. Right, I'm off to get changed – how about I see you down there in about fifteen minutes?" suggested Lorelei.

The others murmured their assent and the four of them disappeared off to their rooms.

"Well, this all sounds way too energetic for me" Peggy remarked. "I'm just going to sit on the sun deck by the lake with a cup of coffee and watch you lot exerting yourselves".

"Sounds good to me – I'll join you" said Irene quickly.

"Me too" smiled Nicky. "Sod all that sporting nonsense – I need a rest after yesterday!"

"I'm going to take a walk round the lake" announced Lucy "then I'll join you afterwards for coffee and spectating. I'm not up for anything too strenuous either".

With that, everyone dispersed to clear up the breakfast things and get ready for the morning ahead.

An hour later, the various sporting activities were getting underway and Peggy, Irene and Nicky were happily installed on the sun terrace with a fresh pot of coffee.

"This is bliss" breathed Nicky, reclining regally on her sun lounger as she sipped her coffee. "I can't think of a better place to enjoy the first real sunshine of the year".

"I couldn't agree more" said Irene. "I never get tired of this amazing view".

"It's nice to see everyone enjoying the place" commented Peggy, smiling contentedly as she watched Emily and Gemma propel their respective craft expertly towards the far side of the lake.

"Ooh look" exclaimed Irene excitedly "here comes Alice on her paddle board!"

The three women watched as Alice emerged from behind the boathouse and glided smoothly away from the shore.

"Oh my goodness, she is so well suited to that paddle board" gasped Irene. "She just drifts calmly along like – I don't know – like a swan or something…"

"Or maybe something even more elegant than a swan" mused Peggy. "Do you remember that old song – how does it go - 'la la la, she looks so fine, like a flamingo'…" Peggy sang.

"Yes – it's called Pretty Flamingo – I remember it" smiled

Irene. "I think it actually goes 'she walks so fine' but I do take your point".

"That's just what she looks like" agreed Nicky "floating along like a gorgeous, willowy flamingo…"

The three women chuckled to themselves as they refilled their coffee mugs.

After a few minutes, a second kayak wobbled into view.

"Oh look, here comes Jane. Not quite as elegant as Alice, I fear" observed Peggy as Jane splashed erratically along, veering crazily from side to side.

"Never mind" said Nicky "as long as she is having fun, which she seems to be, that's the main thing".

The women continued watching as Jane weaved her way towards the centre of the lake. In the background they could hear the repeated 'thunk' of tennis ball hitting racquet, punctuated frequently by loud expletives and hoots of laughter. Clearly the doubles match was proving as chaotic as Lorelei had predicted.

"Oh look, Jane's starting to get the hang of it" Peggy remarked. "She's going a bit faster now, getting into her rhythm. Mind you, she's getting a bit close to Alice – she needs to change course now, and quickly…"

Suddenly, Peggy was on her feet, running towards the edge of the lake and yelling:

"STOP, JANE – STOP NOW!"

The resounding 'crack' of the kayak, as it collided squarely with the side of Alice's paddle board, reverberated across the lake, along with the screams of the three observers. On the lake itself, Jane dropped her paddle and clapped both hands across her mouth as Alice flew into the air and hit the water like an arrow, disappearing instantly below the surface. The only sight Jane had time to glimpse was a swirl of strawberry blonde hair, before it was swallowed up by the dark water.

"JANE, DO SOMETHING! HELP HER!" Peggy was distraught.

"Hang on – look. Here come Emily and Gemma – and there's Lucy. Don't worry – it will be fine" Irene soothed her.

From across the lake Emily, always a strong rower, was rapidly approaching the scene, closely followed by Gemma in her kayak. Lucy, who had obviously heard the commotion whilst on her walk, had stationed herself on the jetty next to the boathouse and taken off her coat, ready to wrap it around Alice once she came ashore.

"Out of my way!" yelled Emily roughly to Jane as she came to a halt alongside Alice's paddle board. Leaning over the side of her rowing boat, she reached down into the weeds that grew abundantly on the bottom of the lake and felt around with both arms submerged. A few seconds later, she abruptly pulled back and Alice's face emerged from the water, contorted with panic as she clutched Emily's arms, gasping for breath. Working together, Emily and Gemma hauled Alice into Emily's rowing boat as she choked and spluttered.

"I...I...was trying to swim to the surface but I must have got...caught in the weeds" she sobbed. "I was so scared..."

"Not to worry – you're safe now" Emily said gently to her friend. "Look – there's Lucy waiting on the jetty with a nice warm coat, and I'm sure Mum will have got the brandy out. Everything's going to be fine".

With that, Emily rowed off with Alice, leaving Gemma and Jane floating in their two kayaks. Wordlessly, Gemma wheeled her kayak around, grabbed Jane's paddle from the water and handed it to her. Tears streamed down

Jane's face.

"I'm s-so sorry" she wailed. "I didn't mean to – I just forgot how to stop – and then I panicked – I didn't know what to do!"

"It's OK – it was an accident; could have happened to anyone" replied Gemma briskly. "Let's head back and make sure that Alice is alright – but I'm sure she'll be fine".

Half an hour later, a slightly subdued group of book club members assembled in the living room at Waterside View. Alice sat in the midst of them, drinking a large mug of hot chocolate laced liberally with brandy and clearly none the worse for her ordeal. Jane, however, was still ghostly pale and stricken-looking. Noticing this, Alice put down her mug, walked over to her and sat down beside her.

"Please don't upset yourself" she said gently. "I'm absolutely fine – no harm done".

Jane, however, was not so easily mollified. Turning to Emily and Gemma, she whispered through her tears:

"I'm just so sorry I didn't help to rescue her. I just sort of... froze".

Emily had heard enough. "Look, we've established that you're no good in a crisis" she said airily "but you're still a Titswiper – you're one of the gang! We're all friends here – and friends forgive each other and move on. Well, maybe they take the piss a little along the way – you had best prepare yourself for that; but anyway, what I mean is – let's put this all behind us and enjoy the final part of our weekend. Shall we have lunch, Mum?"

Smiling proudly at her daughter's adroit diplomacy, Peggy immediately started laying out the copious leftovers that would form the final lunch at Waterside View. The rest of the group, equally grateful to be moving on, quickly joined in to help.

Lunch was a surprisingly fun-filled affair. Not for the first time, the book club demonstrated its ability to get past a crisis quickly and have a good laugh. Jos and Anna, in particular, were in good spirits, having beaten Lorelei and Verity at tennis. However, Anna confessed that she was starting to feel nervous about her daughter Alexandra's wedding, which was now less than a month away. Various members of the book club happily volunteered to help in any way they could; some agreed to put relatives up overnight, whilst others offered their assistance in getting Anna and Kit's large garden ready for the reception, which would take place in a marquee on the back lawn.

All too soon, lunch was at an end and it was time for the members of the book club to head home. Verity, Jos and Gemma, the three designated drivers, herded their passengers into their vehicles and squashed in the final items of luggage which, unaccountably, seemed to have increased in volume, despite the amount of food and drink which had been consumed over the weekend. Peggy and Emily, who were staying behind to do some tidying up, stood in the doorway to wave everyone off.

As Alice was about to climb into Verity's SUV, Gemma passed by on the way to her car and gave her a quick hug. As she pulled her friend close, she whispered:

"Remember what I said to you last night? Well I'm reconsidering now. I think I might have been wrong – about being wrong."

"Let's wait and see" replied Alice calmly.

Gemma squeezed her hand warmly in reply and took her leave. "Coming, you lot!" she yelled to her unruly passengers, who were waiting rowdily for her to drive them home. Eventually, with much waving out of windows and hooting of horns, the convoy of SUVs moved off and disappeared down the driveway of Waterside View, leaving Peggy and Emily behind. The book club weekend was over.

\* \* \*

That evening, Jane sat disconsolately at the window of her cottage, watching the darkness falling over her unkempt back garden and clutching a large glass of wine.

"Oh, crap" she muttered to herself. "What have I done?"

It had all been going so well. Contrary to her expectations and fears, she had actually had a lot of fun. She had even enjoyed that crazy Titswiping game – and the praise she had received afterwards for her performance. Once again, she had felt that she was becoming a valued part of the group – and then she had got over-confident and messed up in spectacular fashion right at the very end. Perhaps it was time to give up on this ill-fated scheme, cut her losses and move on. After all, that was what she usually did when things got a bit difficult in her life.

As she drank her wine, Jane watched a lone blackbird wrestling tirelessly in the twilight to extract a worm from the flower bed. In the time it took her to empty her glass, the epic struggle played out before her and the bird was eventually successful. Somehow it seemed like a sign – a reminder from nature not to give up.

Maybe all was not lost, Jane thought. After all, the book club members were obviously a forgiving bunch – and she still had time to spare. Time to start afresh and deploy a few new tactics. Glancing over at her bookcase in the corner, she spotted her favourite novel of all time and reflected on its indomitable heroine and her final, defiant words. Raising her empty glass, Jane cried to herself:

"Tomorrow is another day!"

With that, she tottered off to the fridge for a refill.

\* \* \*

# CHAPTER 6

*June Book Club*

T he weather that afternoon was remarkably hot and sultry for the time of year. Until recently, however, the village had been subject to an almost daily deluge of rain, so the huge expanse of grass behind Anna and Kit's house had grown abundant and lush. Anna had ample opportunity to curse these ideal growing conditions as she toiled up and down the lawn on her ride-on mower under the sun's pitiless gaze.

"Only a few more rows to go" muttered Anna to herself, staring grimly ahead as the bone-shaking mower inflicted yet more damage on a body already bruised and battered from her campaign to create the perfect lawn. If she kept up her efforts, their beautiful garden would provide an ideal backdrop for Alexandra and Tom's wedding the following Saturday – and that was worth any number of aches and pains. Indeed, she would happily sell her soul to Satan in order to guarantee fine and sunny weather on her daughter's wedding day.

Later that evening, relieved that her gardening was done for the day, Anna crossed the road to the Village Hall for her regular yoga class. Claudine, the yoga teacher, was an attractive Belgian lady whose melodic accent and laid-back vibe were guaranteed to soothe her frazzled pre-wedding nerves. As she entered the hall and breathed in the familiar, heady smell of incense, she felt herself instantly relax a little. Emily, Peggy and Verity were among the group of yogis; Anna waved to them and rolled out her yoga mat.

"Claudine, I have to apologise to you in advance" she called to her teacher. "I have spent so much time on my rickety old lawn mower over the last few days that my body is shot to pieces, so I'm going to struggle tonight, I think".

"Don't worry" Claudine soothed her "just work at your own pace and do what you can".

As the yoga class progressed, it quickly became clear that Anna had not been exaggerating. Her Warrior poses were distinctly un-warlike and her Downward Dog was more of a pooped-out pooch. Never mind, she consoled herself - it was better than nothing and would still count as part of her pre-wedding fitness regime, whilst the vibrations of the ride-on mower were surely more effective than any Power Plate.

* * *

The following day remained hot, but the heat was tempered by a stiff breeze, providing ideal conditions for the sailing trip on Tidston Lake that Jos had organised for Lorelei and Verity. Jos had been a keen sailor for decades but for her, sailing was usually a solitary pursuit. A couple of hours on the lakes in her trusty Osprey, bought when her well-loved Pico started to take its toll on her knees, was an ideal safety valve when the pressures of being a busy GP, wife and mother got too much. The winds across Tidston Lake could be tricky and unpredictable so, as she tacked and gybed her way across the water in all weathers, Jos had no choice but to forget her problems and leave them behind for a while.

Today, though, Jos had company; she was fulfilling a long-standing promise to Verity and Lorelei that she would take them out in her boat.

As a child, Verity had sailed with her father in Cheshire but, as usual, she had played down her abilities when talking to Jos, protesting that she was sure she had forgotten everything. Lorelei had never sailed before but she was a practical soul and a natural sportswoman; a keen equestrian who lived and worked in the countryside and used to ride to the office every day on her temperamental eventer. Jos was confident that, between the two of them and with a bit of instruction, Verity and Lorelei would form a decent crew.

As the morning progressed, it was clear that Jos had been right. The three friends made a good team and the two novices were soon able to relax enough to enjoy the ideal conditions and even share a few, snatched moments of conversation between tacks.

"Ready about!" shouted Verity cheerfully.

"Ready!" Lorelei yelled back.

"Lee-oh!" Verity cried, pushing the tiller firmly away from her.

The women ducked simultaneously and neatly switched sides as the boom swept across the boat, right over their heads. The sails flapped briefly, then filled pleasingly with wind and became taut as the crew hauled in the sheets and the boat headed off in the opposite direction.

"Beautifully done, crew!" called Jos. "I'm really having an easy morning with you two on board! You can probably speed up a bit, Lol – just pull on that sheet – great, that's fine".

"I'm glad our day on the water is proving less eventful than the episode on the lake at Waterside View" observed Verity wryly. "Although I probably shouldn't speak too soon. I mean, what was Jane up to in that kayak? I know I'm clumsy, but even I haven't drowned one of my friends yet" she joked, giving Lorelei, who was perched on the side of the boat, a playful but gentle shove.

"Neither have I; but there's a first time for everything" replied Lorelei, shoving her right back.

"I think she was trying so hard to fit in" said Jos "and she just got it wrong in that kayak. She's not really used to sports – not like you two. From what she told me about her background, when we were talking in our room, there wasn't much room for sports, or for any kind of fun, when she was growing up. I think we need to make allowances for her. Life has dealt her a few low blows over the years and she could do with some friends".

"I wish I were as kind as you" mused Lorelei. "I'm afraid I find her a bit odd and I'm struggling to trust her. Put it this way – I'm glad it's you and me crewing Jos's boat today, Verity, not me and Jane. I think I might have had to plead a headache if she had been coming. After all, it is terribly hot and the heat does give me a migraine sometimes…"

"Sorry to interrupt, ladies, but we'll need to gybe in a minute" Jos announced. "Can you remember how to do that, Verity?"

Verity shook her head in mute horror and Jos set about organising her crew to execute the manoeuvre. The incident at Waterside View was instantly forgotten.

A few seconds later, the boom swung abruptly across the boat with a loud crash, causing a dog walker on the nearby shore to jump in alarm. The sails flapped violently, but settled quickly, then Jos's boat sailed serenely on.

\* \* \*

Satan had obviously taken Anna up on her offer as the morning of the wedding dawned warm and sunny with just a light breeze. The whole of the village was dead quiet, as though it was holding its breath in anticipation of the day's events. Most of the book club members were looking forward to attending, as they were friends with Alexandra and Tom; the exceptions were Lorelei, who lived some distance from the village so did not know the couple, and of course the newcomer, Jane.

Inside Anna and Kit's house, the scene was slightly less peaceful, as was only to be expected, although with several hours to go until 'I do', the hive of activity was still reasonably well controlled. Alexandra, the bride, was having her hair done, the make-up artist was setting out her lotions and potions and the bridesmaids were drinking coffee, chatting and generally faffing about while they waited for their own transformations to begin.

In her bedroom, Anna held up her immaculately tailored mother of the bride outfit, hoping that a few weeks of healthy eating and garden exercise would have reversed the effects of the debauched blowout at Waterside View. Lifting her arms, she carefully slipped the silky, pale blue dress over her head, then reached in trepidation for the side zip and pulled gently. It slid easily right to the top. Next, she shrugged her arms into the matching jacket, did up the three buttons at the front, then looked critically at her slim, auburn-haired reflection in the full-length mirror.

"Yesss!" Anna shouted suddenly, jumping for joy and punching the air with delight. The outfit fitted perfectly and looked exactly as she had intended – stylish, sophisticated and classy. She hoped that her girls, and Kit, would be proud of her. Slipping on her elegant court shoes, she headed off to the bathroom in search of her most expensive perfume to complete the effect. As she reached the bathroom door, it opened suddenly and Caitlyn, her youngest daughter, emerged in her dressing gown, still damp from the shower and with a towel wound around her head.

"Caitlyn, what are you doing?" screeched Anna, her cheerful mood dissolving in an instant. "You're way behind schedule! Go and get your hair blow-dried – now!"

"Chill out, Mum, it's fine" Caitlyn replied calmly. "There's loads of time – it's you who is ready way too early". With that, she wandered off languidly in the direction of the hairdresser, who was now working on Elise's shiny brunette mane.

Anna stared after Caitlyn in frustration, feeling her stress levels rise as she fought the urge to try and control everything around her. "Relax" she told herself sternly as she opened the bathroom door. "Everything's going to be just fine".

With that, she stepped briskly into the bathroom, where her court shoes slipped uncontrollably on the wet tiles. Anna's feet shot out from underneath her and she flew into the air, landing heavily right on her bum. It was all over in an instant and Anna was unhurt, but she had still somehow registered the ominous sound of ripping fabric. Tentatively, she unbuttoned her jacket and felt underneath, checking the side seam of her dress.

"Nooo!" wailed Anna. "This cannot be happening!" The left seam of her dress had come apart, right down the length of her body. To quell her mounting panic, she counted slowly to ten and then took a look, concluding with relief that all was not lost. Thankfully, her sewing machine was still set up in her study, where she had produced what felt like miles of bunting over the last few weeks. With a little help from Elise who, unlike Caitlyn, appeared to be almost ready, she would be able to repair the damage and still get to the church on time. Just as well she had allowed herself plenty of contingency, she reflected, resolving to tell Caitlyn about the incident later and impress upon her the moral of the story.

\* \* \*

Two hours later, the last minute hitches were a distant memory as the congregation waited in anticipation for the bride to arrive at the historic village church, the interior of which had been transformed for the occasion by some helpful friends. Normally, 'shabby chic' was the kindest term that could be applied to the rather dilapidated building, but today it was bright, clean and redolent with the smell of the abundant fresh flower displays which crammed every available surface.

Suddenly, without warning, the expectant hush was pierced by the soaring notes of a solo violin, played with confident expertise. All eyes turned in awe towards the musician standing to one side of the altar. A glamorous figure with long, honey-blonde hair, her eyes closed and her body swaying in time to the music, she was sporting a stratospherically high pair of heels; a brave choice given the uneven cobbles on the floor of the church.

"That's Kit's sister-in-law" whispered Verity to Aidan, her voice wavering slightly with pent-up emotion. "Isn't she incredible?" Aidan, who was standing in as verger and preoccupied with his responsibilities, merely grunted in response. "No blubbing when the bride walks in" he ordered gruffly. He knew from experience that his wife could get a bit teary during wedding ceremonies, which he found intensely embarrassing.

Aidan's orders fell on deaf ears as Alexandra quietly appeared at the door, with a beaming Kit at her side. Indeed, quite a few of the congregation welled up and fumbled for their tissues as the poised and stunning young woman, blonde hair cascading down her back and train swishing regally behind her, glided up the aisle of the church on the arm of her proud father. Behind Alexandra her squad of gorgeous bridesmaids, stylish in matching lilac gowns, also drew many admiring glances. Meanwhile, at the altar, the tall, dark-haired groom, his handsome face suffused with joy, waited to welcome his bride.

Then, as the radiant June sunshine streamed through the church windows and romantic violin music played discreetly in the background, Alexandra and Tom joined hands, looked into each others' eyes as they spoke their vows - and became husband and wife.

* * *

After the service, Aidan the replacement verger grabbed the collection box and moved swiftly to intercept the first of the guests as they left the church. Many friends and family members, impressed by the venue but conscious that a bit of remedial work wouldn't go amiss, happily proffered paper money, but some of the younger guests, accustomed to London's largely cashless society, were unable to oblige. Aidan, true to form, did not let them off lightly. "No, I'm afraid we don't take contactless!" he jested. "The 21$^{st}$ century has not yet reached Oak Welby

– did no-one tell you? Shame – if you haven't got cash, there'll be no beer for you later on…"

As the downcast youngsters made their way down the hill towards Anna and Kit's house, Verity took her husband to task. "Stop torturing them, Aidan" she chided "and hurry up – we need to get down to the house for the aperitifs and the wedding breakfast".

"Will there be beer?" enquired Aidan.

"I don't think so" replied Verity "but there will be lots of fizz I imagine – plus red and white wine with the meal".

"So no beer, then" concluded Aidan gloomily.

Verity tapped his skull gently. "Just the one track operating in there today, I see?" she smiled. "Come on – we're going to be late".

The two of them hurriedly checked the church, locked up and followed the rest of the congregation in search of a refreshing celebration drink.

Later, after aperitifs on the expertly mown lawn and a delicious meal in the spacious, stylishly customised marquee, it was time for the speeches. Kit demonstrated his solidarity with his wife by delivering his father of the bride speech with a large split in his trousers, having suffered his very own wardrobe malfunction whilst walking back from the church. Thankfully, nothing untoward was revealed during his speech and one of the ushers had a spare pair of trousers in his car, so Kit hurried out to get changed as soon as the speeches had finished. Aidan noticed his friend depart and wasted no time in taking advantage of the opportunity afforded by his absence.

"Hey Verity, I'm gasping for a beer. I'm going to nip over to The Mallard for a quick one while they're clearing the tables and setting up for the band. Cover for me? I'll only have the one – I promise".

"That's a bit bloody out of order Aidy – at a wedding?" Verity was not impressed, but Aidan was undeterred. He looked pleadingly at his wife and then gave her the cheeky smile that had got her to agree to so much over the years – usually against her better judgement. Sighing deeply, Verity caved in – as Aidan knew she would.

"Oh – go on then; just the one. But be warned – if you come back and I am making a fool of myself on the dance floor, you have only yourself to blame". Verity's enthusiastic but ungainly disco dancing had often caused her husband to hang his head in shame. Aidan just beamed at her in reply, gave her a quick peck on the cheek, then disappeared.

Looking around her, Verity spotted Emily, Peggy, Gemma and Lucy, who had commandeered a few bottles of white wine from various tables and were wandering out of the marquee onto the lawn to enjoy the early evening sunshine. Grabbing her bag, Verity trotted out to join them.

✻ ✻ ✻

Aidan wandered into the bar of The Mallard, where a few of the die-hard regulars – Rick, Dave and Melvin, to be precise – were enjoying a quiet Saturday evening drink. In the corner, a group of regular diners were deep in conversation as they waited to be called to their table. From the kitchen came the distant sound, and delicious smell, of frying chips.

"Pint of Abbot, please, Toby" called Aidan as Toby returned from his culinary duties.

"How's the wedding going?" asked Toby as he pulled Aidan's pint.

"Great so far" replied Aidan "but I just really needed a

beer, you know – after all that champagne and wine".

Toby nodded in mock sympathy. "I'll be seeing you there later on, actually" he remarked. "I have been invited to the evening do".

"Excellent news" smiled Aidan "I'll be sure to save you the first dance".

"I'll look forward to it!" laughed Toby, moving away to serve his dinner guests.

A few minutes later, the pub door opened and in walked Jane, dressed smartly in a straight black skirt, black top and high heels. Spotting Aidan at the bar, she immediately made a beeline for him. "Hi Aidan, good to see you" she began. "Hi guys" she added as an afterthought, waving distractedly at Rick, Dave and Melvin. "Can I buy you a beer, Aidan?" she enquired. "I actually wouldn't mind a quick chat, if you could spare a minute".

"Sorry, not at the moment" replied Aidan firmly, downing the last of his pint in haste. "I promised Verity I'd only have one pint – I have to get back to the wedding. I'll catch up with you another time". With that, he placed his empty pint glass back on the bar and swiftly headed out of the door.

Jane gazed after Aidan's retreating figure with a look of annoyance, then quickly regained her composure. Leaning over the bar, she ordered her usual from Toby and bought a round of drinks for the regulars, who were happy to include her in their conversation.

\* \* \*

Returning to the wedding, Aidan was pleased to see that the band had not yet started playing and that, consequently, Verity was a safe distance away from the dance floor, laughing and chatting happily with her book club pals and their husbands. "Wow – that was quick!" remarked Verity as her husband joined their group. "Don't tell me you actually only had one pint – I don't think that's ever happened before!"

"Well, you can just put it down to my animal magnetism" announced Aidan proudly. "That new girl of yours – Jane, is it? Well, she came into the pub and tried to accost me! She offered to buy me a drink and said there was something she wanted to discuss with me. There was only one possible explanation – clearly the woman fancies me. I didn't want to disappoint her, so I downed the rest of my pint and scarpered".

The whole group burst out laughing at Aidan, who looked slightly miffed. "Everyone fancies you, my darling – in your opinion" giggled Verity.

"Mind you, we were just saying that Jane was a bit of a fruit loop" added Emily, nudging Aidan playfully and earning herself an angry stare from her mother.

"Well, thanks for the vote of confidence, so-called mates" pouted Aidan.

"Don't take it personally" Edward consoled him, patting his friend on the back. "Let me buy you a beer".

"There's beer?" said Aidan hopefully, perking up all of a sudden.

"Yes" replied Edward "look over there. Kit has set up an outdoor bar with several types of real ale for us, plus lots of rhubarb gin and prosecco for the laydeez".

"Well, happy days!" cried Aidan cheerfully. "I'll come with you and see what's on offer".

❋ ❋ ❋

Back at The Mallard, Jane was on her third glass of chardonnay and her feelings of rejection at Aidan's sudden departure were fading rapidly as the alcohol took hold. In fact, she was rather enjoying being the centre of attention and making Rick, Dave and Melvin laugh with stories of mishaps at The Mill, where she had earlier finished her lunchtime shift. One of the young waitresses had dropped a bowl of sherry trifle in the lap of a local councillor, who was having lunch with a group of his cronies. The councillor's very vocal complaints had caused her great stress at the time but now, in the pub, Jane managed to use them to great comic effect. She was just pulling her purse out of her bag to buy another round when Toby leaned over the bar and announced:

"Sorry everyone, but I need to ask you to drink up now. As I mentioned to you earlier in the week, I'm shutting the pub for the rest of the evening so that I can go across the road to the wedding – I have been invited to the evening do".

"No problem, mate" replied Rick "I was just off anyway". As the diners settled their bill and thanked Toby for another lovely meal, the three regulars got ready to leave. Jane, however, was not happy with the news, as she had been at work every evening that week and was therefore unaware that the pub would be closing.

"Oh, that's such a shame!" she wailed tragically. "The evening was just getting going, and I have got tomorrow off, so for once I can stay up late. Just my luck". Her shoulders sagged miserably as she watched her three drinking pals disappear through the door of the pub.

Looking around the bar, which was now empty apart from Jane, Toby suddenly had an idea. "Look, Jane" he began somewhat nervously, twisting a tea towel in his hands. "I don't know if you'd be interested, but my invitation was a plus one, and I don't have a partner to go with me. Would you like to join me? I'm sure Anna and Kit wouldn't mind".

"I'm hardly dressed for a wedding" protested Jane, waving a hand to indicate her black outfit. "I haven't been home yet, so I'm still in my work clothes".

"Nonsense – you look fine!" Toby reassured her.

"Well, if you're sure" replied Jane softly, a smile creeping across her face.

"Course I'm sure – let's go!" cried Toby, grabbing her hand and leading her towards the door of The Mallard.

As the two of them stepped outside the pub, their ears were immediately assaulted by the roar of an unseen motorbike, revving loudly. Pointing at the house opposite, Toby yelled over the din: "we have to put up with this every weekend! Our neighbour is something of an enthusiast, I fear".

Before he had even finished speaking, a lilac-clad whirlwind of rage emerged from Kit and Anna's driveway. Elise, who had clearly had enough of the cacophony, was storming towards the neighbour's house. Seeing Toby, she yelled: "He promised he would shut up – just for one sodding day! How hard can it be?" Not waiting for a response, she stomped up the steps to the neighbour's front door and leaned on the doorbell. As Toby and Jane continued up the driveway towards the lawn and the marquee, the bike noise suddenly ceased.

"Hell hath no fury like a bridesmaid scorned" mused Toby to himself.

\* \* \*

At that very moment, the wedding guests were treated

to a far more welcome sound – that of the band striking up. Most of the guests were veterans of numerous weddings so were not expecting much from the music, having endured countless mediocre wedding singers, lacklustre bands and dodgy discos over the years. However, from the very first track it was clearly that they were going to be pleasantly surprised. The band excelled at every genre of music, from rock and indie to reggae and even jazz, delivering old favourites and contemporary hits with real musical flair and skill. Gemma, Alice, Lucy and Emily immediately hit the floor, followed soon afterwards by Verity and her inept attempts at disco dancing.

As Peggy and Jos watched the action from a nearby table, they were joined by Jane, who appeared to be in high spirits.

"Good evening, ladies!" she announced, swaying slightly on her high heels and plonking herself heavily on a chair.

"Hello Jane" replied Peggy, looking confused. "I didn't know you were coming".

"I wasn't" agreed Jane "but I was in The Mallard when Toby was shutting up shop, and he invited me as his 'plus one'. Wow – isn't this band brilliant? Look at the bass player – he's lush. I'm going to chat him up when they take a break". Peggy and Jos looked at each other in alarm.

At that moment Toby appeared, carrying a large glass of white wine for Jane and a soft drink for himself. In common with many landlords, he very rarely drank.

"Hi, Toby!" called Jane. "I was just saying to Peggy and Jos how fabulous this band are – don't you think? You know, I used to sing with a band once, in a previous life. I'm going to have a word with them when they take a break – maybe they'll let me sing with them!"

At the end of their next song, almost as though he had

heard Jane speak, the lead singer announced:

"We're going to take a short break – we'll be back very soon. Don't go away". Ignoring his plea, and the canned disco music that replaced the live performance, the guests immediately abandoned the dance floor in droves, mostly heading in the direction of the bar. Meanwhile, Jane rose unsteadily to her feet and took a large swig of her wine.

"Right – here goes nothing!" she proclaimed.

As she turned towards the stage, Toby attempted to restrain her, saying: "Are you sure this is a good idea, Jane?"

"Yeah – don't worry – it'll be fine" laughed Jane, flapping a hand lazily in Toby's general direction and tottering off towards the stage, where the band were busy tuning up for their next session.

Toby shrugged and sat back down with Peggy and Jos plus Mack and Stan, who had just wandered back from the bar. "Toby" ventured Jos gently "did you intend this to be a date – you know – between you and Jane?"

"God, no" replied Toby quickly "I just felt sorry for her. She had nowhere to go this evening apart from back to an empty house".

"Well, it's very sweet of you to invite her" added Peggy "but you had better keep an eye on her. It looks like she's had a few". Peggy pointed over at Jane, who was talking animatedly with the bass player and waving her arms around.

"I'll do my best" promised Toby, nervously clinking the ice cubes in his Diet Coke.

A few minutes later, the band resumed with a superb cover of a popular indie anthem, much beloved by most of the book club and their husbands, plus many of the other guests. In an instant, the area nearest the stage was transformed into a temporary mosh pit full of sweating, leaping bodies of all ages, screaming the lyrics and punching the air. Jane, however, remained immune to the general mayhem, sitting quietly to one side with her legs crossed, sipping her wine.

After a couple more high-intensity tracks, the band fell silent and the audience became still, taking the welcome chance to get their breath back and gazing expectantly at the lead singer as he gripped the microphone stand and prepared to make an announcement.

"And now, ladies and gentlemen, for something a little more soulful. We have an unexpected treat for you tonight. One of your fellow guests, a former singer, has offered to perform for you. With us as her backing band, she is going to cover a classic track from the late, great Amy Winehouse. So tonight, singing the iconic 'Back to Black', I give you – Jane!"

"Oh my good God" gasped Peggy. On the dance floor, Anna gave a small squeak as she spilled her gin and tonic down the front of her dress. Emily, Gemma and Alice stared in horror at each other as Jane walked unsteadily to the front of the stage, wobbled momentarily in her high heels and grabbed the microphone stand for support. Then something changed. Standing before the audience in her black outfit, complete with laddered tights and smudged, panda-eye make-up, Jane suddenly looked like completely the right person to cover the song. Glancing imperiously behind her, she gave the bass player a discreet nod and the band launched into the introductory chords. Right on time, Jane came in with the vocal.

"He left no time to regret…" she began in a low, gravelly voice, clutching the microphone and still teetering precariously on her heels.

As the song progressed, the members of the book club

heaved a collective sigh of relief. "Actually, she's not bad" conceded Gemma.

"Kind of a cross between Bonny Tyler and Alice Cooper" observed Verity.

"Ah, don't be so mean" scolded Lucy "you can see that the words of the song really mean something to her..."

"I died a hundred times; you go back to her and I go back to..." Jane intoned huskily, bending over as if in pain and veering dangerously near to the front of the stage.

"I actually think that, if she can stay on her feet until the end of the song, she's nailed it" declared Emily. "I just hope that the family aren't too upset by her impromptu performance".

"Look – there's your answer to that" replied Lucy, pointing towards the other side of the dance floor where the bride and groom were swaying, arms around each other and phones held aloft, with the torch app switched on. As the women watched, more and more phones were added until the marquee was aglow with little points of light.

As the final notes of the song died away, the marquee fell silent for an instant and Jane peered in confusion at the myriad lights. Then, the wedding guests erupted in a huge wave of noise as they cheered, waved and stomped their feet in appreciation. Smiling shyly, Jane stood uncertainly on the stage until Toby gallantly stepped forward, took her arm and helped her back to the table where Peggy and the others were sitting.

"Well done, Jane!" cried Jos warmly. "You certainly were – brave".

"I don't know about anyone else, but I need a large gin" proclaimed Peggy. "I'm going to the bar".

"I'll come with you" said Jane. "I need some more wine after all that singing".

"Are you really sure you should…" began Toby, but it was too late. Jane had already staggered off after Peggy.

"A large rhubarb gin – with a Mediterranean tonic, please" said Peggy emphatically to the barman. "It's not quite a Titswiper's Tipple, but it's the closes thing I'm going to get" she explained to Jane.

"Sorry, we're all out of gin at the moment" replied the barman apologetically.

"What?" Peggy exclaimed. "You mean we have drunk every last drop of gin in the place?"

"Yes I'm afraid so" confirmed the barman "but we've sent one of the staff over to the Newgate Hotel in Oultonshore to buy up their spare supply".

Emily, who had just joined her Mum and heard the end of the conversation, burst out laughing. "So what you mean to say is - we have drunk all the hard liquor in the place and we're making a 20-mile round trip to get in fresh supplies. Amy Winehouse would be proud of us! Let's buy a few bottles of wine while we are waiting, then everyone can have a glass". A few minutes later, loaded up with bottles and glasses, the three women headed back to the marquee.

By the time the emergency gin supplies arrived, the band was in full swing and most people had returned to the dance floor. Jane, glass in hand, was swaying about on the periphery of the dancers when she spotted Sandy nearby and had a sudden flashback to the incident on the lake at Waterside View. "Shandy!" she yelled and began weaving her way towards him.

"Shandy! I've been looking for you everywhere! I jusht wanted to shay – I'm shorry for nearly drowning your wife" slurred Jane, looking up at Sandy forlornly, her panda eyes slightly out of focus.

"Don't worry; it was just an accident" replied Sandy. Moving quickly to grab Jane's arm and steady her as she threatened to topple over, he looked around in alarm for someone to help. As if by magic, Toby appeared at his side.

"Hi Sandy – I think Jane's had just about enough" he observed. "She's my plus one, so I think I ought to see her home. I don't suppose – I mean, would you mind helping me? It's just that – I don't want to be accused of…"

"Of course" Sandy cut in "I totally understand. You can't be too careful in this day and age. Stan!" he called out as Stan walked past with a tray of drinks. "Could you tell Alice that I'm just helping Toby to take Jane home? We won't be long".

"No problem!" called Stan, giving the two men a look of sympathy as they each took one of Jane's arms and ushered her out of the marquee. Jane opened her mouth to protest, but from somewhere in her brain came a small voice of reason that overrode the impulse and told her it was best to go quietly.

An hour later, the band finally left the stage after two encores amid noisy protests from the guests, who would happily have danced all night. Their disappointment was replicated all around the village, where residents had been sitting, and indeed dancing, in their gardens for hours, enjoying the impromptu concert and the warm summer evening. Reluctantly they returned to their houses and, even more reluctantly, the wedding guests said their goodbyes and departed in mini-buses or on foot. A superb day was at an end – but it would never be forgotten.

❊ ❊ ❊

Unbelievably, the sunshine reappeared the next day.

Wedding fever had somehow also survived the night, persisting despite sleep deprivation, hangovers and sore feet. By lunchtime, both families had reconvened on Anna's lawn along with various friends, to swap wedding stories and polish off the leftover food and drink. Verity was happily demolishing a large wodge of cheesecake when Anna came over to ask her a favour.

"You wouldn't happen to be passing Jane's cottage over the next day or so, would you? I think she left her scarf behind last night, and I'm going to struggle to find time to take it round. If you could drop it back to her, it would be a really big help." Anna held up a long, tasselled black scarf. "I'm pretty sure it's hers because the bass player found it on stage after she had finished singing – and she was the only one wearing black".

"No problem" mumbled Verity through a mouthful of cheesecake. "Aidan and I will sort it out on our way home".

An hour or so later, Aidan and Verity rang the doorbell of Jane's cottage. As Jane opened the door, Verity gave her a friendly smile and held out the scarf.

"Hi Jane! Anna gave me this scarf to bring round - she thinks it might be yours. Did you leave it behind at the wedding last night?"

"Yes, it's mine" Jane answered quickly, taking the scarf from Verity and giving Aidan a sidelong glance. "Thank you for returning it". With that, she shut the door firmly in their faces.

"That's odd" remarked Aidan. "I thought she might have asked us in, particularly as she said she wanted a word with me about something".

"I guess it's probably because I'm with you" observed Verity with a cheeky grin. "Clearly I'm cramping your style!"

With that, the two of them wandered off down the road, giggling and nudging each other like kids. From her bedroom window upstairs, Jane stood silently and watched them go.

\* \* \*

The following week, the book club held its June meeting in the beautiful, oak-beamed drawing room of Jos and Mack's lovely old house. Naturally, most of the gossip centred on the wedding, with the women clamouring to show Lorelei various different wedding photographs on their phones. One photo in particular caught her eye.

"That's such a beautiful picture, Jos!" cried Lorelei, pointing at a shot on Jos's phone of the bride and groom leaving the church amid a shower of rose petals thrown by the guests.

"It's funny you should pick that one out" replied Jos. "I was actually thinking of painting it as my next project for Sim's art class".

The Village Hall calendar of events had recently been enhanced by a series of art classes run by Sim, a talented Dutch artist who had come to live in the village. Jos, and other villagers with an artistic streak, were finding that their paintings were now of a higher standard than they had ever dreamed possible, thanks to Sim's expert tuition.

Jos had already produced a couple of very pleasing watercolours. The first depicted the wheat fields behind her house, whilst the second portrayed the beautiful wildlife pond in her back garden. Her latest project, an oil painting entitled 'Still Life with Quinces' had also garnered a lot of praise, so she now felt confident enough to try her hand at figures.

"I hope I'll be able to exhibit my wedding painting at the art class exhibition in August, alongside the rest of my stuff – if it's good enough" Jos explained to the group. Promising to attend the exhibition, and inspired by Jos's creative efforts, the book club felt motivated to move on and discuss this month's book.

The book in question was a popular, recently published thriller focused on an anti-heroine who is obsessed with a seemingly perfect couple she observes during her daily commute. As the book progresses it transpires that, as is so often the case, nothing is as it seems. Her real, far more dangerous obsession lies elsewhere and the perfect couple's idyllic lifestyle hides a dark secret from the past. Even the commute is an illusion.

The different members of the book club had a variety of perspectives on, and opinions about the novel, which provoked a lively and interesting discussion. Irene observed that, whilst she had found the novel quite gripping, she had actively disliked every one of the characters in it.

"It did prove to me that it wasn't necessary to like the people in a book in order to enjoy the book itself" she observed "but it did mean that I didn't care what happened to any of them. They could all have been finished off with a corkscrew to the neck and it wouldn't have bothered me!"

"I enjoyed the book as well" added Alice "but I made the mistake of reading the book reviews first, and I have to say I found them quite annoying. I should have avoided them and just concentrated on the book itself. In particular, I was irritated by the way they just over-simplified things by labelling the woman an alcoholic, which I'm not sure she was. I think she was more of a problem drinker..."

"I agree!" Jos cried. "I think she could have just been a normal, social drinker, if events in her life had not caused her to become over-reliant upon drink as a coping mechanism and develop a problem".

"That interpretation makes the novel more powerful, I agree" added Verity "as it enables us to relate more closely to her. For instance, back when I was drinking, I was rather partial to a can of G&T on the train home of a Friday night, just like she was – to celebrate the start of the weekend and make the commute more bearable. So I can look at her and think that on one level, I could have ended up like her, if my life had turned out differently".

"So, Verity, are you saying that we are all potential alcoholics?" teased Peggy.

"Well, Mum, they did run out of gin at the wedding, and had to make a 20-mile emergency trip to buy more!" laughed Emily. "Just saying…"

The group all laughed heartily at the joke apart from Jane, who looked distinctly uncomfortable.

"Well, as a non-drinker clearly I am safe" jested Verity, putting on a mock-smug expression "but seriously, I think drinking is just a side issue. The root cause of that woman's problems, in my opinion, is her obsession with her ex, and by the end she is over that, so she is able to start tackling her drink problem and the book ends hopefully. On the other hand, anyone who commutes when they don't have to, like she does when she pretends to have a job, is plain barmy I think. Beyond hope."

"And before you get too smug" added Lucy with a smile "I think that Jos is probably safe as well, due to her art classes. A student of mine has just completed a fascinating dissertation showing that art therapy can be really helpful in treating drink problems and other types of obsessive behaviour".

"Well I'll drink to that!" cried Nicky, holding out her empty glass to Jos, who was dispensing refills of prosecco.

"Me too, and pass the cheeseboard while you're at it!" giggled Irene. "Might as well be hanged for a sheep as a lamb..."

As they finished off the prosecco, cheese and chocolate cake, the group agreed that the thriller deserved an overall score of 15 for a storyline that was quite gripping although, like an old sofa, it did sag a bit in the middle. They also agreed that, although they generally liked a drink and a few of life's other pleasures, they hoped that they were more likeable and less obsessive than the characters in the book.

* * *

Returning home from the book club meeting, Jane dropped her bag on the hall floor of her cottage, hung her coat over the bannister and made her way to the kitchen. Once there, she opened the fridge door as usual and reached for a half empty bottle of chardonnay. However, as she was about to pour herself her usual large glass, something stopped her in her tracks.

Reflecting on her last few weeks in the village, Jane concluded that she had made progress in her year-long quest and found out some new and useful information. The wedding had been an unexpected bonus and she had, on the whole, enjoyed her evening, including the way that the guests had cheered her rendition of Back to Black. However, she had to face the fact that drink had brought her close to making a fool of herself that night, and it could derail her plans if it caused her to mess up over these crucial next few months.

The earlier book club discussion about problem drinking

had served as a timely reminder, thought Jane. From now on, things would need to change. A couple of glasses of chardonnay in the pub was fine – but the solitary drinking at home would have to stop if her plan was going to succeed. After all, she did not want to become like the woman in the book, whose obsessions were far too close to home for her liking.

Slowly, bottle in hand, Jane walked over to the kitchen sink. Before she could change her mind she unscrewed the cap, upended the bottle and poured the golden, fragrant white wine down the plughole.

✽ ✽ ✽

A couple of weeks later, Jos and Mack were enjoying a drink in The Mallard early one Saturday evening whilst having a friendly chat with Rick, Dave and Toby. All of a sudden, the pub door opened and in walked Gemma and Robert. Greeting their friends, they bought a round and were quickly absorbed into the general conversation. Rick was talking about one of his current work projects, which involved repainting the exterior of a large house further up the road.

"Ooh, that reminds me" said Gemma excitedly "how's your new painting coming along, Jos – the one of Alexandra and Tom at their wedding?"

"Very well" smiled Jos "Sim is such a big help. I'll definitely be able to display it at the exhibition in August, if everything continues to go according to plan. Also, what's more, we have a new addition to the group. You'll never guess who joined us, for the first time, at art class last week?"

"I've no idea – who?" enquired Gemma, intrigued.

"Jane" replied Jos.

\* \* \*

# CHAPTER 7

*July Book Club*

**U**nbelievably, the hot sunny weather continued into July, much to the delight of the children in the village, who were starting their summer holidays. For the Mums in the book club, this presented the annual challenge of how to transform oneself into a cross between a Butlins Redcoat and a short order cook for the next six weeks whilst still attempting to juggle a job, a marriage and a home. Some days, wine o'clock could not arrive quickly enough for these poor beleaguered women.

However, the school holidays did provide some respite for Anna and Gemma, the two teachers in the book club. Anna, especially, needed a break after all her hard work organising Alexandra's wedding. First, though, she was hosting the July book club meeting, which she had volunteered months ago to organise, despite the protestations of her friends in the club. As she pushed her heavily laden trolley around Tesco a few days before the meeting, she remembered Nicky laughingly calling her a masochist. She definitely has a point, admitted Anna to herself as she grabbed an armful of baguettes and stacked them in her trolley alongside the prosecco.

As she gazed wearily at the cheese counter, struggling to decide which varieties to buy for the cheeseboard, she felt a tap on her shoulder and jumped back in alarm. It was Gemma, pushing a far more manageable trolley containing depressingly healthy food.

"Hi Anna, what excellent timing!" cried Gemma. "I was going to drop you a text today but now I can save myself the trouble and have a chat with you I.R.L, as Tabitha would say. Have you got a minute?"

"Sure" Anna replied "this cheese isn't going anywhere. What's on your mind?"

"You'll never guess who called me yesterday" whispered Gemma excitedly.

"I can't even seem to choose a block of Cheddar today, so you're right – I'll never guess" responded Anna with a sigh.

"Arabella!" announced Gemma triumphantly. "Her contract in Dubai is coming to an end earlier than expected. She explained that the client is very happy with her work but there has been a change of strategy, so her services are no longer required. She didn't sound too glum about it, to be honest. Anyway, she is flying home tomorrow and wondered if she could come back to book club. Obviously we'll have one too many people, but what can you do? I can hardly throw Jane out at this stage, when she is just finding her feet. I guess we'll have to run with it until the end of the year, when Jane heads off to her new job in France, but I wanted to let you know and check that you're OK to cater for one more person at the meeting on Thursday".

"That's fine by me" smiled Anna. "One extra body won't make any difference food-wise and it will be lovely to have Bella back. I'm glad you caught me while I was in the shop, though – I'll buy a few more bottles of prosecco, so that we can celebrate her return in true book club fashion – with loads of fizz!"

\* \* \*

Later that same day, Jane parked her car in front of Nicky's salon. Inside, Nicky was in an excellent mood, as she and Bill had just booked a holiday in a glamorous all-inclusive resort in the Greek islands, complete with infinity pool, health spa, à la carte seafood restaurant and a secluded private beach. As she waited for Jane to arrive, Nicky bopped energetically around the salon, tidying up her products and putting on a pot of coffee.

"I'm walking on sunshine, yeah, and don't it feel good!" sang Nicky as she rearranged the bottles on their shelves, with her back to the door. As she turned around she jumped in alarm to see the unsmiling figure of Jane, standing silently in front of her.

"Oh my goodness, Jane, you gave me a shock – I didn't hear the door open! Come on in and take a seat – let's get you some coffee, then we'll do your consultation". Recovering quickly, Nicky brought in Jane's cafetière and mug and set them down in front of her.

"So, what are we doing today?" she enquired. "Same again – or something slightly more daring for summer?"

"Actually, I was thinking of something a bit more radical" replied Jane. "Could I go for an undercut pixie – and if possible, could we dial up the red a bit?"

"An undercut pixie, you say" repeated Nicky. "I'm sure I can do one – I'm just not sure I know what it is. I've never been asked for one before – a shoulder-length bob is as daring as my clients usually get. Hang on a sec – let me Google it. Here we go..."

Nicky held out her phone to Jane, showing her a photograph of a woman with short, vibrant, chilli-red hair, shaved closely at the sides and back.

"Yes, that's it. The model's a lot younger than me, though. Do you think that look would work on me – or am I too old to carry it off?

"Of course not!" cried Nicky, delighted. "It's really exciting to have a client who is willing to take risks and, as I have said before, you have the right face shape to complement a fashion forward hairstyle, what with your killer cheekbones!"

"It wasn't always like that" confessed Jane. "At school they use to call me 'Moonface'. In fact…" she tailed off and lapsed abruptly into silence.

As usual Nicky came to the rescue with her irrepressible charm. "Well, no-one could say that now, could they?" she soothed in a friendly tone of voice. "A slim thing like you – come on, let's get you shampooed".

As she applied Jane's bright new colour, Nicky attempted to resume their conversation.

"Actually" she began "I think that this radical look will go well with your new artistic persona! I hear you have joined the art class. How are you finding it?"

"It's great" replied Jane "really therapeutic. It certainly helps me get some things out of my system…" again Jane broke off and fell silent. Nicky, applying the last of her colour, ran out of ideas on how to revive their chat. Abandoning her efforts, she handed Jane a bundle of magazines and busied herself with other tasks whilst Jane's colour developed.

An hour later, Nicky had completed Jane's fiery red, undercut pixie and was proudly spritzing it with finishing spray when the salon door opened and in walked Rick.

"Hi Rick – you've arrived at exactly the right time" said Nicky warmly. "I'm just finishing off Jane's new look. What do you think?"

"Yeah – I really like it" mumbled Rick, obviously uncomfortable at being asked to express an opinion about hair. "It makes you look – well, all young and trendy".

"Thanks, Rick" smiled Jane. Briskly she tapped her PIN number into the card machine, said goodbye and trotted cheerily out of the salon.

"Nicely done, mate!" said Nicky, clapping Rick on the back. "That's the first time that woman has cracked a smile since she arrived. Quite the ladies' man these days, aren't you?"

Rick blushed and hurriedly took his seat for his six weekly restyle.

\* \* \*

The next day, Alice pushed open the door of the salon. Hearing the bell, Nicky came rushing through from the back to greet her friend.

"Good afternoon, my lovely!" she cried, giving Alice a warm hug. "I'm just making us a nice pot of Earl Grey. How are you doing?"

"I'm fine now that I am about to get my colour done" Alice replied, bending her head. "Would you look at these roots? It's my own fault, I know, for postponing my appointment".

"Not to worry" Nicky soothed her friend, ushering her towards her work station. "We'll soon sort you out – just take a seat. Right, before we mix your colour up, I thought you might fancy something a bit more daring this time. After all, you have been sporting your natural-looking strawberry blonde colour for quite a while now. I've just taken delivery of this new range called Punk Princess – take a look" she urged, plonking an eye-wateringly bright colour chart on her friend's lap. "You could go for one of these blues – or an acid green – or maybe even a vibrant red…and I could shave your hair a little bit too – just about there…"

Alice stared at the colour chart in shock, but only for a moment. Glancing up at Nicky, she smiled slyly.

"Ah – nice vibrant red, you say? Let me guess – you have been doing Jane's cut and colour, haven't you?"

"Yes – you saw right through me!" Nicky giggled. "She came in yesterday. That new colour chart is pretty scary though, isn't it? Same colour as usual, I assume?"

"Yes please" replied Alice "but you can put a few extra layers in my bob when you trim it – like you suggested last time. I'm feeling a bit braver after surviving my near-death experience at Waterside View – let's go for it!"

"Yeah – live dangerously" teased Nicky, heading off to mix up Alice's colour and pour out the tea.

Nicky had just finished applying Alice's colour when Peggy walked in.

"Great timing, Pegs! I can do your cut and blow dry whilst Alice's colour is cooking. Same as usual for you too, I take it?"

"Yep – same as ever" confirmed Peggy, sitting down at the basin.

"Conservative, aren't we, Peggy…" called Alice from across the salon "with our tasteful, subtly highlighted blonde bobs. Nicky was trying to tempt me with a green buzz cut earlier, but I respectfully declined" she smiled. "I'll leave that sort of thing to Jane!".

"She has gone for an even more radical look this time" said Nicky "but I have to say it really suits her. She was in a right funny mood, though, when she came in. I could hardly get a word out of her! I find her pretty hard to talk to – which is rare for me, as you know!"

"I struggle as well, but we shouldn't rush to judge her" warned Alice. "Jos mentioned to me that she had quite a troubled childhood".

"Well that was a long time ago" Peggy retorted briskly. "I get so annoyed when people blame their childhoods for their problems or their anti-social behaviour. They should just man up and move on, in my opinion! Mind you, I did hear another bit of gossip about her the other night at Knit and Natter in the Village Hall. I was sitting next to Mo, who said that Dave had been giving Jane the third degree down at The Mallard, like he does. She was pretty tight-lipped apparently – no surprise there – but Dave got the impression that there were a few skeletons in that particular cupboard and that she might even have been involved with some sort of cult. I told Mo that it was probably rubbish; after all, Dave is inclined to embellish his stories when he can't uncover the truth. Who knows, though? There might be something in it".

"Well – it's amazing what you learn at Stitch and Bitch!" laughed Nicky. "I must dig out my knitting and come along. Now, how's that water for you, Peggy? Is it about right – or a bit too hot?"

\* \* \*

That Thursday evening, Anna was hard at work in her large, rustic kitchen as she awaited the arrival of the book club posse. Artfully she piped thin strips of icing over a nut-free lemon drizzle cake that she had baked specially to celebrate Arabella's return.

In the dining room next door, the table was completely obscured by a lavish cornucopia of canapés, cheese and biscuits, bread, paté, crisps and olives whilst in the fridge, the large consignment of prosecco, generous even by book club standards, was waiting to be drunk.

As she was applying tiny sprigs of lemon thyme to the finished cake, the doorbell rang. Wiping her hands, Anna answered the door to be greeted by Lucy and Gemma, who had run into each other whilst walking up the road.

"Gemma was just telling me that Arabella's back!" said Lucy, giving Anna a hug. "Great news, isn't it?"

"Certainly is" agreed Anna. "I have made a celebration cake and bought in extra prosecco so that we can toast her return liberally!"

"Sounds perfect" replied Lucy "and, if I am not being too cheeky, maybe we can make it a double celebration."

"Why is that?" asked Anna, intrigued.

"Well – I received a letter from the lawyers earlier today, informing us that our offer for The Mallard has been accepted!" announced Lucy proudly.

"That's brilliant news!" cried Anna "well done! I just hope we've got enough fizz to do justice to a joint celebration!"

Over the next ten minutes, Peggy arrived with Emily and Irene in tow, followed closely by Nicky, Alice, Jane and Jos. Shortly afterwards, the doorbell rang again and Anna ushered Lorelei into the hallway. No sooner had she placed a glass of prosecco in Lorelei's hand than the bell rang yet again.

Rushing to the door, Anna flung it open to be greeted by a tall, tanned, glamorous figure, resplendent in a tropical printed T-shirt, pristine white pedal pushers and tasselled Todd's loafers, with a large pair of Gucci sunglasses perched on top of her impeccably coiffed hair.

"Arabella!" shrieked Anna "it is so good to see you again. You look absolutely marvellous. Come on in – nearly everyone is here. We're all so excited to have you back".

As Anna led Arabella into the kitchen where the book club members were gathered, there was instant uproar as the women jostled around the new arrival, hugging her repeatedly and all talking at once about how amazing she looked and how great it was to see her again.

Anna pressed a large glass of fizz into Arabella's hand and the group drank a toast to their friend. Eventually, when the hubbub had subsided a little, Irene asked:

"So how was Dubai, Bella? I'm sure it can't compare with the excitement of Oak Welby" she finished drily.

"Well, obviously I was working most of the time, but we did manage to enjoy ourselves as well" Arabella began. "The weather was lovely, of course, and we spent most of our weekends at the beach. George even learned to water ski – after a fashion! I've got the videos to prove it. I'm seriously thinking of sending them in to 'You've Been Framed' and bagging myself two hundred and fifty quid. We went wadi bashing in the desert, made new friends and got invited to some pretty lavish parties but to be honest, you can't beat the social life in our crazy little village! It's good to be back."

"I'll drink to that" said Lucy. "Welcome back. We're also celebrating some more good news – hot off the press. A group of us has put in offer to take over The Mallard and run it as a community pub. I just heard today that our offer has been accepted, so we'll be taking over the running of the pub from September. In fact, we'll be timing the opening night to coincide with this year's Oak Welfest. It's going to be a sci-fi and superhero themed night – I'll explain why later on" she finished, in response to Bella's puzzled expression.

"Well I don't know – I go away for just a few months and it all starts kicking off!" complained Arabella. "It seems as though I have missed such a lot – typical".

"You're right" observed Jos "we do have a lot of news for you, to bring you up to speed. Obviously there was Alexandra's fabulous wedding last month and then the month before, we had a very eventful weekend at Waterside View. Oh, and I almost forgot – how very remiss of me! We must introduce you to our newest book club member".

Jos held out her hand towards Jane, who had been standing unobtrusively at the back of the group, obscured from Bella by some of her friends.

"Arabella" said Jos "meet Jane".

"Lovely to meet you!" exclaimed Arabella, confidently holding out a beautifully manicured hand, festooned with sparkling rings.

"Um – good to meet you too" mumbled Jane, holding out her own hand with its bitten nails and chipped black nail varnish. She shook Bella's hand but failed to look her in the eye. There was a brief, awkward silence, until Irene observed:

"I've just noticed that Verity isn't here. Has anyone heard from her?"

The women looked at each other and shook their heads.

"That's odd" Lucy remarked "she usually lets us know if something has come up and she can't make it. I guess something urgent must have happened at work, and she hasn't had time to text yet".

"Shall I WhatsApp her?" asked Anna.

"No, I'd leave her to it" advised Emily. "Let's not disturb

her if she is under the cosh. I'm sure she'll turn up if she can".

"OK fair enough" Anna replied "let's move through to the dining room and make a start on the food".

The women happily complied and began filling their plates with Anna's delicious fare, whilst continuing to bring Arabella up to speed with what had been happening in the village during her absence. Jos explained to her about Sim's art classes and the eagerly anticipated art exhibition that was planned for August. She proudly announced that she would be exhibiting a selection of watercolour landscapes and still life oil paintings along with her latest creation, the wedding portrait of Alexandra and Tom.

Smiling teasingly at Jane, Jos remarked:

"Jane has produced a few paintings already, even though she only joined the class recently, but she is being secretive – she won't show them to anyone apart from Sim! The rest of us will have to wait until August to view them. You're very sensitive about your work, Jane – a sure sign of a true artistic temperament!"

Jane blushed but did not reply. As Jos turned away to speak to Irene, Jane stared fixedly after her until interrupted by Anna offering to refill her glass.

Lucy then regaled Bella with an account of the latest Village Hall quiz, which had taken place the previous Saturday. The quizmaster came to the village from Rushton Green several times a year and took great delight in torturing the poor villagers with a set of cryptic, challenging and unpredictable questions. As a consequence, each contest was closely fought and Lucy and Edward always fielded a strong team, which had won on more than one occasion. This time, though, they had been beaten into second place by a bunch of egghead quiz buffs from Lower

Bragbury.

However, Lucy's team was somewhat consoled by their victory in the Best Team Name contest. No other team could hope to match the ingenuity of 'Auntie Josie's Tartan Zip-Up Slippers'.

Peggy's team had surprised themselves by coming third, helped partly by last minute entrant Rick, who had joined their team to make up the numbers and proved himself to be unexpectedly knowledgeable, particularly whenever a history question came up. Those who did not attend the quiz expressed their surprise.

"To my knowledge, Rick has never attended a village event before – and who knew that he was so good at history?" observed Irene. "Perhaps Pat could employ him as her glamorous assistant when she delivers her lecture next week".

The latest in the successful series of Village Hall lectures was due to be held the following week. This time, the lecturer was amateur local historian Pat, a long-time resident of the village who was a good friend to most of the book club members.

Pat was a cultured, intelligent, incredibly knowledgeable but rather reserved lady. The villagers had therefore been surprised to see, from the posters displayed around the village and the leaflets posted through their doors, that her lecture was entitled **WOW**, which stood for **W**icked **O**ak **W**elby. In the leaflets, Pat promised to explore the darker side of village history including murder, prostitution and especially witchcraft.

"I ran into Pat the other day while she was walking her dog" said Alice "and I asked her about her choice of subject matter. She said that she had been inspired by the Horrid Histories series of children's books that her friend Marge had been buying for her grandchildren the last time they were in Oultonshore bookshop together".

The book club members agreed that the lecture was a must-see, if only to observe how Pat, with her gentle disposition, dealt with such grisly subject matter.

At this point the doorbell rang and Anna disappeared into the hallway, returning a moment later accompanied by Verity, who looked pale and unusually subdued.

"Sorry I'm late, everyone" she began "I've been helping Aidan pack. He's had to go away for work at very short notice – in fact he has just left".

"Why has he gone – what's happened?" asked Lorelei.

"Well – did you hear the reports on the news this morning about those two little boys who have gone missing in Manchester?" began Verity.

Everyone nodded.

"So Aidan has been asked to join a special task force assigned to the investigation – as he has such a lot of relevant experience from our own similar case a few years ago not far from here – do you remember?"

"Yes we certainly do" replied Peggy gravely and the group nodded in sympathy, remembering the two little girls whose photo captured the hearts of the nation and who would never be coming back.

"Do they think that this case will turn out the same way?" asked Alice.

"It's too early to tell" Verity answered "but in the meantime, they want to get the best people onto it straight away, which is why I'm going to be home alone for a while".

"How long will Aidan be gone for, do you think?" enquired Irene.

"That's anyone's guess" sighed Verity "he worked on the

last case for two years and I didn't see much of him during that time. Let's just say that I don't expect our paths to cross very often for the next few months, unless I make the trip to Manchester".

"Right, we need to cheer you up, you poor thing" said Nicky. "Anna's got some nice elderflower cordial ready, for all the good that will do. Maybe it's time to rethink this silly non-drinking business and join your mates in a glass of lady petrol. In the meantime, there is cake – and you can admire Jane's bold, trendy new haircut – to mark her emergence as Oak Welby's newest and most mysterious artistic talent!"

Verity looked over at Jane, smiled and made mock 'down with the kids' hand gestures.

"Radical, dudette!" she laughed. "Seriously, though – that's a really good look – suits you".

"Thanks" mumbled Jane, embarrassed as usual when on the receiving end of a compliment.

"Right, you lot" announced Gemma. "While we're on the subject of artistic talent, maybe it's time to review the book?"

This month's book was a historical novel set in the Netherlands in the seventeenth century, the golden age of Dutch painting. It featured a mystery painter who produced tiny, exquisitely executed portraits which appeared to reflect, and even influence, the lives of the characters portrayed in the pictures.

"As one of our resident artists, Jos, would you like to start?" asked Gemma.

Jos was very happy to go first as she had really enjoyed the novel. She described in detail how she had loved its deeply visual nature and beautiful descriptive passages, which she likened to a Dutch painting. She could easily imagine the deep blue and gold hues, the delicate lace that adorned the character's elaborate outfits and the dark, brooding menace of their canal-side house. She also found it very refreshing to read a serious novel in which the leading characters, who drove the plot forward and made the key decisions, were all women.

Irene was up next. She had also enjoyed the book, but found the closing chapters frustrating, as the mystery surrounding the identity of the portrait painter was never fully resolved or explained.

"I was expecting a big reveal, or a clever plot twist, towards the end, but it never happened. Now I know that some of you are quite comfortable with an inconclusive ending, but I like to have all the loose ends tied up by the time a book finishes, if you know what I mean."

Peggy and Emily, who both admired a well-crafted and robust plot, nodded in agreement.

Lucy was next. Like Jos, she thought it was refreshing to see female characters driving the plot, but she questioned how realistic it was for a novel set in the seventeenth century.

"In reality, it was the men who called the shots back then" Lucy asserted. "It felt to me as though she was overlaying twenty first century values onto a historical setting, which didn't ring true. For instance, the main character is incredibly tolerant when she discovers that her husband is homosexual and when her sister in law has a mixed race baby. I don't think people were that enlightened back then, personally. I still enjoyed the book, though".

The rest of the group broadly agreed with the points already made, until it came to Jane, who was the last to give her opinion. Tearing her ciabatta roll into tiny pieces as she spoke, she put forward the theory that the book was all about revenge.

"If you consider the image of the man being thrown into the water to drown, surrounded by his family, friends and adversaries – that was an incredibly powerful and disturbing portrait of people taking the ultimate revenge. I also thought it was a book about the deadly sins, such as lust, greed, gluttony, sloth – and particularly hypocrisy".

Jane fell silent as she looked around the room and took a large gulp of wine.

"Well, I think we're all guilty of at least some of those sins – thank goodness!" laughed Nicky.

"I quite agree" Gemma added quickly. "There's not much left of this wonderful food that Anna has prepared for us and I'm definitely guilty of gluttony when it comes to that cake! So, before we all add sloth to our list of sins, shall we score the book?"

The group gave the book a very respectable score of 16 out of 20 as they had generally enjoyed it, but had been disappointed by the way the mystery remained unresolved at the end.

As the women pushed back their chairs and prepared to leave, Peggy reminded everyone about the Wicked Oak Welby lecture the following week.

"Pat would really love it if you were there to support her" she urged the group.

"I wouldn't miss it for the world" said Irene. "I do love a bit of village gossip, even if it's hundreds of years old!"

The others agreed and most of them arranged to meet in the Village Hall just before the lecture. Then, after exchanging goodbye hugs, they headed off down Anna's driveway.

Gemma and Arabella were the last to leave.

"Shall I walk you home, my sweet?" asked Bella, putting an arm around Gemma's shoulders and giving her a squeeze.

"That would be great" replied Gemma "I have missed you".

As soon as the others were out of earshot, Arabella whispered:

"So, what's the deal with this new girl Jane? She seems rather odd to me – all this talk of revenge and sin. Not your usual book club topics of conversation! Is she just socially awkward, or is there something else going on there, do you think?"

"Oh, I'm so glad you said that!" cried Gemma with relief. "Some of us have been asking ourselves the same question. There have been quite a few weird moments like that since she joined book club. We have given her the benefit of the doubt so far, but I for one can't help worrying that she might be harbouring some more sinister intentions. I haven't told anyone else what I am going to tell you now – can you keep it a secret?"

"Of course, darling!" answered Bella.

"Well – when we were at Waterside View, there was an accident on the lake" began Gemma. "Jane was in a kayak and she paddled right into the path of Alice's paddleboard and hit it really hard. Alice fell into the lake and was under the water, out of sight, for nearly a minute as she got tangled in the weeds. She could easily have drowned, but Emily got her out, with a bit of help from yours truly – the two of us were boating just across the lake at the time. But get this – all the time we were struggling to rescue Alice, Jane did not move a muscle to help. She made out later that she was in shock and that it was all an accident, and she did seem genuinely upset at the time. Nevertheless, I can't help feeling that there might have been more to it than that."

"You mean – you think she might have done it deliberately?" gasped Bella in hushed tones.

Gemma nodded.

"But why?" mused Arabella. "What possible reason could she have for wanting to harm Alice?"

"I don't know" Gemma admitted. "That's why I haven't spoken up. Also, I don't think Alice is the only person who could be in danger. I have caught Jane looking at some other members of the book club with what I can only describe as real venom. Did you see the way she glared at Jos, when she teased her about her secret paintings? And she's always giving Lucy dark looks – plus a few of the others like Lorelei, Irene and even Peggy. I just can't work it out, and neither can the others who harbour similar suspicions. Lucy, Alice and I had a chat about it a few months ago when we first suspected that something was not quite right. In the end we agreed just to keep a careful eye on things."

"That sounds very sensible, my lovely" concluded Arabella. "I'll do the same. As I have been away for a while, perhaps I'll be able to look at the situation with fresh eyes and spot something that the rest of you might have missed. Right – that's me!" she said briskly as the two of them reached her house. "I'd invite you in, but there's stuff everywhere; I haven't remotely finished unpacking yet".

"Don't you worry" Gemma reassured her "it's late and I have got to get home. See you soon, old friend" she said warmly, giving Bella a big hug. "I can't tell you how good it is to have you back". With that, Gemma turned away and marched purposefully down the road towards her own house.

\* \* \*

Jane slammed the door of her cottage and angrily threw her bag onto the floor. Marching into the kitchen, she flung open the fridge in search of a bottle of chardonnay. Resolutions be damned, she cursed, reflecting upon the promise she had made to herself after last month's book club. This was an emergency. Sadly, there was no wine in the house as Jane had not bought any more since she poured her last bottle down the sink after the previous book club meeting and had managed, until now, to stick to her resolution not to drink at home.

"Shit!" yelled Jane as she began a frenzied search through her kitchen cupboards "there must be some booze around here somewhere". She knew that she could not drive to Sparkford Services to pick up some emergency supplies, as she was well over the limit after the book club prosecco fest earlier. Eventually, at the back of the cupboard, she discovered a dusty bottle of Bacardi that she had received the previous Christmas in the Secret Santa organised by the staff of The Partridge. She hated Bacardi, but she did have a few cans of Diet Coke in the fridge and needs must. Cracking upon the bottle and the first can, Jane mixed herself a very stiff Bacardi and Coke and sat down to think about what to do next.

No doubt about it, she thought to herself, this is a set-back, but it's not game over just yet. What she needed to do, she concluded, was to refine her 'Plan A', work out the finer details and be ready to execute it at the first book club meeting when the opportunity presented itself. She would also need to devise a 'Plan B' to have up her sleeve, should the opportunity to implement 'Plan A' never arise. 'Plan B' would have less of an impact, but it would still be preferable to doing nothing.

In the meantime, Jane reflected, there was nothing for it but to stay in touch with village life, work on rebuilding the trust of the book club members – and get to know the newcomer, Arabella.

"She has got sharp eyes, that one" said Jane to herself as she mixed herself another Bacardi. "Something tells me that Arabella could be trouble!"

* * *

The following week, Jane got held up in traffic during her drive home from work, so she only reached the Village Hall just in time for the start of Pat's Wicked Oak Welby lecture. As she walked into the room, she noted that most of the book club seemed to be in attendance, along with a fair number of their friends and family members. Looking around the crowded hall for a spare seat, Jane was pleased to see Lucy waving to her and pointing to a vacant spot between herself and Nicky. Emily and Arabella were immediately in front of them, whilst Peggy and Irene were just across the aisle.

Nicky gave Jane a quick hug as she sat down.

"A few of us are going to The Mallard afterwards if you fancy coming along" she offered. "It was my idea, I admit. Listening to people giving lectures isn't really my thing, so I think I'll need a stiff drink afterwards!"

Before Jane had the chance to reply, Pat walked onto the stage and the noise level in the room gradually diminished. Pat's tiny figure was dwarfed by the large projection screen next to her and she wrung her hands nervously as she waited patiently for the last few people to stop talking. Eventually, she walked to the front of the stage and made a start.

"Good evening everyone – and welcome to the first in my short series of lectures entitled Wicked Oak Welby – or WOW for short. As the name suggests, I will be focusing on the evil deeds and sinister events that have taken place in our beloved village over the centuries. Tonight, we will be taking a look at the period between 1650 and 1700 – a time when prostitution, murder and especially witchcraft were rife."

Nicky sat up straight in her chair and suddenly started paying attention.

By now Pat had overcome her nerves and her clear enthusiasm for the subject matter was shining through. As she talked, she began clicking through a series of images that would make a Hieronymus Bosch painting look tame and which were depicted in all their gruesome glory on the big screen.

Pat first told the tale of two farmers, Jethro and Edmund, who had been locked in a ferocious dispute over the ownership of a patch of land on the outskirts of the village. Jethro's hay bales mysteriously caught fire at the end of the harvest and he blamed his rival Edmund, although there was no evidence to place him at the scene of the crime. The following week, Edmund was found lying on his back in his barn, with his throat slit from ear to ear. Jethro was convicted and executed at a public hanging in the market square in Hanningford.

Next Pat recounted the sad story of a wife in her thirties who was in despair at discovering that she was pregnant for the tenth time. Although only six of the children had survived, she could not cope with a seventh, so she drowned the newborn in the village stream under cover of darkness. Afterwards, unable to cope with the guilt, she confessed to her husband, who promptly turned her in to the authorities. Like Jethro, she too provided an entertaining spectacle for the crowds in Hanningford.

But the most captivating tale by far was that of Molly, Anne and Maud –the three witches of Oak Welby. Molly was the first of the three to be accused of witchcraft, although she was youngish and pretty, so did not fit the stereotype of the snaggle-toothed old crone with the hairy upper lip.

Following the death of her husband, Molly struggled to make ends meet, so she resorted to prostitution. She was pursuing several local clients for non-payment of their debts, but the men joined forces and denounced her to the witch hunters. Molly was secured by ropes and thrown into the River Nass at Waterborough where she sank and drowned, thereby proving her innocence. Clearly this verdict was no consolation to the unfortunate woman.

The second woman, Anne, was older and looked much more like a witch was supposed to look, with her long, greasy grey hair and warty face. She was said by some in the village to have the evil eye and she also had a cat, which was enough to persuade the witch hunters of her guilt. Poor Anne was tortured with thumb screws before being burned at the stake outside the village church.

The third woman, Maud, was old and cantankerous. She also sported a bristly moustache, which was said to alarm the village children. Maud had an active mind, though, and made a number of prophecies which were said to predict the invention of the aeroplane and the motor car, among other things. Needless to say, the witch hunters could not get rid of Maud fast enough and she ended her life with her head in a noose.

The various members of the book club sat captivated and open-mouthed throughout Pat's lecture. Afterwards, over drinks in The Mallard, they all expressed their amazement at how unexpectedly dark and entertaining the lecture had been.

"Who would have thought that Pat had it in her?" Emily

remarked. "It's always the quiet ones, let me tell you!"

"Well it has certainly made me feel very grateful to be living in the twenty first century!" laughed Nicky.

"Me too" agreed Peggy. "In fact, I doubt that any of us would have survived for long in the fifteenth century – the witch hunters would have had a field day with us lot!"

The women laughed and topped up their glasses of prosecco. When their laughter subsided, Lucy added:

"It seems like the only way to guarantee your longevity in those days was to turn on your friends and neighbours and denounce them to the witch hunters. Survival by incriminating your mates, if you like. That's not how I would have liked to live".

"Excuse me" mumbled Jane, standing up hurriedly and almost knocking over the small round table in their midst, which was covered with bottles and glasses. "I have to head off – I'm on the early shift tomorrow".

As Jane rushed for the door, Arabella looked over at Gemma and raised one perfectly groomed eyebrow, before turning back to the rest of the group.

"Right" she cried "which of you old witches would like another drink?"

\* \* \*

# CHAPTER 8

*August Book Club*

The weather in Oak Welby that August had segued almost imperceptibly from hot and sunny to humid and oppressive. The trees, which had been so lustrous and vibrant in early summer, were now drooping wearily from the unrelenting heat and lack of rain. Similarly, as the school holidays entered their final weeks, parents' enthusiasm for spending quality time with their offspring was starting to wane and tempers were fraying.

Further south, the weather conditions were no different. On the day of the August book club Lorelei, that month's host, stood alongside her faithful Labrador, Clipper, in a large open field and prayed in vain for a cooling deluge. The field was dotted with strategically placed, brightly coloured obstacles including fences, tunnels, lines of evenly spaced, vertical posts and, at the centre, a large seesaw.

With the temperature pushing 31 degrees, today's dog agility class was not exactly going to plan. The dog owners, who normally enjoyed competing alongside their pets, were all complaining and sweating profusely; meanwhile, some of the dogs were taking advantage of their lack of energy by misbehaving at every opportunity. Coco, a wayward Spaniel/Husky cross, had taken off after a rabbit halfway through her round and had still not been recaptured whilst Butch, a muscular Staffie, had also finished his circuit prematurely in order to traumatise Trixie, a nervous and vulnerable Pomeranian.

Lorelei and Clipper were up next. Clipper was an eager competitor who bounded away happily as soon as the whistle blew and gave Lorelei none of the problems suffered by some of the other owners. Lorelei was proud of her but, as she panted and sweated her way through her dog's clear round, she could not help but think longingly of the cold jugs of Pimms that she planned to serve later at book club. Those refreshing drinks could not come soon enough, she sighed to herself, mopping her brow with a sodden handkerchief.

By early evening, though, things were looking up. The temperature had dropped slightly and, over to the west, the sky was tinged with the golden and pink promise of a spectacular sunset. Lorelei, refreshed after a cool shower, was pottering around the shady conservatory at the back of her farmhouse, carefully laying out canapés and glasses on the large table around which the book club would shortly be gathering. In the kitchen next door her partner, Lenny, whistled softly to himself as he tipped a cascade of ice cubes into a large jug of Pimms and mixed up a pitcher of Seedlip and tonic for Verity and the other designated drivers.

Suddenly, the peace was disturbed by sound of a car horn and the familiar small convoy of SUVs appeared on the driveway. Clipper bounced out to greet the new arrivals, followed at a more sedate pace by Lorelei and Lenny.

The book club posse was slightly diminished during this holiday month as Nicky was away with Bill on their luxury trip to the Greek Islands, whilst Irene was in Cornwall with Judd, plus their children and grandchildren. The remaining members of the book club were happy to escape from their cars after the half hour drive to Lorelei's house, which stood in splendid isolation, surrounded by golden wheat fields and leafy orchards.

Most of the book club knew Lenny but did not see him very often, so they happily rushed over to greet him and give him a hug. Lenny, resplendent in a scarlet pinny emblazoned with the slogan: 'Mr Good Lookin' is Cookin' gladly soaked up all the attention from the different women as he and Lorelei ushered them into the conservatory. A couple of his favourites were treated to a tour of his prized apple orchard before sitting down, but soon enough the whole crew was seated and ready to begin. Lenny quickly dispensed large glasses of Pimms and Seedlip before disappearing back into the house and leaving the book club to it, which was always the best option for any husbands and partners who chose to remain on the premises during meetings.

As soon as the women were alone, Anna excitedly announced:

"I was waiting for us all to be together before I told you. It's been a real struggle to keep it to myself, but I'm delighted to announce that we're going to have another wedding in the family! Elise and Ted have just announced their engagement although, luckily for our bank balance, they're not going to be getting married for another year or so".

The book club happily raised their glasses to toast Anna and Kit's lovely second daughter and her long-term partner.

"You know, I always thought that Caitlyn would beat Elise to it for some reason" Lucy reflected "but it's great news – Ted is such a sweet guy".

"That's not all, though" added Emily. "Elise has asked Billie to be her bridesmaid! Billie is over the moon – she can't stop talking about it".

Elise had often babysat for Billie and her brother Dan when they were younger, and the two girls had grown close over the years.

Verity raised her glass in a toast. "Well, here's to another beautiful bride – and her gorgeous bridesmaid. No doubt I'll be blubbing like an idiot again on the big day and showing Aidan up as usual. I do always seem to embarrass him on special occasions".

"There's nothing wrong with a bit of emotion" Peggy stated firmly. "Aidan needs to get over himself and be proud, rather than embarrassed. Maybe some time away in Manchester will help him appreciate what he has got!"

"Talking of proud" interjected Emily "I'm feeling pretty chuffed with my lot overall, for a couple of reasons. First of all, Dan has been named the Under 13s Regional Batsman of the Year. It's the first time an eleven year old has won the award – all the previous winners have been pushing thirteen. Not only that, he has won a place at the National Fast Bowling Academy, against some really tough opposition. Loads of talented young players competed to get in, so Dan has done amazingly well to be selected, I think".

The group agreed and passed on their congratulations to Dan who, like his sister, excelled at all kinds of sports. He was a really useful rugby player and a talented skier, but cricket was his true passion, so the women were delighted to hear that he was progressing so well.

"One of these days" remarked Anna "when Dan opens the bowling at the first test in the Ashes series, we'll all be able to boast that we knew him when he was young and just starting out on his playing career!"

"Hang on, though - you haven't heard all our news yet" Emily continued. "I'm also really proud of Josh, as he has been named as one of the three finalists in this year's Arable Farmer of the Year contest! The award is sponsored by Fabulous Farmer magazine and we get to go to a glitzy gala dinner in London in October, but that's not the point, really, although I do like a nice posh do now and then. The main thing is that it's a prestigious industry award so it's a huge achievement for Josh to have reached the final three".

"Is there a public vote?" asked Alice. "If so, we all need to make sure we vote for Josh".

"No, unfortunately it's not like Strictly" laughed Emily "text 1 for Josh, 2 for Albert and 3 for Eugene. It's a panel vote by industry experts, so you can't do anything to influence the outcome, I'm afraid".

"Oh I don't know" smiled Lucy "maybe we can arrange for the other two nominees to meet with a nasty accident or something".

The rest of the group burst out laughing apart from Jane, who remained resolutely stony-faced.

Once the laughter had died down, Gemma ventured:

"I'm so happy for all the good news, but as I'm among friends, can I confess to feeling just a little bit down at the moment? It's only because Tabitha is off to university in a few weeks and I'm going to miss her so much. I know she's going to have a brilliant time and there's nothing to worry about, but I just can't help feeling a bit sad".

Alice got up from her seat, walked round to Gemma and gave her a hug.

"I feel just the same about Beatrice" she confided "the

house will feel so quiet without her, but we need to just let them fly the nest and be there for them whenever they need us, as they inevitably will!"

"And if any of you need any advice about being home alone, you can always come and talk to me!" added Verity with a wry smile. "We can binge watch some box sets together".

"I take it there's no prospect of Aidan returning home any time soon?" Arabella enquired.

"Not while those little boys are still missing" Verity replied gloomily.

At that moment, as if he sensed that they all needing perking up, Lenny burst into the conservatory, holding aloft two trays of delicious smelling baked canapés, fresh from the oven.

"Watch out, ladies – hot stuff coming through!" he cried.

"Thanks, darling" laughed Lorelei "now if you wouldn't mind mixing up some more jugs of Pimms and Seedlip, that would be lovely".

"Yus, m'lady" replied Lenny, doffing an imaginary cap and putting on his best 'Parker' voice.

As Lenny disappeared back into the kitchen Gemma quickly called the group to order.

"Shall we start reviewing the book while we are waiting for a refill?" she suggested.

Everyone around the table readily agreed. They were all intrigued to discover what their friends had made of this month's curious book. An incredibly long saga, it charted the action-packed adventures of an ex-convict as he journeyed through the Indian sub-continent. In this autobiographical account the hero, who could not count modesty among one of his virtues, practically saved the entire region on several occasions by fighting wars, cholera epidemics and organised crime. With a blatant disregard for cliché, he also embarked on a passionate love affair with a woman whose green eyes were depicted using every simile and metaphor known to man.

Jos was the first to comment. She had particularly liked the sensual aspects of the narrative; the evocative and often poetic descriptions of the sights, sounds and smells of the region, which brought it so vividly to life.

Peggy, on the other hand, found the lengthy descriptions tedious; for her, they obscured the plot and were largely superfluous. Overall, she felt that the book was long-winded and self-indulgent, so in the end she gave up and did not finish reading it.

Emily managed to plough her way through the huge tome, but thought it far-fetched. She could not believe that one person could have lived through all the experiences depicted in the book.

"I felt the same" agreed Arabella, "but I kept reminding myself that it was an autobiography and should therefore bear at least some relation to the truth, shouldn't it?"

"I have an answer to that" began Lucy quietly "if you could all just indulge me for a moment while I put my professional hat on. I have thought long and hard about this and I believe that the author is suffering from what is known as Narcissistic Personality Disorder".

Arabella raised an eyebrow and gave Lucy a sceptical look.

"It's a genuine psychological condition, backed up by lots of reliable research studies and listed among the personality disorders in the Diagnostic and Statistical Manual, which is the clinical psychologist's bible" asserted Lucy in response. "The episodes in the book might be hugely exaggerated, as most of you have mentioned, but the author genuinely believes them to be true. His condition distorts his view of reality, giving him an arrogant sense of superiority and an erroneous belief that he is special compared with everyone else. This tends to be combined with extreme self-absorption and a lack of empathy. For instance, compare his 'look at me' approach with your own stories earlier, when you were talking of your pride in the achievements of your loved ones. This guy would never focus on others, except in relation to himself. He is preoccupied solely with bigging up his own achievements".

"I'm not sure I agree with that" remarked Jane from across the table, with a slight tremor in her voice. "After all, the author does talk about episodes in his life where he failed; for instance, when he was sacked from his job and when he was injured during the war. He doesn't always come out on top".

"You're right, he doesn't" agreed Lucy, "but these events illustrate another aspect of this personality disorder that does sometimes manifest itself". Taking a large gulp of Pimms, she continued:

"Sometimes, when a narcissist like this is exposed as not being superhuman after all, he becomes fixated with proving how bad the person who injured him is and how wonderful he is in comparison with them. People with Narcissistic Personality Disorder can harbour and nurture a perceived injury like this for years and become obsessed with avenging it, just like the author does with his former boss and his enemies from the war".

While Lucy was speaking, Jane's face had turned red; but then it was warm in the conservatory. Holding tightly to her tumbler of Pimms, her knuckles turning white, she stared fixedly at Lucy and retorted:

"Well I don't buy your theory; I don't think you can use psychology to explain away the mysteries contained in a work of art. I for one really liked the book as I felt that the author was baring his soul to his audience and at the end of the day, isn't that what art is all about?"

Lucy returned Jane's gaze with equanimity but said nothing more.

Lorelei was the last to comment. The host briskly brought the book review to an end by declaring that she had found the author's soul pretty hard going, bare or not, especially during the final quarter of the book, and had only just managed to finish reading it.

"Well, that was an interesting discussion" concluded Gemma tactfully "and quite educational, if I may say so. Shall we score the book?"

As Gemma worked her way round the table and collected the scores, it quickly became clear that this was going to be quite a low-scoring book. In the end, the book received an average score of 12 and was judged to have been enjoyable in parts, but generally both overlong and overblown.

At that point, Lenny reappeared carrying fresh jugs of Pimms and Seedlip, each piled high with cucumber slices, strawberries and sprigs of fresh mint. Smiling with relief, Lorelei refilled everyone's glasses and most of the women happily forgot about the book as they settled down for more gossip. While they chatted and laughed, behind them the burning red disc of the sun finally dipped below the horizon, washing the darkening sky with flaming jets of orange and red in a dramatic farewell gesture to a long, hot day.

Later on, when night had finally fallen and the book club was getting ready for the drive home, Jos reminded her friends about the art exhibition which was due to take place the following week in the Village Hall.

"It would be great if you could come along and support us" she urged. "We'd really appreciate it, wouldn't we, Jane?"

Jane nodded.

The women agreed that it would make a change from their usual leisure activities, which centred mainly around drinking and eating.

"Hang on, though" said Arabella quickly. "Let's not go mad. How about we meet in The Mallard for a drink first, before this onslaught of culture?"

Everyone agreed that this was a great idea, particularly as The Mallard had just starting stocking a couple of local craft gins, which could only enhance their cultural experience.

"Oh, sorry – just one more thing before we go" added Jos apologetically, as people stood up and grabbed their bags. "There's so much going on at the moment; I almost forgot to remind you. If you can, please come back to the Village Hall at the end of the month for the Fashion Show, in aid of the church restoration fund. I'm going to be modelling, along with quite a few other people from the village."

"Including me, but don't let that put you off!" laughed Verity.

"I've told you before – will you stop putting yourself down!" Peggy admonished her.

"You haven't seen what I have to wear" replied Verity "but point taken all the same".

"Henry has been asked to model some of the children's clothing" said Lucy proudly "so I will definitely be there".

"Excellent" smiled Jos "and, as if seeing your friends strut their stuff on the catwalk is not enough, we can offer the added incentive of a 20% discount on all items ordered during the show!"

This was enough to ensure the attendance of most of the women in the book club. They all loved new clothes – and they loved a bargain even more.

By now it was getting very late. Conscious of the fairly long drive home, the women hugged Lorelei and Lenny, thanked them for a fantastic evening, then piled into their SUVs. As the convoy disappeared up the road into the darkness, Lorelei put her arm around Lenny and murmured: "Thanks, Mr Good Lookin'. You came in with the Pimms at just the right time. Tonight wasn't the easiest book club discussion".

"Creative tensions?" Lenny enquired.

"Something like that" answered Lorelei vaguely as she turned and walked back towards the house.

*  *  *

Jane, Anna and Jos were travelling home in Verity's car. As Verity focussed on negotiating the unfamiliar, narrow country roads in pitch darkness, Jos took the opportunity to ask Jane a favour.

"Jane" she began cautiously "I have been sorting through the clothes for the fashion show and there's one beautiful dress that's really slim fitting. I think that you and Alice are the only ones who could possibly get into it – sorry ladies" she added quickly, looking anxiously at Verity and Anna, who smiled and flapped their hands dismissively to indicate that no offence had been taken. "Anyway" Jos continued "Alice is going to be away on holiday and to be honest, I think that the dress is more your style anyway, so I wondered if you would do the honours and model it for us?"

"Oh – I don't know about that" protested Jane. "I mean, I've never modelled before – I don't think I'd be any good".

"Nonsense – you're great in front of an audience!" cried Anna. "Look at how well you performed at Alex's wedding – you brought the house down! This will be a cinch in comparison to that. You'll walk it – quite literally!"

"Oh, go on then" said Jane, flattered in spite of herself. "I'll give it a go".

"That's brilliant" breathed Jos, smiling gratefully at Anna in appreciation of her help in persuading Jane. "The models get an extra 10% off, by the way, in addition to the customer discount – they're practically giving the clothes away!"

∗ ∗ ∗

When Lucy got home from book club, her house was in darkness and deadly quiet. A quick check upstairs confirmed that Edward and the boys were fast asleep in bed. Lucy knew that she should go to bed too – it was late and she was undoubtedly going to be tired when she went for her run and then dialled into her conference call the following morning. Right now, though, her mind had gone into overdrive and she realised that she was unlikely to sleep in her current agitated state. Instead she walked quietly into the kitchen, resisted the urge for a cheeky G&T and switched on the kettle instead.

Sitting down at the kitchen table a few minutes later, armed with a mug of supposedly relaxing herbal tea, Lucy replayed her earlier conversation with Jane.

"There's no doubt about it" she reflected "the gloves are definitely off. But what, exactly, is she up to?"

Half an hour later, Lucy concluded that she could waste

a lot of time and energy trying in vain to decipher Jane's plans and motives. There was only one thing for it – make like a Boy Scout and be prepared. As she finished her tea, she resolved to fire up her laptop extra early tomorrow morning and make a start on the preparations after her run but before her conference call. Feeling calmer now that she could see a way forward, Lucy popped her mug in the dishwasher and headed off to bed.

❋ ❋ ❋

The following morning dawned as hot and humid as the morning before – and the one before that. Standing outside her house in her most sweat-wicking running gear, Lucy waited for Gemma to appear. The two running partners had brought their training run forward by half an hour in a bid to outwit the heat, but the heat clearly had other plans and had easily matched their new start time. Lucy was sweating profusely before she had even finished her stretching exercises. As she looked up from a hamstring stretch, Gemma came jogging round the corner and stopped beside her. Although her house was only just down the road from Lucy's, she was already breathing heavily.

"Morning love" she panted. "There is a fundamental flaw in training for an autumn half marathon, isn't there?"

"You mean – having to do your training runs during the hottest part of the summer?" Lucy raised an eyebrow.

"Precisely". Gemma wiped the sweat from her forehead with her wristband.

"What's the alternative, though? Training for a spring half marathon during the depths of winter!" replied Lucy with a smile.

"Dead right – so how come we have signed up for the Bronford Heath half marathon next March, as well as Rushton Green this October?" asked Gemma.

"Because we're masochists, that's why. Come on – let's do this". Lucy trotted off up the hill and Gemma took her place alongside her.

For most of their run, the two running partners kept a companionable silence, conserving their oxygen to help them cope with the temperature that was still rising without remorse. It was not until they were nearly home, and on a downhill stretch, that Gemma found the energy to broach the subject of the previous night's book club.

"Now Lucy, I know you'll tell me if I am reading too much into this, but I get the distinct impression that Jane isn't your biggest fan, after what she said last night".

"For once I'm not going to accuse you of exaggerating" Lucy panted. "I do actually feel as though she has got it in for me. I'm going to keep a close eye on her from now on, but I'm determined not to change my behaviour. I'll go to the art exhibition and the fashion show as planned and see what happens. I'm fairly sure I can cope with anything she throws my way".

"I'm sure you can" Gemma agreed. "If you can handle training runs in this heat, you've got to be pretty determined – in fact, we both have. Talking of which – take a look at this!" Gemma triumphantly held out her wrist to show Lucy her training watch as the two of them slowed to a halt outside Lucy's house.

"That's nearly a 30-second improvement on our previous time for that route! A bit of adversity is clearly good for us!" Gemma winked at her friend.

"That's great – well done us!" replied Lucy, wishing that she felt more enthusiastic. As she waved goodbye to her friend and headed indoors for a cool shower, she felt vaguely guilty for not revealing more to Gemma about the preparations she was making. For now, though, she was inclined to keep her own counsel. It just felt like the wisest thing to do.

\* \* \*

The following week, the various members of the book club gathered in The Mallard to sample the new varieties of gin that Toby had got in stock and consume a few bottles of prosecco before the art exhibition. As they were enjoying their first round of drinks, Rick wandered over. The women stared at him in surprise; Rick usually avoided large groups of women in the pub, particularly when they were laughing and making noise, which was invariably the case with the book club.

"Hi Jos" muttered Rick awkwardly. "What time does the exhibition close tonight?"

"It's on until nine" replied Jos.

"OK thanks; I'll come along later and take a look".

As Rick turned and headed back to the bar, the women stared at each other, puzzled.

"What has got into that guy?" whispered Irene. "I wouldn't have thought an art exhibition was his thing".

"Damned if I know" answered Nicky. "I've asked him about it in the salon, but he's playing his cards very close to his chest".

"Right, we had better head off, Jane" announced Jos suddenly. "We need to make sure that our pictures are displayed correctly before our public arrives!"

Jane quickly downed the remains of her wine, then stood

up and followed Jos out of The Mallard and over to the Village Hall next door.

Half an hour later the other women, feeling cheery and lively after a few gins and glasses of fizz, decided that they had better head over to the Village Hall and take in the exhibition, before the evening descended into a full-scale piss-up.

As the giggly group entered the hall and took in the first few paintings, they were suddenly very glad that they had dragged themselves away from the pub. Sim, the art teacher, had exhibited some of his own recent paintings and the women fell silent as they gazed in awe at his superbly executed interpretation of their little village.

"Wow, that guy is seriously talented" gasped Arabella. "I'm not surprised to see a few 'Sold' tags on his paintings. I'm going to talk to George about buying some of his work – I reckon it could be a good investment".

The group then moved on to look at Pat's paintings, which included competent and colourful images of her beautiful garden plus a cute portrait of Dolly, her friendly little dog.

Jos's paintings were next. Her friends exclaimed with delight as they took in her detailed and skilful watercolour landscapes and noted with satisfaction that her 'Still Life with Quinces' was already sporting a 'Sold' tag. The jewel in the crown, however, was undoubtedly her stunning portrait of Alexandra and Tom outside the church after their wedding. Nervously, Jos looked over at Anna, who met her gaze with tears in her eyes.

"Oh Jos, you have done them proud" Anna whispered. "This must have taken you forever to paint – and you have captured the two of them perfectly".

"You don't know what a relief it is to hear you say that"

breathed Jos. "I was so worried that you might not like it".

"I love it so much that I want to be able to look at it every day" Anna reassured her. "I would like to buy it, please; I don't care how much it costs".

Without speaking, Jos held up a tag attached to the painting, which bore the words 'Not for Sale'. Then, seeing Anna's crestfallen face, she quickly turned the tag over to reveal the words 'Reserved for Anna and Kit – Free of Charge'.

Anna grabbed Jos and hugged her tightly. "Thank you so very much" she whispered. "That's the best present ever".

"Let's go and have a look at Jane's paintings" suggested Irene, pointing to the far corner of the Village Hall where Jane stood, encircled by a group of paintings facing inward, so that visitors had to make a special effort to see them.

The women walked across the room towards Jane. "Watch out Jane – the critics are coming!" called Nicky cheerfully. Nudging each other and giggling, they jostled their way into the centre of the circle, then abruptly fell silent.

The pastel and vibrant colours used by the other artists were absent in Jane's work. In stark contrast to the rest of the paintings, hers were brutally rendered in violent shocks of red and black. Tortured images of faces in agony, reminiscent of The Scream by Edvard Munch, filled every canvas, whilst the background to each painting was raw and industrial. Smoke billowed from towering, ominous chimneys and tiny, insignificant figures tumbled into the gaping jaws of fiery, gluttonous furnaces. Jane's paintings were a world away from the gentle landscapes and sympathetic portraits produced by the other members of the art class, but there was no denying their raw, visceral power.

The women stood in silence, unsure of what to say. Peggy, always one to speak her mind, was the first to comment.

"I must say, these really pack a punch" she ventured. "Well done, Jane, for doing something different and being so brave!"

"Yes I agree" added Lucy. "After all, you said yourself at book club that art was all about baring your soul, and these pictures really feel incredibly – how can I put it - honest".

Jane glared suspiciously at Lucy, unsure about how to interpret her remarks. The group collectively held its breath, and the tension was such that they did not notice a new spectator quietly joining them among the circle of paintings, until the newcomer broke the silence by asking:

"Er – that painting over there – I really like it. I mean, I like all of them, but that's my favourite. Can I buy it, if that's OK?"

"Yes of course, Rick" smiled Jane.

Walking over to the largest picture, she proudly attached a 'Sold' tag, which dangled over the canvas, obscuring one of the eyes in the scarred and tormented face.

* * *

Towards the end of the month, most members of the book club reassembled for the fashion show hoping for a relaxed and entertaining evening with no drama, after the tense episodes at both book club and the art exhibition. Arriving only a few minutes before the first models were due to grace the catwalk, they quickly grabbed some drinks and sat down together in a group near the front, ready to bag themselves a few bargains.

The show began with a lively performance by various young people from the village, including Edward and Lucy's eldest son Henry, who looked cool and self-assured in a series of hoodies, T-shirts, jeans and trainers.

"Very hip and trendy!" whispered Nicky to Lucy as Henry slouched past them, stepping in time to a gangsta rap soundtrack that neither of them remotely recognised.

The teenagers were followed by the men of the village, starting with George, who looked stylish and sophisticated in a series of nautical-inspired outfits. Next up were Mack, Stan and Judd, all dressed in a smarter version of the country clothes they usually wore every day. The men had no problem with the clothes, but were struggling with the accessories they had been allocated, which included fancy gloves and hats, jaunty scarves and even a couple of man bags.

"I need a beer" growled Mack to Stan as the two of them attempted to saunter casually down the catwalk. "Me too" grumbled Stan, pushing his hat out of his eyes and shoving the shoulder strap of his man bag back into place. "How the bloody hell did we get talked into this?"

Backstage, the women were getting changed in preparation for their set. Jos, who was all ready for the catwalk in an elegant, full-length evening gown, was helping Verity, dressed in tight jeans and a leather biker jacket, to put on a pair of pointed stiletto boots.

"This outfit is not a good idea, believe me" grumbled Verity, slapping a dollop of Grubby Putty on her head and combing her short hair back into a slick DA. "I can't walk in heels – it'll all end in tears, let me tell you".

"Nonsense" Jos soothed her "you will be fine. Just take it slowly".

As the two were talking, Jane disappeared behind the

modesty curtain to get changed into her slim-fitting, bright red cocktail dress. A minute later, she cried out to Jos in dismay:

"I can't wear this, Jos! You never told me that it was backless!"

"That's precisely why I picked you to wear it, Jane" replied Jos firmly. Conscious that Jane was susceptible to a little flattery, she quickly added:

"You are the perfect person to carry off a slinky, skimpy dress like that. Not many people could wear it, but you definitely can!"

Without waiting for any further objections, Jos sashayed out onto the catwalk to introduce the women's set, which would form the final, climactic part of the show.

In the end, the women's fashions drew enthusiastic applause from the audience and numerous orders were placed for the different garments, modelled with varying degrees of style and glamour by the women of the village. Jos remained poised and elegant throughout several costume changes but Verity, as she predicted, had a few mishaps when modelling her tight biker gear, as she wobbled and stumbled on her high heels like Bambi on ice. However, she recovered well and made the audience laugh with a couple of strategic bum wiggles.

Jane was the last model, tasked with bringing the fashion show to a dramatic conclusion. As she waited anxiously for Jos to finish showcasing the penultimate outfit, she kept a blanket wrapped tightly around her shoulders. Then, as Jos left the catwalk to rapturous applause, she defiantly threw off the blanket and strode haughtily down the runway with her head held high.

The audience clapped and cheered as they took in the front view of Jane's scarlet, shiny, figure hugging dress, which looked sensational on her skinny figure. Then, as Jane passed them by and they saw her from the rear, their expressions instantly changed. The backless gown revealed two large tattoos, which covered most of Jane's back. The first took the form of an enormous dagger, with blood dripping from its tip. The second was a large red heart, jaggedly torn apart into two broken pieces.

* * *

# CHAPTER 9

*September Book Club*

As the summer in Oak Welby drew towards a close, the weather turned cooler and fresher but remained mostly dry and sunny, fuelling the new found air of optimism around the village. For the many villagers whose lives had always revolved around the academic calendar, September felt like the real New Year – a time of anticipation, fresh starts and clean slates. Children were gearing up for their return to school, whilst those moving on to University were preparing for their new adventure and the Bacchanalian festival of indulgence otherwise known as Freshers' Week.

At the same time, the village was busy making preparations for its own unique festival; the annual three-day party and drinking spree known as Oak Welfest. Traditionally, proceedings kicked off on Friday night with Mallard Mayhem, a raucous pub night with German food and a quiz with a Teutonic theme, plus karaoke. The main event, Oktoberfest, followed on Saturday night in the Village Hall and the festival culminated in a bike ride and barbecue on the Sunday. This year, though, was special, as the investor group was officially taking over the management of The Mallard on that same Friday. To mark this change, and as promised by the group earlier in the year, Mallard Mayhem was going to be reimagined as a sci-fi and superheroes night for this year only, in honour of Edward's now well-known spoof.

* * *

In Peggy and Stan's cottage, Irene and Peggy were meant to be spending the morning sorting through the boxes of old clothes in the attic in search of garments that they could repurpose into sci-fi costumes for the Friday night. However, Irene the master baker had brought a ginger cake with her, still warm from the oven, and the two old friends were taking some time out first to enjoy a few slices with a cup of tea, before climbing the loft ladder and getting stuck in.

"Well I don't think I have ever seen anything like it – at least, not in Oak Welby" said Peggy as she removed the tea cosy and poured the tea.

"Oh I don't know" countered Irene "Ron's got quite a few large ones on his legs and arms – you can see them in the summer, when he comes into The Mallard in his shorts and T-shirt".

"That's true; but I meant on a woman. And I'm not just talking about the size of the tattoo – it's the design as well. A big knife, and all that blood – whatever was she thinking, when she had it done?" Peggy mused, slicing into the cake.

"I've no idea, but I have a feeling she regrets it now. Jos said that she didn't want to model that dress once she found out it was backless. I think Jos feels a bit bad for pushing her into it but in my opinion, Jane shouldn't feel embarrassed about her tattoo" Irene concluded firmly.

"Why do you say that?" enquired Peggy through a mouthful of cake.

"Well you know what – I think Jane has shaken us all up a bit, what with her hairstyle, her paintings, her tattoos – and her challenging ideas about some of the books we have read this year. That's no bad thing in my view. It's got to be good for us to be made to think differently about things, otherwise we could just get too set in our ways. I mean, think back to the things that you and I used to wear – and do – back in the '70s, before all this political correctness started up. We didn't care what people thought back then, did we? Jane has reminded me of how we used to be – and I think it's time we recaptured some of that spirit. Come on Pegs; let's go up into the loft and see what we can find to dress up in. It's high time we gave our younger friends a bit of a surprise!"

"Have you been drinking, Irene – or did you put something in that cake?" laughed Peggy as she got to her feet and followed her friend out into the hallway to get the loft ladder down.

An hour later the two women, covered in dust and cobwebs, were starting to despair of finding anything suitable.

"I wouldn't bother with this bag, Irene" sighed Peggy "it's just got some of Stan's old work clothes in it".

"Let me have a quick look, just in case". Irene pulled the bulging bin liner towards her and delved into its contents. After a minute or so, she triumphantly pulled out a malodorous grey garment. "This will do just fine!" she cried.

"That's one of Stan's old work overalls" said Peggy, looking puzzled. "Whatever are you going to do with that?"

"You'll see" replied Irene with a smile. "I have a cunning

plan".

Peggy shrugged, then opened up a battered suitcase and waved a jaunty felt hat at her friend. "Now this really does take me back. Do you remember that '60s theme night we went to at the rugby club – it's got to have been when Mum was still alive. I thought we had thrown our outfits away but here they are. I don't know about you, but I feel a bit of time travel coming on. You're right – maybe Jane isn't the only one who can make a few waves around here!"

"That's the spirit!" laughed Irene. "Let's go back down, have some more tea and cake and finish sorting our outfits out. I'm starting to look forward to this sci-fi night!"

*  *  *

For the busy investor group, the sci-fi evening came upon them very quickly, as they had all been busy with the handover preparations. However, they had still found the time to give the pub a comprehensive sci-fi makeover and, with only half an hour to go until opening time, Lucy and Alice were busy putting the finishing touches to the temporary décor.

The whole interior of the building, including the toilets, was plastered with classic sci-fi film posters and blown-up illustrations from well-known books and computer games. Women wishing to powder their noses would be doing so under the watchful gaze of Darth Vader and Iron Man, whilst men paying a visit to the Gents would be able to look upon Barbarella and Wonder Woman. In the bar a large, polystyrene Dalek, donated by Sandy's mate who worked in the BBC Props Department, took pride of place, and every available surface was adorned with sci-fi paraphernalia, loaned by all the closet village geeks and their friends.

As opening time approached, Toby finished labelling the various food items that made up the huge buffet laid out in the games room. Villagers would be feasting on his specially created concoction named Chewbacca, apparently a type of tuna and cheese bake, plus other dubiously named items, such as Superman sausage rolls. Toby also loved to invent lethal cocktails for festive occasions, and tonight was no exception. Customers would be plied with mind-altering beverages such as Kryptonite, which contained industrial quantities of vodka and Kahlua, plus the Pangalactic Gargleblaster, a gut-busting brew that seemed to be made up of all the spirits on the top shelf of the bar that Toby and Tim had been wanting to get rid of for years.

"Five minutes to go!" called Alice in a voice quavering with nerves, as she switched on the themed soundtrack and set it at a discreet background volume. Lucy, meanwhile, finished laying out copies of her Quantum Power Quiz on the tables in the bar. She and Edward had enjoyed devising the questions for the quiz, and the fact that they could not compete relieved some of pressure on her, leaving her free to worry about whether anyone was actually going to turn up.

Finally it was time to open the doors. Toby, Alice and Lucy gathered together in the bar and made some final adjustments to their costumes. As described in Edward's spoof, Toby was dressed as Han Solo and Lucy had transformed herself into a glamorous Princess Leia complete with Danish pastries, although she had opted for the white dress rather than the gold bikini, despite being called a chicken by Edward. Alice, in the meantime, was a slinky leather-clad Catwoman.

"So there you all are!" Bridget, Toby's diminutive business partner, appeared all of a sudden behind the bar, looking cute in her Betty Boop costume. "Ready to rock and roll?"

"Yes I guess so" answered Toby, walking over to unlock the door. "Here we go, ready or not…"

Immediately the doors opened, the four of them were joined in solidarity by the rest of the investor group apart from Aidan, who was still in Manchester. Each person in the group was wearing an impressive sci-fi costume so that the theme would be clearly apparent, even if none of the customers chose to dress up. Sandy, the self-confessed Trekkie was, not surprisingly, dressed as Mr Spock, whilst Kit was sporting an ingenious dual-faced costume whereby he was a bespectacled Clark Kent when seen from the front, but when viewed from the back he was Superman. Next through the door was Anna, almost unrecognisable as Trillian from Hitchhiker's Guide to the Galaxy, followed by Edward, who made a very convincing Yoda and was clearly going to enjoy speaking in his best Yoda voice for the rest of the evening. Verity, the last of the group to enter the pub, was dressed as an Ewok.

As it turned out, the investor group need not have worried about the lack of guests or of costumes. Very soon The Mallard was full to bursting point; the village had turned out in force along with regulars and occasional visitors from other villages, and even some brand new customers.

Most of the book club members were there to support their friends in the investor group and some were sporting stunning sci-fi costumes. Nicky, with her shiny dark hair, looked gorgeous in her Wonder Woman outfit, whilst Irene had really gone to town, transforming herself into a tough and very convincing Ripley from Alien. Emily, meanwhile, was blonde and glamorous as Buffy the Vampire Slayer whilst Arabella, her short hair slicked back, was suitably foxy as Trinity from The Matrix. It was Peggy, though, who stole the show in her ingenious retro 1960s outfit, topped off with a sassy brimmed hat. Most people had no idea who she was, however, until she took them back to their childhoods by revealing that she was Sarah Jane Smith, the Time Lord's faithful sidekick from Doctor Who.

Jane had been working late that evening, carrying out a stock take at The Mill, so she did not arrive until Mallard Mayhem was in full swing. As she pushed her way into the pub, dressed in her black work outfit, she was astonished to discover that most of the customers were in fancy dress. A few minutes later, once she finished saying hello to a few of the regulars and managed to find a space at the bar, she found herself alongside Ripley, aka Irene, who was in the middle of ordering a large round of drinks.

"Hi, Jane!" shouted Irene, attempting to make herself heard above the general hubbub. "Would you like a drink?"

"Thanks, that would be lovely. I'll have a white wine" Jane replied. Looking around her, she remarked:

"I can't believe how many people have dressed up! I feel distinctly underdressed in my work clothes. I wasn't expecting such a big effort – on the posters and leaflets it said that fancy dress was optional, so I didn't think that many people would bother".

"You had better get used to it" warned Irene "people like a bit of dressing up in this village. If you come along to Oktoberfest tomorrow you'll see lots of people in Lederhosen and Bavarian costumes, but I predict that the really big fancy dress opportunity will be Gemma's birthday party next weekend. People are intrigued by the idea of dressing up as their musical hero, so I think that's when they will really pull out all the stops".

"Thanks for the heads up" said Jane "I'm very grateful. It's too late for me to get hold of a Bavarian costume for Oktoberfest tomorrow, but I'll make up for it by creating a really outrageous outfit for Gemma's party".

"Well, I for one will look forward to seeing what you come up with" smiled Irene, squeezing Jane's arm. "But now if you'll excuse me, I must take these drinks over to Judd and his friends – I can see them looking antsy through lack of beer! See you later".

In the end, the pub's opening night was successful beyond the wildest dreams of its new owners. The Quantum Power Quiz was a popular and closely fought contest, which was won by a margin of just two points. The victorious team was called the Chocolate Chip Wookies, more usually known as the Abbott crew from Westford, a group of men united by their love for real ale. As their team name suggested, they had each dressed up as Chewbacca or one of his relatives, which did not require a huge sartorial departure from their normal attire.

The karaoke contest proved just as popular as the quiz. Almost every customer in the pub had a go on the mike, with those who had sampled Toby's cocktails particularly keen to show off their dubious skills. It was generally agreed, however, that the most entertaining performance came from a trio comprising Jan who, like Lucy, was dressed as Princess Leia, plus Claudine, who made a sexy Lara Croft, accompanied by one of the Westford Wookies. Their rendition of 'I Will Survive', although not exactly tuneful, was so funny and energetic that the audience was soon clapping along and joining in with the mauling of the 70's disco classic.

Alice found herself standing next to Jane, who was watching the antics with her mouth open in shock.

"You've got to admit" ventured Alice "we're not afraid to let our hair down and look a bit uncool in this village, if it helps people to enjoy themselves and have a laugh. I think we've got something really special here, actually".

"That's one way of putting it" replied Jane drily. "It's not every day you hear Gloria Gaynor covered by a pissed-up Wookie and a Tomb Raider with a Belgian accent; I grant you that".

❊ ❊ ❊

The next day, there were a few sore heads in Oak Welby and the surrounding villages, but nevertheless a huge crowd assembled in the Village Hall for the ever-popular Oktoberfest, the main event at the heart of Oak Welfest. The hall, which had been transformed into a vague approximation of a Bavarian Bierkeller, quickly filled up with people whilst others, eager to take advantage of the unseasonably warm and dry night, settled down at the picnic tables in the adjoining playground or grouped together under the various gazebos that had been erected in front of the building in honour of the occasion.

Several members of the book club had key roles to play in the Oktoberfest proceedings. Peggy and Anna, dressed in their bespoke black festival T-shirts with the iconic Oak Welfest sunshine logo, were tasked with selling Bratwurst and Pretzels to the masses whilst Lucy, looking demure in the most tasteful Bavarian costume of the evening, was helping to run the bar alongside Emily. Meanwhile Verity, looking rather less sophisticated than Lucy in a Bavarian Wench outfit fashioned from Amazon's finest polyester, spent most of the evening on top of a table, leading the singing of the most popular Oktoberfest drinking songs and demonstrating the actions that accompanied them.

As the evening wore on and the beer, prosecco and gin flowed freely, the ability of the audience to speak German and dance to the Oktoberfest tunes miraculously improved by leaps and bounds. Nicky and Irene looked on in amusement as Verity led the unruly mob in yet another rendition of 'Ein Prosit', apparently the Oktoberfest number one.

"I worry for her safety" said Nicky to her friend as Verity jumped up and down on a rather rickety wooden table, yelling the lyrics and twirling her yellow polyester plaits. "We need to keep her away from the kitchen - or any naked flame, for that matter – one stray spark and she'll go up like a bloody Roman Candle!"

In a far corner of the hall, Jane stood watching the action, wearing jeans and a biker jacket and drinking her customary large glass of white wine. Although she had already drunk a fair bit, she felt no inclination to join in, but was content to observe the antics of others and chat to people she knew from The Mallard and from book club. Earlier, as she was teasing Lucy's Edward about his very authentic Lederhosen, it had suddenly occurred to her that, contrary to all her expectations, she was actually having quite a good time. Now, however, she felt like fleeing, as she saw danger approaching in the form of a long and chaotic Conga – but it was too late. She had already been spotted by Jan who, as she knew, was not one to take 'no' for an answer.

"Come on, Jane!" yelled Jan. "No point in looking too cool for school – you've got to join in!"

Before she could object, Jane was grabbed and subsumed into the Conga, slotted in between Lucy and Edward's son Henry - who had a remarkably high embarrassment threshold for someone his age – and, surprisingly, Rick.

"I didn't know you went in for this sort of thing" Jane said to Rick as they Conga'ed off towards the stage at the front of the hall.

"I don't, as a rule" replied Rick. "Sometimes, though, there's nothing for it but to go with the flow, forget about your image, or whatever, and just relax and have a good time".

"Fair enough; I'll take your advice - just this once" Jane answered. "What the hell".

As she danced around the room, with strangely dressed people swaying and clapping all around her, Jane could not suppress the smile that crept across her face. It was a huge relief to leave her planning and scheming behind, if only for one night. After all, she reasoned, everyone deserved to have a little fun once in a while.

* * *

The following week, Irene pottered happily around the stylish, rustic kitchen in her warm and welcoming house on the edge of Lower Bragbury, with its stunning views across the fields to the south. As the weather had turned slightly colder, she was busy making some hot snacks to welcome her book club friends who would be arriving shortly for their September meeting. Right on cue, the oven pinged. Irene pulled on her oven gloves, removed two delicious smelling trays of herby cheese scones and arranged them carefully in neat rows on a large cooling tray.

A few minutes later, as she was easing the cork out of a chilled bottle of prosecco, the first of the book club guests arrived in the form of Peggy, Lucy and Emily, who had driven over together in Peggy's SUV. Over the next ten minutes, the rest of the gang showed up in small groups. Glasses were filled, hugs were exchanged and then, as ever, it was time for a good old gossip.

Unsurprisingly, the main topic of conversation was Oak Welfest and the drunken antics of those who had taken part in the festival. True to form, the group was not short of anecdotes. They all enjoyed the story of Don, a handsome man from neighbouring Clayford whom most of them had not met before and who had played an active part in Oktoberfest, clad in a very fetching pair of tight leather shorts. After working his way through the extensive range of German beers, Don had decided that he was unable to make it home, even on foot. When the Village Hall closed he had managed to stagger as far as his van, which was parked in the playground. Still clutching his final beer, he had crawled into his vehicle and slept there until late the following morning, when he judged that he was finally under the limit and able to drive home.

Don later described his long night out in a Facebook post, complete with incriminating photos of him in his leather shorts. The post was promptly picked up and shared by a number of villagers, including Claudine, generating a passionate response from one of her friends over in Belgium who propositioned Don from afar, offering to cross the Channel immediately if he was single. Sadly, Don was already spoken for, so the international hook-up was unfortunately a non-starter.

Not all the book club had taken part in Sunday's events, which were always rather more low-key. A pleasant barbecue in the car park of The Mallard was preceded by a bike ride organised by Tad (short for Tadeusz) a super-keen club cyclist who did not always realise that most of the other villagers who took part in the ride were not as committed as he was. This year, for the first time, Nicky and Emily had decided to join in, as they were both trying to get fit. After a few miles, however, their initial enthusiasm had waned and they rapidly got left behind as they were chatting, giggling and not really concentrating on the route. Before long the inevitable happened – they took a wrong turn and became completely separated from the other cyclists.

Initially dismayed by this turn of events, Nicky and Emily quickly cheered up when they realised that they were only a mile or so away from The Partridge. By the time Josh arrived in his Land Rover to rescue them, they had each consumed several Bellinis plus a large bowl of apple crumble and custard. The fitness campaign was temporarily put on hold and the trio returned to the village just in time to catch last orders at The Mallard.

"Right, I think we have all dissected Oak Welfest enough for one year – what do you think?" enquired Gemma, taking advantage of a rare lull in the conversation.

"Yes I agree – let's get on and discuss the book" replied Peggy firmly. "I'm dying to find out what everyone thinks!"

The author of this month's book was not exactly the modest type. In this macho, two-fisted roller coaster of a thriller he took the reader on a breathless, action-packed tour of the world's terrorist hot spots, as the hero raced against time to foil an attack that was ingeniously concealed and which threatened the survival of the entire world.

"Can I go first?" asked Peggy. "I just want to say that, like the tome we reviewed last month, I found this book incredibly long, but the similarity ends there. This time, I couldn't put the book down – I loved every single page and binge-read the whole lot! I think it's one of the best thrillers I have ever read and, as you know, I have read an awful lot of thrillers. I know some of you might disagree, but that's my view" she finished defiantly.

Strangely enough, the opposition that Peggy had anticipated did not materialise. As Gemma worked her way around the table seeking the views of each person, it quickly became clear that they had all been caught up in the action, even those in the group who generally preferred more character-driven novels. Even Nicky, who had been known to abandon quite a few book club offerings, particularly the longer tomes, had devoured every page.

"I could hardly keep reading when I got to that bit with the eyeball" she confessed, and the rest of the group winced in recollection of what was a particularly gruesome scene. "But I had to carry on, as by then I was hooked! Any writer who makes me stay up reading until the early hours when I have a diary full of appointments the following day has got to have done his job, I reckon".

"Ah – so that's why my layers were a bit wonky this time" joked Alice. "Just kidding!" she added quickly as she noticed Nicky's crestfallen face.

Jane was the next to comment.

"Aren't we forgetting something?" she began quietly.

The group of women looked at each other with some trepidation. None of them wanted more conflict after last month's showdown in Lorelei's conservatory.

Here we go, thought Lucy to herself.

"OK, it was exciting; I get it. But can you all really have overlooked the Islamophobia, the racism, the misogyny and the rampant American nationalism? The one thing that really surprised me, when I read the author's biography on the inside cover, was that he is not, in fact, an American! That, for me, was more of a big reveal than the plot, which I found quite predictable. I'm sorry to disagree with everyone, but I have to speak as I find". Jane grabbed her wine glass and drained the remaining contents in a single gulp.

Lucy was the last to comment. Taking a deep breath, she ventured carefully:

"Actually I have to agree with Jane about the Islamophobia etc. – it is a little unpalatable in places".

Jos and Anna nodded in assent.

"I don't agree with you about the plot, though" Lucy continued. "Like the others, I too found it really gripping; so much so that I was willing to forgive him for his occasional lack of political correctness!" she finished, looking over at Jane in expectation of a response.

The group collectively held its breath.

"Well, clearly you are a much more forgiving person than me" replied Jane, smiling thinly in Lucy's direction.

The other women inwardly heaved a sigh of relief and Gemma immediately took advantage of the benign atmosphere by starting to gather the scores for the book. In the end, the thriller received an incredibly high average score of 18.5 – the highest that anyone in the club could remember. Clearly the rest of the group shared Lucy's forgiving nature.

* * *

Next Saturday night Gemma, Robert and Tabitha waited nervously in their kitchen for the first guests to arrive for Gemma's birthday party. When it came to fancy dress, the host family had set the bar incredibly high. The birthday girl was stunning as Agnetha, the 'blonde one' from Abba, in a glittering body-con jumpsuit. Her husband, meanwhile, dressed in a matching jumpsuit and fetching 70s wig, had contrived to look more attractive than the real Bjorn from Abba ever did, even in his heyday. Not one to be outshone by her parents, their daughter Tabitha had managed to retain her teenage cool by looking more classy than Ginger Spice in her replica of the iconic, sparkling Union Jack dress.

The family's anxious wait for their first guests was mercifully short. Only a few minutes after the official start time, the doorbell began ringing repeatedly and the house quickly filled up with guests. Despite a few protestations beforehand from those who claimed not to like fancy dress, almost every person had wholeheartedly embraced the challenge to transform themselves into a musical hero from their youth.

Nicky, one of the first to arrive, had complemented Gemma's outfit beautifully by dressing as Anna-Frid, the 'brunette one' from Abba – again in a shiny, form-fitting jumpsuit. Emily, meanwhile, looked suitably kooky as Cyndi Lauper, complete with a scene-stealing pink wig. Lucy made a realistic and funky Amy Winehouse whilst her husband Edward was uncannily lifelike as Freddy Mercury.

Some costumes required a little more musical knowledge to decipher the identity of the musician in question. Sandy, wearing an under-sized school uniform complete with shorts and a cap, was delighted when anyone recognised him as Angus Young from AC/DC, whilst many of the younger guests also failed to decode Simon and Garfunkel.

Some of the guests were in such deep disguise that Gemma, opening the door to them, could not actually tell who they were in real life. Always the perfect hostess, she made the decision to smile politely and let all these strangers in. She figured that, if they had made such a big effort, they must be friends. She could solve the mystery of their various identities later on, when she had a bit more time.

One guest in particular made Gemma physically jump in alarm when she opened the door. She had no difficulty in recognising Jane, despite the fact that tattoos covered every inch of exposed skin on her arms, legs and even her face. Given that Jane's outfit consisted solely of a skimpy, tattered black tunic, belted around the waist, plus a distressed pair of pixie boots, there was plenty of space for the tattoos in question. Recovering her poise quickly, Gemma felt compelled to compliment Jane on her appearance.

"Wow, that's quite a costume, Jane" ventured Gemma. "I must confess I am puzzled, though – who are you?"

"You'll have to guess" replied Jane enigmatically, handing Gemma a gift and a card. "I'll be very interested to see who knows enough about music to work it out". With that, she stalked off towards the bar.

"Well, that's put me in my place" remarked Gemma to her husband Robert, who had come over to greet the new arrival and caught the last part of the conversation.

"Don't take it personally, love" said Robert "as you have said yourself, she's just socially awkward. You should feel sorry for her". He nodded discreetly towards the bar where Jane had grabbed the biggest wine glass she could find, filled it nearly to the brim and was swigging it nervously.

Jane scanned the room, her heart thumping in her chest. She always found parties a challenge and was glad that she had pre-loaded with a couple of drinks before leaving home, otherwise she would be really anxious by now. Strangely though, her outfit was helping, along with the wine. The clothes and tattoos provided a comforting barrier behind which she could hide, making her feel a little less exposed than she normally did at parties. Quickly, to avoid losing her nerve, she turned back to the bar to refill her glass before setting out to join one of the happy, laughing groups around the room.

Jane cautiously approached a group that included Emily, aka Cyndi, plus Alice, who was a dead ringer for Sandi Shaw in a 60s mini-dress. Both women noticed her and drew her into their circle, introducing her to their friends. Unexpectedly, no-one seemed to be fazed by her tattoos. People were just trying, unsuccessfully, to guess the identity of her musical hero when Lucy the Amy Winehouse clone wandered over to join them.

"Hi everyone – oh, hi Jane" she said with a friendly smile.

Jane's tattoo'ed face darkened in anger as she took in Lucy's fancy dress costume, including the classic black beehive and the tattoos on her arms. Drawing Lucy away from the group, Jane hissed:

"Are you taking the piss?"

"What do you mean?" answered Lucy, genuinely puzzled. Then the penny dropped.

"Ah I see – you think that I dressed up as Amy Winehouse to tease you, after your performance of Back to Black at the wedding. Well, I've got news for you. Contrary to what you seem to believe, the world does not revolve around you. I just happen to like Amy Winehouse – OK?"

With that, Lucy marched off.

Mortified by her blunder, Jane quickly retreated to the bar for another drink, relieved that no-one else appeared to have witnessed the unfortunate exchange. As she was refilling her glass with her back to the room, she suddenly felt a tap on her shoulder and wheeled round in surprise.

Standing behind her was a woman with waist-length dark hair, wearing a huge, floppy-brimmed hat, a sleeveless fur gilet and preposterously long, patterned flares. On her arm was a huge heart, drawn using lipstick, with the name 'Bobby' in its centre.

"Let me guess" drawled the woman in a rather dodgy attempt at a laid-back Californian accent. "You're Ari Up from The Slits – am I right?"

"Yes, you are!" gasped Jane, astonished. "You're the only person to have guessed correctly so far."

"It's the same for me" confided the mystery women. "No-one seems to know who I am, either. Can you guess?"

"I'm ashamed to say I can't" admitted Jane, looking flustered. "Who are you?"

"Don't sweat it" drawled the woman with a smile. "I'm not surprised that you don't know, if punk is more your thing. I'm Janis Joplin."

"No, sorry – you misunderstand me" stammered Jane. "I mean – who are you – in real life?"

The mystery women grinned at her. "I think I had better leave you to work that out – Jane" she murmured, moving away towards the buffet table.

Everyone agreed that Gemma's party was an incredible success. As night slipped seamlessly into early morning, it showed no signs of slowing down; in fact, people laughed, drank and danced more and more, with fewer inhibitions, as the hours wore on. Even Jane found herself on the dance floor with lots of partners, her earlier awkwardness forgotten as, for the second weekend in a row, she unexpectedly had a really good time. She was just leaving the dance floor after a particularly energetic dance to Tiger Feat with a Marc Bolan lookalike when she spotted the mysterious Janis Joplin talking to Peggy and Emily. Intrigued, Jane walked over to join them.

"Isn't it incredible that they found those two little boys

alive?" Peggy was saying as Jane wandered up.

"Yes I agree; it's very rare for things to turn out that way" replied Janis. Jane noticed that Janis had dropped her American accent.

"Does that mean that Aidan will finally be coming home?" asked Emily.

"Not right now" answered Janis "they still have a lot of work to do. They have to prepare and catalogue the evidence, for instance, and that takes quite a bit of time. Aidan has been told that he will be released from the task force by mid-October, so I should be more cheerful by the next book club meeting, as he will be home by then!"

"Well I am slow on the uptake, aren't I?" remarked Jane, to announce her arrival. Peggy and Emily turned to look at her, with a confused look on their faces.

"Sorry ladies, I should explain" Jane continued. "I didn't recognise Verity earlier when I was talking to her – that fancy dress costume is a very effective disguise and her American accent totally fooled me! I feel like such an idiot. Anyway, Verity, it's great news that Aidan is coming back. I'm so glad that I'm hosting the October book club – I'll organise some special treats to celebrate you no longer being home alone. Seedlip cocktails all round!"

At that moment the women were distracted from their conversation by a roar of laughter and a round of applause from the dance floor. They hurried over to see what was happening, whereupon they were treated to the sight of Lucy's Edward, aka Freddy Mercury, clutching the host family's Dyson and comprehensively stealing the show with his high camp rendition of 'I Want to Break Free'. As she clapped and sang along with the others, Jane noticed that Lucy had come to stand beside her. Plucking up her by now substantial store of Dutch courage, Jane decided to make amends. Tentatively she reached out her hand

and squeezed Lucy's arm in a gesture of friendship.

"I'm sorry about earlier, Lucy" she whispered. "You're right – I am hugely oversensitive. You must think I'm completely crazy. Can we forget it ever happened?"

Lucy wordlessly turned around, looked at Jane with a smile and enfolded her in a hug. Jane stood stiffly in her arms, amazed and relieved by this sudden display of affection from a woman with whom she had crossed swords on several occasions over the last few months.

"It's fine – don't worry about it" Lucy whispered gently in Jane's ear. "I'm totally cool with crazy people. After all, look at what I have to live with!" she laughed, releasing Jane from her embrace and pointing towards the dance floor. Edward/Freddy was still gyrating energetically as the audience immortalised his antics on their phones, ready to upload onto social media. Behind him, through the window, a few pale pink ribbons trailed across the velvet darkness of the sky, heralding the imminent arrival of the dawn.

* * *

Jane finally stumbled into her cottage around five in the morning. Slamming the front door behind her, she tottered towards the kitchen for a final, solitary nightcap. On the way, she caught sight of her reflection in the hall mirror and gasped in horror. She looked a total mess; her temporary facial tattoos had melted in the heat of the party and were running in rivulets down her cheeks, whilst her heavily gelled Mohican had collapsed into a sticky bird's nest on top of her head.

"Who cares!" cried Jane defiantly to herself, wobbling unsteadily in front of the glass. "This calls for a celebration – even if I do look like crap".

Wandering into the kitchen, she spotted the empty wine bottle on the counter – she had forgotten that she had finished it when she was pre-loading earlier before the party. Not to worry, she though to herself – there was still some of that Bacardi left from the other week.

Not even bothering to open a can of Diet Coke, Jane poured the last of the Bacardi into a tumbler and raised the clear liquid aloft in a dramatic toast to herself.

"Game on!" she cried.

❋ ❋ ❋

# CHAPTER 10

*October Book Club*

Outside The Mill at South Napton the waterwheel turned slowly and relentlessly, launching sparkling drops of water onto the chill autumn breeze. The last of the lunchtime customers tried to dodge them on their way to the car park, but inevitably their coats and jackets were freckled with droplets by the time they said their goodbyes and thanked each other for a wonderful lunch.

Back in the restaurant, Jane was preparing to finish her shift when she spotted Andy, the Hotel Manager, heading in her direction, laptop in hand. As he approached, her stomach did an automatic backflip as her body reminded her that approaching bosses usually meant trouble. This time, though, her boss, usually a hard taskmaster, was smiling broadly.

"Jane, I've just been reviewing our Trip Advisor scores" he began. "They're well up on last year and they have improved steadily as the year has gone on. You get a lot of mentions in the review comments as well – look at this". Andy held out the laptop so that Jane could see the screen.

"A big thank you to Jane and the team for making our Nan's birthday so very special" Andy read out. "And here's another one – 'nothing is too much trouble for Jane and her crew – they really go the extra mile.' It's clear to me that these higher scores have a lot to do with you, Jane" he finished, smiling at her as his flipped the laptop shut. "I was just wondering if you would consider renewing your contract when it ends in December?"

Jane hesitated, but only for a moment.

"It's very kind of you, Andy, and I am flattered, but I'm committed to my new job in France next year. I do love working here, though, and I'll try and pass on all my knowledge to the team before I leave, so they can carry on without me".

"Well, you'll be sorely missed is all I can say" replied Andy. "If you ever change your mind and want to come back, there will always be a place here for you – and a warm welcome". With that, he turned on his heel and quickly walked away.

Jane headed towards the staff room, glowing inside from the positive feedback from her boss. Compliments had always been a rare occurrence in her life; in fact, she reflected, she had received more in the last year than in the previous two decades. Ironic, isn't it, she thought to herself with a wry smile as she opened her locker and removed her bag, car keys and phone.

As she took her phone off silent, Jane noticed that there were 23 WhatsApp messages waiting for her. Something must be going on with the book club group, she concluded as she clicked on the green icon, eager to find out more.

The first message was from Lorelei, who had posted a picture of a bottle of prosecco, accompanied by a short caption:

"Staying with Peggy on book club night, so I'll be able to drink this!"

Peggy had swiftly replied to her sister-in-law:

"More good news Lol – Stan has offered to give you, me and Emily a lift – and Bill is dropping Nicky and Irene off, so we can all partake for a change. Happy days!"

A number of the other book club members had sent encouraging replies to Lorelei and jokey reminders to Jane, telling her to make sure she had enough fizz in stock. Jane posted a quick response and continued scrolling.

Further down, she encountered a picture of an attractive young woman holding a small, red-faced baby. It was from Jos, who had written:

"Welcome to the world, Cian! Our little grandson (nine pounds seven ounces!) is doing well, but Esme is very tired after a long and difficult labour, so I'll be staying with her for a while as planned, to help out. Sorry to miss book club, but I'm sure you understand. I'll send comments on the book separately – lots of love".

A long list of congratulatory comments followed below. Jane added hers and made sure that she sounded suitably excited, although in reality she wasn't remotely interested in other peoples' babies. As she dropped her phone in her bag and headed out towards her car, she smiled to herself.

"Thanks, ladies" she murmured. "Your timing could not be better".

\* \* \*

That same morning, the cool autumn breeze provided ideal conditions for Lucy and Gemma as they completed the final mile of the Rushton Green half marathon. Nevertheless, while the benign weather offered some relief to the two weary runners, it couldn't ease their aching legs, nor could it combat the sense of utter depletion which told them that their glycogen stores were well and truly spent.

Lucy rooted around in her bum bag as she ran. Grabbing a handful of jelly babies, she wordlessly tapped her running partner's arm. Gemma duly held out her hand for what felt like her hundredth sugar fix and, as she did so, she spotted their race time displayed on the screen of her sports watch. Quickly cramming the jelly babies into her mouth and holding out her hand towards Lucy she tapped the screen, then gave her a mute thumbs-up as she hurriedly chewed and swallowed her sweets.

"We're finally going to do it, I think!" Gemma gasped as soon as she was able to speak. "By my reckoning, we're on track to finish in under two hours!"

The two women had completed quite a few half marathons together, but neither of them was a particularly fast runner and they had never succeeded in recording a sub two-hour time. On a couple of occasions they had narrowly missed out, finishing in less than two hours and one minute, so the two-hour milestone had acquired great significance for both of them.

Neither Gemma nor Lucy had expected to break two hours at Rushton Green as, on the whole, their times had been pretty slow during the summer months. Now, however, as they crested the brow of the final hill and saw in the valley below them, about half a mile away, the spire of the church next to the finish line, they both felt a surge of energy that had little to do with the sweets they had just eaten. The two women smiled at each other and, breathing heavily, Gemma said:

"Are you up for a strong finish, my lovely?"

Lucy nodded. "Let's go for it!" she panted.

Running in step, they both picked up their pace and raced down the hill together, ignoring the protests from their worn-out thigh muscles as they passed several other runners and eagerly anticipated their first sight of the finish line. Suddenly, they rounded a corner and there it was at the end of the road – a garish archway fashioned in the corporate colours of the main sponsor, a local engineering firm. The digital clock on top of the archway read 1:57:42.

"We're going to smash it!" yelled Lucy, grabbing Gemma's hand and urging her forward in a sprint finish.

The two friends crossed the line together in a time of one hour and 58 minutes. Laughing and hugging each other, they fumbled with the foil capes that the marshals had pressed into their hands and tried to disregard the lactic acid that was flooding into their exhausted legs.

A few minutes later with capes on, medals round their necks and finishers' packs clutched in their hands, the runners were joined by their husbands and children who had been watching near the finish line and now gathered round to congratulate them.

"Time for a celebration lunch in The Partridge, I feel" suggested Robert "once you have both cleaned up".

"But first" said Gemma's daughter Tabitha, who was home from university for the weekend "look what I brought you both, to toast your success!" From behind her back, she produced a familiar green bottle, still covered in condensation from where she had carefully stored it in her father's cool box. "I do believe it's your favourite..." Tabitha murmured, shooting her mother a conspiratorial look.

"Fizzy lady petrol! Can't beat it – thank you darling, that's so thoughtful of you". Gemma expertly eased the cork from the prosecco and handed the bottle straight to Lucy, who grabbed it and took a hefty swig.

"Thanks, Tab" Lucy said gratefully, wiping the prosecco froth from her mouth. "We definitely deserve this".

* * *

The next evening, Jane bustled merrily around her little kitchen, putting the finishing touches to the canapés that she had made herself, plus several trays that had been left over at work and that she had been permitted to bring home. She felt confident that the food and drink she planned to serve would stand up well against the best that others had offered. Clearly, though, her living room could not compete with the larger, better appointed rooms in the other houses she had visited for book club, but she had done her best to make it cosy with an array of throws, cushions and scented candles plus a couple of beanbags, all purchased hastily from Dunelm the previous day.

Jane did not have to wait long for her book club guests to show up. First to arrive was the family group comprising Emily, Peggy and Lorelei, who had been dropped off punctually by Stan. Jane ushered them into the living room and presented them each with a large glass of prosecco.

"Let me take your coats" she offered. "I'll put them upstairs in the bedroom – to give us a bit more space, as this room is so small".

"It's lovely and cosy in here" remarked Peggy tactfully when Jane returned. "Isn't it, Em?"

"Wh-what's that? I wasn't really listening" Emily admitted.

"Are you still thinking about the result?" Peggy asked. "If you are, I suggest you stop – there's nothing you can do about it. We all agree Josh deserved to win, but there were other factors at work – you know that".

"I don't understand" said Jane, puzzled.

"You remember that Josh was nominated for that award, by Fabulous Farmer magazine?" Peggy reminded her. "Well he didn't win, I'm afraid, and we suspect that the winner was chosen for, shall we say, political reasons, rather than on merit. But what can you do about it?" she asked rhetorically. "That's the way of the world sometimes – and we did have a brilliant time at the awards do. I didn't drink for nearly a week afterwards – it took me that long to detox!"

"Well, I'm glad that you are all back in the saddle now" said Jane warmly as she topped up their glasses, which were already nearly empty. "We couldn't have you abstaining on book club night. Please pass on my commiserations to Josh, though" she added to Emily. "I for one know that life is not fair, and this is just another example to confirm it. But if he perseveres, I'm sure he'll win in the end".

"Funny – that's pretty much what I said to him myself" said Emily, looking at Jane in surprise.

At that point the doorbell rang again and, over the next few minutes, Jane was kept busy welcoming her guests, pressing large glasses of fizz into their hands and taking their coats upstairs. Eventually, the whole group was assembled, cooing over the latest baby photos and toasting Jos's new grandson with prosecco. The only exception was Verity, who was clasping a large tumbler full of Seedlip cocktail.

"Now do you have reason to celebrate as well, Verity?" asked Irene. "Have you got Aidan back yet?"

"Yes – he returned a couple of days ago" smiled Verity. "He's exhausted, though – it was such a hard case. He's done nothing but sleep since he got home. Still, it's an improvement on last time – he wound up in hospital then as he was totally burnt out".

"Well, it's great news that he is back safe and sound this time" remarked Jane, topping up everyone's glasses again.

"I had better pace myself", said Peggy "I'm still not sure I have recovered completely from that awards ceremony!"

"Nonsense" scolded Jane "let's all sit down and have some food – that'll help soak it all up!"

"Before we do, Jane" said Irene, "can I just propose a toast to our two successful runners? A little bird told me that you both ran a personal best at Rushton Green last Saturday and finished in under two hours for the first time! I'd just like to say well done. I can't even run for a bus, so I can't imagine how you can run 13 miles without stopping. I think I speak for us all when I say that we are very proud of you both".

The women gathered round Gemma and Lucy to offer their congratulations, then obediently filled their plates with the food laid out on the sideboard before settling themselves in the various chairs around the room, with Verity and Lucy braving the new bean bags. Once they were all seated, Gemma spotted an opportunity to begin the book review.

"Shall we make a start, now that we are all sitting comfortably?" she suggested, and the group nodded in agreement, especially Verity. She wanted to avoid a late night as Aidan was back and also wondered privately how long she would be able to survive on the beanbag. She hadn't sat on one since she was a student and her body was reminding her in no uncertain terms that her undergraduate years were long gone.

This month's offering, a gentle memoir about the Royal family, was a world away from last month's hard-hitting thriller. It had been written by a genuine insider, an aristocratic woman who grew up with the Royals, so the book club members had been eager to discover what new insights the author would provide.

Irene was the first to comment.

"I though it was a lovely, relaxing read" she began. "It reminded me a bit of Downton Abbey, except it was true. It gave me an interesting view on a world that has pretty much disappeared".

Lorelei was next. Taking a large swig of prosecco, she remarked cheerily:

"I found it really entertaining, and the bit I enjoyed the most was where the author was talking about the Queen Mother's drinking habits, and how she didn't really drink very much, in her opinion! Well, I don't know about anyone else but from her description, I think the QM put us all to shame – and that's saying something!" she laughed, accepting a top-up from Jane, who was once again doing the rounds.

Anna was a little less enthusiastic.

"I quite enjoyed it, but I was a little disappointed, to be honest" she began. "I was expecting some new revelations about the Royals, but the book didn't tell me anything I didn't already know. It was pretty clear that it had received Royal approval – and had undergone Royal censorship".

"I agree!" cried Arabella. "I wanted more goss! In reality, the book was more about the author's life than that of the

Royals and, to be frank, she was not that interesting to me".

Peggy was next in line. Hastily putting down a golden brown choux bun filled with Gruyère-flavoured mousse, she said:

"Before I start, can I just compliment you, Jane, on this lovely food. Like you I have worked in the catering trade, so I'm not easily impressed, but this is really excellent – well done!"

"That's nice of you, Peggy" replied Jane, colouring slightly. "Just remember to save some room for pudding. Spoiler alert – it has got lots of chocolate in it!"

"Sounds wonderful" smiled Peggy "and now for the book. Like Irene I really enjoyed it. I thought it was an affectionate and realistic view of the Royals, from one who really knew them. What did you think, Verity?" she enquired, looking down at her neighbour who was sitting below her on her beanbag, knees in the air.

"I can't say I enjoyed it, I'm afraid" answered Verity, shifting uncomfortably. "I agree with Arabella that the author's own story was not that interesting and, as Anna said, she revealed nothing new or exciting about the Royals. As for the book itself, I found it badly written and poorly structured. In my opinion it should have remained a private memoir – to be read only by her immediate family, not by the world at large".

"Harsh words, Verity" added Lucy "but I'm afraid I have to agree with you". Looking at her phone, she continued "and Jos says pretty much the same thing in her review, which she just sent on WhatsApp".

"Well I found it a pleasant, harmless tale – and yes, I did finish it!" said Nicky triumphantly. Jane, who was busy clearing away the canapés in preparation for dessert, cast her a dark look as she disappeared into the kitchen.

While Jane was gone, the women continued reviewing the book, but all thoughts of its literary merit were driven from their minds as their hostess came back into the room, holding aloft a stupendous chocolate cake. As they watched in delighted anticipation, Jane sliced it up and handed around the heavily laden dessert plates.

Gemma, who had been mid-way through giving her opinion, raised her fork in the air.

"The only thing I want to say in conclusion is that the book is sweet – much like this delicious cake. Now please leave me alone while I devour the rest of my slice and think about seconds!"

Everyone laughed, and Lucy pointed at Jane with her fork.

"You haven't had a go yet, Jane" she observed. "What's your opinion?"

"Well I'm sorry to be negative, as I so often seem to be" she began "but, in my opinion, the book is anything but harmless – sorry, Nicky. It describes an Upstairs Downstairs kind of world that, for me, can't disappear fast enough. I guess I'm biased because I am a republican by nature and…"

"Jane I'm sorry to interrupt, but ladies, I don't feel too well all of a sudden", gasped a breathless voice from the other side of the room. All eyes turned instantly towards Gemma. Her lips had swollen up and hives were starting to break out all over her face, which was red and shining with sweat.

"Oh God, I think she must be having an attack – you know, her anaphylaxis – her nut allergy?" babbled Lucy. "She always keeps her kit in her bag, with her EpiPen in it, so we just need to keep calm - Gemma, where is your bag?"

"It's right here" Gemma panted, bending laboriously towards the floor "down by my feet". A second later she raised her head, her face showing the first signs of panic.

"That's funny, it's not here. I can't see it anywhere. I always have it with me – my bag, where's my bag?" Gemma shouted, her eyes now wild with fear.

Emily rounded on Jane.

"What was in the cake, Jane?" she demanded. "Are there nuts in the fucking cake? You knew all about her allergy – how could you be so careless?"

"I bought the cake" confessed Jane "and nobody said it had nuts in it. You tasted it yourself – there's no nuts in there".

"Ground almonds, I'm willing to bet" said Peggy grimly. "For texture. Anyway, there's no point blaming Jane at this point – we have to help Gemma. Has anyone found that bag yet?" she called out.

Shouts of "no" came from all over the house, where the women had run in different directions and were frantically searching in every room for Gemma's bag.

"Right then, we need to get her to hospital now" ordered Peggy. "I'll call an ambulance".

"Not quick enough!" cried Lucy. "When Henry broke his arm the ambulance took over half an hour to arrive. We need to drive her ourselves – now".

"I'll take her" announced Verity "after all, I'm the only one who hasn't been drinking – but I walked here, so I don't have my car with me".

"Take mine" said Lucy, tossing her the keys. "Good job my legs are still so sore after the half marathon so I decided to drive instead of walk. Let's sit Gemma on the back seat and prop her up with a few cushions – I read somewhere that people should stay upright during an attack, I think".

"I'll come with you Verity, so you can concentrate on driving while I sit in the back with Gemma and look after her" offered Anna.

"And I'll call ahead to A&E, so they can prepare for her arrival" added Peggy.

Quickly the women rushed Gemma out to Lucy's Discovery and sat her on the back seat of the SUV, propped up by some of Jane's recently purchased cushions. As soon as the door shut, Verity took off like Lewis Hamilton.

"The roads should be clear at this time of night" remarked Nicky. "At least, I bloody hope they are, the way she is driving".

The remainder of the book club regrouped in Jane's living room, their faces full of concern. Once again, in a grim reminder of the Sunday at Waterside View, Jane's face was pale and streaked with tears.

"I didn't mean to!" she sobbed. "Oh God – she is going to be alright, isn't she?"

"We'll find out soon enough" answered Emily, who was not inclined to let Jane off the hook like she did in May.

"I suggest that the three of us go round to Gemma's house, talk to Robert and tell him what has happened" said Peggy firmly, looking at Emily and Lorelei. "I'll text Stan and ask him to pick us up from there". With that, the three of them retrieved their coats and took their leave, without the usual goodbyes. At that moment, there really seemed to be nothing more to say.

"I think I'll call Bill and ask him to pick us up" said Nicky. "Is that OK with you, Irene?" Her friend nodded gratefully in Nicky's direction. Clearly both women were keen to leave Jane's house.

"In that case, shall we walk home together?" suggested Lucy, looking pointedly at Alice and Arabella, who both murmured their assent.

At that moment everyone's phones pinged apart from Nicky's, as she was on the phone to Bill. It was Anna, sending them a WhatsApp message with the welcome news that they had just arrived safely at the hospital and that Gemma had immediately been rushed into A&E for treatment. Verity and Anna were planning to stay at the hospital with her and wait for Gemma's husband Robert to arrive.

"Wow that was quick!" cried Lucy, breathing a sigh of relief. "I wonder how many speeding tickets V picked up on the way. Right, time to go". The next three women headed off, clearly eager to be gone.

Jane, Nicky and Irene sat together for a tense and awkward few minutes until the doorbell rang, heralding Bill's arrival.

"Will you be OK here on your own, Jane?" enquired Irene gently. Jane nodded miserably, unable to reply, and Irene pressed her arm in a discreet, silent gesture of sympathy, as she and Nicky took their leave.

* * *

Lucy, Alice and Arabella walked quietly back down the dark, unlit road that led away from Jane's cottage towards the centre of the village. As they neared Alice's house, Lucy broke the silence.

"Would you two mind coming back to my house with me, just for a little while? I think I might need your help".

Without missing a beat, Arabella replied:

"You think she's up to something, don't you?"

"I can't be sure" Lucy admitted, "but I do have my suspicions".

"A few of us have had our doubts about her, for several months now" explained Alice to Bella.

"I know; it was Gemma herself who mentioned it to me, in fact; and from what I have seen so far, I share your concerns" Arabella answered.

"Right, come on then" urged Lucy. "If I'm right, we need to hurry; we can't hang about here".

With that, the three of them continued briskly up the road towards Lucy's house. When they arrived, Lucy unlocked the door and ushered her friends in quietly, in case Edward and the boys were asleep - only to encounter her husband in the hallway, wearing pyjamas and holding a mug of tea.

"You're back earlier than usual" he remarked, raising a quizzical eyebrow as he spotted Alice and Bella standing behind Lucy in the darkened hallway. "Let me guess – is something happening with Jane?"

"Yes I think so – it was bound to come to a head sooner or later" replied Lucy. "I suggest you leave us to it for the moment – we're just going to sit in the front room with the lights out, so we can see what happens outside in the street. I'll let you know if anything kicks off".

"Well in that case I'm not going to bed" replied Edward in a tone that made it clear this was non-negotiable. "I will be upstairs in my study. Call me if you need me – and don't do anything rash".

A few minutes later, as the three women sat together in darkness, looking out of the window onto the main road, their phones again pinged simultaneously with a second WhatsApp message from Anna. She explained that Gemma was doing fine and responding well to her medication, but the doctors had decided to keep her in overnight, just in case she had a second attack. She and Verity were planning to stay with her for a while, until her husband arrived with her overnight bag plus Tabitha, who was at a friend's house but had insisted on being picked up as she understandably wanted to make sure her mother was OK.

"Wow – that's a relief" whispered Alice.

"Certainly is" agreed Lucy, then she abruptly fell silent and pointed towards the window. "Hang on a minute – look. There she is – just across the road".

As their eyes adjusted to the darkness, Alice and Bella spotted Jane's diminutive figure walking up the street. As she reached the Village Hall, directly opposite Lucy's house, she turned into the car park and headed for the Clothing Bank in the corner. In her hand she held a rectangular object. As the three women looked on, Jane reached up, opened the hatch, deposited the item into the Clothing Bank and closed the hatch firmly.

"I'm willing to bet that was Gemma's handbag" muttered Bella grimly. "Christ, she's evil".

"Not evil in my opinion – but she does need help" Lucy replied.

"But how could she hurt Gemma like that – and why?" whispered Alice.

"Stick with me and we'll find out. Look..." said Lucy, pointing towards the window.

Jane was on the move again, heading out of the car park. As she reached the street, she looked anxiously in both directions then, instead of turning left to head back towards her house, she began walking rapidly in the other direction, up the hill towards the opposite end of the village.

"Where on earth is she going now?" cried Arabella. "We've got to follow her and find out".

Lucy placed a restraining hand on Bella's arm.

"Trust me" she said, quietly and firmly. "We will find out. Let's just wait fifteen minutes, then we'll go after her. I'm pretty sure I know where she's headed".

Jane hurried up the hill, shining her torch app behind her repeatedly to ensure that no-one was following her. In a couple of minutes she had reached her destination. She hesitated for a moment, then marched resolutely towards the house, her footsteps crunching on the gravel driveway. Quickly, before she could change her mind, she pressed the doorbell. A few seconds later a man appeared, unshaven and dishevelled.

"Hello Jane" Aidan said gruffly, as he took in the sight of his unexpected night-time caller. "Where's Verity? Is she OK?"

"She's fine" Jane replied in a pleasant and reassuring voice. "She had to take Gemma to hospital as her nut allergy flared up and she was the only person who was sober enough to drive, so she will be back later than usual. I just thought I should let you know".

"That's kind of you" answered Aidan, "but you didn't have to walk up here alone in the dark. Verity would definitely have texted me if she was going to be really late. The only reason she hasn't contacted me so far, I'm sure, is that she knew I would be asleep and didn't want to disturb me".

"So sure of her, aren't you?" taunted Jane, her eyes narrowed and her voice suddenly malicious and spiteful. "It's so touching – how much you trust her. Well you're right – I didn't have to walk up here tonight. I chose to come here because I thought it was time you found out the truth about your supposedly *harmless* little wife".

"Well in that case you had better come in" replied Aidan in a neutral tone, holding the front door wide and motioning Jane to enter.

Aidan led Jane into the couple's large, open plan kitchen and pointed to one of the hard, grey bench seats surrounding their minimalist dining table.

"Take a seat" he said pleasantly. "Would you care for a glass of wine? I have got an nice bottle of Kistler open. It used to be Verity's favourite, back when she was drinking. You can share it with me". Aidan placed a bottle and two chilled glasses of white wine in front of them and sat down on the bench seat opposite Jane whose hostile, almost savage expression remained unchanged.

"Verity" Jane spat. "Truth. Unusual and interesting name – but totally inappropriate for your wife. In my experience, your precious Verity has very little regard for the truth".

"Why don't you tell me what this is all about?" invited Aidan, a faint smile playing around his lips.

"You won't be smiling when I've finished" snarled Jane. "Let me tell you a story. Once upon a time, when I was young, I was in a happy, committed relationship with the love of my life. We were so in love – we were even planning our wedding. Then, guess what happened next? Some little girl makes a false accusation of rape against him and the next thing I know, he's up in court. Eventually the girl admits that she has been lying all along and he's acquitted, but by then it's too late – the damage has been done. He fled abroad without saying goodbye and I never saw him again. My whole life was ruined. I have never met anyone since who matched up to him; all my relationships have failed, so I have missed my chance for a husband and a family. That wicked little slapper wrecked my life. That's why, when I came across her again, years later, I vowed that I would do the same to her".

"And that – what was it – wicked little slapper would be my wife Verity?" enquired Aidan, a look of shock on his face.

"That's right" Jane hissed "the very same. She was the one who trashed my life with her lies".

"Well, what a revelation!" Aidan gasped. "I had no idea that Verity was capable of such a heinous crime – she never told me! I must divorce her forthwith! I'm so grateful to you for your honesty – I'll talk to her as soon as she gets home. In the meantime – have some more wine".

As Aidan topped up her glass, Jane stared at him, a confused but hopeful expression on her face. Aidan stared back at her, his own expression slowly changing from one of shock to one of dark, barely controlled rage. Slowly he lifted his wine glass to his lips, drank deeply from it, then placed it carefully back on the table before speaking.

"You nasty, evil little bitch" he growled. "It's time someone sorted you out once and for all, and it seems like that someone has got to be me".

Jane's eyes widened in horror and she jumped up from the bench, but Aidan was too quick for her. Leaping to his feet, he grabbed her shoulders and pushed her back down.

"Sit the fuck down and listen to me!"

"First of all" he seethed "I know".

Jane stared fixedly at him, a look of incomprehension on her face.

"Well, you weren't expecting that, were you?" Aidan said quietly, a bitter grin on his face. "You thought she would have kept it quiet, as it was all so long ago. After all, that's what you would have done in her situation – but she didn't; she told me. It's called love – and trust – two things you clearly don't know much about".

Aidan drained his glass and refilled it.

"Second; unlike you, with your rose-tinted view of this man – what was his name?"

"Jason" mumbled Jane.

"That's right, Jason" Aidan continued "unlike you, I can tell the real story. Once upon a time, a notorious sleaze-bag and serial womaniser called Jason convinces his immature and gullible girlfriend that he is going to marry her. Then, one night, he is out without her and, as is his wont on such occasions, he tries it on with another young, impressionable girl – buying her drinks in the nightclub and fooling her with his charm and his lies. He offers to walk her home and, on the way, he makes a pass at her. When she rejects his advances, as he is moving too fast for her, he drags her into the park near her home and commits a very serious sexual assault which falls just short of rape, as she manages to fight him off and run away. When she gets home she is, understandably, in a very distressed and confused state, and she tells her parents that she has been raped. They immediately call the Police and the guy is apprehended pretty quickly".

Aidan paused for some more wine, then continued.

"So, as you know, the rape case comes to court. As it progresses, the victim wrestles with her conscience, eventually admits to her lawyer that it was not technically a rape and asks for all charges to be dropped. Her lawyer begs her to reconsider as he wants to press for a prosecution on the grounds of sexual assault, for which your dream guy would almost certainly have received a custodial sentence, but she is adamant – she wants all the charges dismissed. So Jason walks free and, realising that he has had a lucky escape, heads off pretty sharpish to begin a new life abroad, with no thought for the girlfriend who had stuck by him throughout the case. And there the story ends".

Jane sipped her wine, a sly smile on her face.

"So that's the version Verity cooked up for you, is it? Well if you believe that – more fool you".

"It's not just Verity's account" Aidan replied "it's the version documented in black and white - in the Court records".

"But you weren't working on the case" said Jane in confusion. "In fact, you can't even have been a Police Officer at the time – you were too young!"

"That's right" Aidan growled. "But when Verity told me what happened back then, I wanted to check for myself, before I married her. Trust only goes so far, you see, and I have been married before, so I wasn't going to make a mistake a second time. I checked up on her and her version was 100% consistent with the Court records".

Jane's eyes narrowed. "But how did you gain access to that information? I do believe some of it's confidential".

"I have been in this game a long time and let's just say - I know the right people" replied Aidan.

Jane smiled thinly. "What you did was illegal" she snapped. "I could have you prosecuted".

"Yeah, but something tells me you're not going to, are you?" snarled Aidan, fixing her with his malevolent gaze. "After all, nut allergies don't just 'flare up' – now do they?"

At that moment the doorbell rang.

"Don't move" ordered Aidan as he walked into the hallway to answer the bell. Opening the front door, he was greeted by Lucy, Alice and Arabella.

"Ah – would this be the No.1 Ladies' Detective Agency?"

he smiled.

"Something like that" Lucy replied. "Is Jane here?"

"Why yes she is – how did you know? Come on in and join us in a glass of wine". Aidan ushered the three women into the kitchen and went to the cupboard for more glasses.

When she saw her fellow book club members, Jane's face turned pale and she stared at them in shocked silence as they took their seats around the table.

"What the hell are you three doing here?" she asked eventually.

"Well, we have had our suspicions about you for a few months, and tonight I suspected that you were up to something when Gemma had her attack. Your reaction just didn't seem authentic to me" Lucy explained. "Thanks, Aidan" she added as she accepted a glass of wine.

"Here's our take on things" Lucy continued. "Tell me if I'm right. For some reason, you have been trying to have a private chat with Aidan since earlier this year. You tried to collar him at the wedding but that attempt failed – and then he was sent away to Manchester, so your plans had to be put on hold. Then, when Verity had to take Gemma to hospital, you spotted your opportunity and came to see him, while she was out of the picture. We figure that you must have it in for Verity, but we don't yet know why. We're also not quite sure why you disposed of Gemma's handbag after you found it, but I'm sure you'll enlighten us. That's as much as we have worked out so far. Our big question is – why? What have you got against Verity?"

Aidan smiled. "Good going. You've pieced together quite a few elements of the story – the finer details can wait for another time. Meanwhile, perhaps Jane and I can explain to you exactly how Verity has supposedly ruined Jane's entire life".

After Jane and Aidan had finished speaking, Alice and Bella looked at Lucy, wordlessly imploring her to respond on their behalf. Lucy nodded in agreement then stood up, walked round the table and sat next to Jane on the bench. Taking Jane in her arms, she held her tightly. Jane burst into tears.

"You poor thing – you have been through a lot, haven't you?" soothed Lucy. Jane nodded as she continued to weep on Lucy's shoulder. "But can't you see that Verity was a victim too? The real villain of the piece is that loser who you were engaged to – what was his name again?"

"J-Jason" sobbed Jane.

"Right, so it was Jason who injured you and Verity. You were both his victims, but the difference between you is that Verity has put it behind her and moved on, but you haven't been able to. Don't worry, though – I know people who can help you with that, but it won't be easy, I warn you. Tell me – are you up for it? Do you want to take control and finally rebuild your life?"

"Yes" whispered Jane. "I do. Help me – please."

"OK, good – let's start now" began Lucy firmly. "Why don't you begin by telling us your real name?"

"Martine" said Jane quietly. "My name is Martine".

At that moment a key turned in the lock and the front door opened. Everyone around the table turned to look as Verity walked into the room.

"Hi, V" said Aidan affectionately. "Is Gemma OK?"

"Yes she's fine" replied Verity, looking in confusion at her friends and at Jane's tearstained face. "They're keeping her in for observation overnight but she going to be perfectly alright. Not being rude, but why are you guys here – and what's wrong with you, Jane? Why are you so upset?"

"Darling – can I introduce you to Martine?" said Aidan pleasantly, pointing at Jane. "I believe the two of you know each other – but it was rather a long time ago".

"Martine?" Verity stared at Jane, a look of confusion on her face. "I only knew one Martine, back when I was a teenager. But she was quite a chubby girl – in fact, the girls in her year at school used to call her Moonface. Also, she had long, dark hair, and a West Country accent – and..." Verity tailed off as she saw Aidan looking at her in wry amusement, one eyebrow raised.

"Oh my God – it's you!" exclaimed Verity, looking at Martine/Jane in astonishment as the penny dropped.

"My sweet" continued Aidan gently. "As we have said on more than one occasion, it's a bloody good job that I am the detective in this family and not you!"

"Could you be just a little bit more patronising, please?" Verity retorted, albeit with a slight smile on her face.

"Lucy, on the other hand; I'll happily give you a job if you can just stop believing in peoples' innate goodness" Aidan continued.

"Thanks all the same, Aidan, but I would rather stick to psychology if you don't mind" answered Lucy. "Right everyone, I suggest we all sit down and agree what we are going to do next". Looking at Bella and Alice, she continued:

"Feel free to duck out at this point if you like – it is very late, after all. Otherwise, if you decide to stay, I suggest you text your other halves – I predict we're going to be here for a while".

"We're going nowhere" said Bella firmly as she and Alice both grabbed their phones.

"I'll go and get another bottle of wine" added Verity.

❊ ❊ ❊

Some time and several bottles later, the group had agreed an outline plan. Martine had undertaken to embark upon a series of counselling sessions that Lucy would arrange via her contacts. Verity had consented to attend one or more of these sessions along with Martine, if she was asked to do so. The first few sessions would be timed to take place before the November book club, to prepare Martine to explain the situation to her book club colleagues and attempt to make her peace with them. In the meantime, everyone in the room agreed to keep the night's impromptu gathering a secret and only release some key information to selected members of the book club, in order to give Martine the chance to begin her recovery without undue disruption.

Finally it was time for Lucy, Alice, Bella and Martine to return home for some much needed sleep. As the four women were putting on their coats, Bella suddenly remembered something.

"We never agreed who was going to host the next book club meeting" she reminded them. "Also, we never decided on which book to read".

"I'll do it" offered Alice. "I'll be sure to order in lots of lady petrol – and an industrial supply of tissues. I'll also tell Sandy that it might be a good idea to arrange a work do in London for that evening. As for the book, I can think of a perfect choice, given what we have just been discussing. It's called – 'Six Months to Get a Life' ". Alice put her arm around Martine, smiled at her and gave her a hug.

"Sounds perfect!" cried Bella as the little group made to leave. "Night my lovelies" she called, waving an arm casually behind her as the four women headed off down the driveway.

Aidan put his arm around Verity's shoulders as they waved goodbye to the book club posse. "You OK, love?" he asked.

"Yeah, I'll be fine" replied his wife. "I wish that you could be a fly on the wall at the November book club meeting, though, because one thing is for sure. If I know Martine, we haven't heard half of the story yet".

"Funny – that's exactly what I said to them earlier" agreed Aidan.

With that, the two of them shut the door firmly on a long, difficult night and headed upstairs to bed.

＊ ＊ ＊

In the middle of that same night, the security lights at Gemma's house blazed into action in response to a small figure who tentatively approached the front door, glancing nervously in all directions. As the neighbours slept soundly, oblivious to the lights, and the owners of the house remained miles away at the local hospital, the figure placed a small carrier bag behind a plant pot next to the front door and then retreated, unseen, into the darkness.

＊ ＊ ＊

# CHAPTER 11

*November Book Club*

G emma stood at her living room window, clutching a comforting mug of coffee and gloomily contemplating her beloved garden. Until recently it had clung on to some remnants of the summer's colour, but November had announced its arrival with a sharp frost and the last few brave flowers had quickly succumbed to the freezing cold. Since then the weather had turned damp and windy, so the lawn was now almost obscured by a sodden, orange-brown coating of fallen leaves. Gemma knew she should rake them up for compost, but on this miserable Saturday morning she couldn't be bothered.

Just then, the living room door opened quietly behind her and Robert came in, holding the coffee pot.

"Are you alright, love?" he asked gently. "Would you like a top up? Also, I'm just about to make myself a bacon sandwich – do you want one?"

"No thanks; I'll get something later – I'm not hungry right now" replied Gemma, holding out her coffee mug. "But I'm fine – please don't worry".

Since she returned from hospital a few days ago, Robert had been working from home so that he could look after his wife. His kindness and care were touching, but Gemma was secretly looking forward to Monday, when they would both be going back to work and life would return to normal – or as close to normal as they could get, given the circumstances.

As Gemma settled herself on her comfy, L-shaped sofa with a stack of magazines and books, her phone pinged to indicate a WhatsApp message. Glancing at the screen, Gemma saw that the message was from Lucy. The book club WhatsApp group had been unusually quiet over the last few days, thought Gemma, once everyone had reassured themselves that she was going to be fine. It was almost as though no-one really knew what to do next. Perhaps this message from Lucy would change all that.

"Hi – any chance I can pop round for a coffee this morning?" Lucy's message began. "I don't want to intrude if you're busy – but I do have cake...seriously though, I could do with a chat if you're free".

"Come on round" replied Gemma "I'll be at home all morning".

Gemma wandered into the kitchen where Robert was busy assembling a large bacon sandwich.

"Lucy's coming round in a bit. I guess she might have an update on what happened at book club – after I was taken to hospital".

"Well I'm going to do some gardening after I've finished this – so I'll leave you both to it" said Robert. "There's more work to do on the patio and those leaves need raking up".

"You're an angel" replied Gemma. "She's bringing cake, by the way – we'll be sure to leave you some".

Shortly afterwards the doorbell rang and Gemma opened

the door to find Lucy half-hidden behind the enormous bunch of flowers she was holding in one hand, whilst the other clutched a large cake tin.

"Come in – what gorgeous flowers. You really didn't have to bring a bouquet and a cake – but it's nice that you did!" exclaimed Gemma.

"They're from all of us" Lucy explained. "We have all been thinking of you, obviously, hence the flowers and cake, but we thought we'd give you a bit of space after you got back from hospital. I imagine, though, that by now you're keen to know what has been going on".

"Yes, you're right" said Gemma. "Let me pour you some coffee, then we'll go in the living room and catch up over that cake. I told Robert earlier that I wasn't hungry, but I can always find room for cake – and something tells me I'm going to need it".

Once the two women were settled at opposite ends of the sofa with two large slices of cake, Lucy turned to her friend and began to speak the words she had been rehearsing constantly in her head since the night of the October book club.

"The first thing you should know is that Jane made the cake that she served at book club – and she put a small quantity of ground almonds in it deliberately, to trigger your symptoms. However, the second thing you should know is that you weren't her ultimate target. It might be hard for you to believe, but Jane didn't want to hurt you; the person she wanted to injure was actually Verity. Her ploy was to get Verity out of the way so that she could go to her house and confront Aidan. She plotted to do this by engineering a trip to hospital for you, so that Verity would have to drive you – as she was the only sober person".

"Bear with me a moment". Gemma wiped her eyes with a

tissue and smiled as Lucy shuffled over to give her a hug. "I'm fine, honestly. I have had a bit of time to think about this over the last few days and I had already concluded that Jane probably did do it deliberately but, at the same time, she didn't mean to cause me any real harm".

"How did you figure that?" asked Lucy, puzzled.

"Well, first of all, I didn't believe her when she said she thought the cake was nut-free" began Gemma. "She's not exactly going to win any BAFTAs for her acting and, as you know, I have never really trusted her. However, I do think she is clever and meticulous, so I suspected that she had done her homework beforehand and used ground almonds as she knew that they would bring on some alarming symptoms almost immediately – but without causing a full-blown anaphylactic attack. If she had really wanted to hurt me, she would have used peanuts – that would have been far more serious."

"Clearly she isn't the only clever one" murmured Lucy.

"Thanks. Also, I twigged that she must have hidden my handbag somewhere in her house, so that I couldn't use my emergency kit and had to be taken to hospital".

"Yes – you're right about that too, Sherlock" said Lucy. "The bad news is that we saw her dump your bag in the Clothing Bank outside the Village Hall, just before she went up to Verity and Aidan's house. It's lucky that your phone wasn't in there, or it would have caused you loads of hassle. Alice said that she was sure she saw it on the table before you were taken ill."

"No - she's wrong about that. My phone was in my handbag – along with my house keys and my wallet, containing all my bank cards."

"I don't understand – how come you have got your phone now?" Lucy asked, a confused expression on her face.

"The morning after we got home from hospital, Robert was just coming back from the shops when he noticed a small carrier bag tucked behind the plant pot next to the front door" Gemma explained. "In it was my phone, wallet and keys. That also made me think she didn't mean me any real harm – or she wouldn't have bothered to return my stuff".

"I guess that she must have decided to dump your bag in a place where it would not be found, so no-one could prove she had hidden it in her house" Lucy mused. "But at the same time, she didn't want to put you to the trouble of cancelling your cards and buying a new phone! She's actually quite considerate, in a twisted kind of way!"

The two women looked at each other and laughed.

"I must say, you're taking this very well" observed Lucy.

"I'm probably not quite as composed as I look" confessed Gemma. "In fact, the whole episode has shaken me up quite a bit – and it has affected Robert and Tabitha as well. We'll all be fine, though, don't worry. At the moment, though, the person I'm most concerned about is Verity. If Jane is prepared to go to these lengths to harm her, are we sure that V's OK – and what are we doing to keep her safe? Also, what can she possibly have done to make Jane hate her so much?"

Lucy took a deep breath before continuing.

"This is where I am going to ask you a big favour" she began. "I can tell you part of the story now, and I obviously wanted to make sure you knew the truth about the nuts in the cake, but I am going to ask that you wait until book club to let Jane tell you all the details. She is a woman with a lot of problems, but I have arranged for her to have professional help and, to her credit, she has grabbed the opportunity with both hands. She's having counselling already and she should be able to update us at book club. I think she deserves the chance to give you her side of the story in her own words, as does Verity. Essentially, the two of them knew each other as teenagers and Verity did something that made Jane blame her for ruining her life. Then, when Jane ran into Verity quite by chance at The Partridge during last year's Christmas do, she started hatching a plot to get her revenge, which is why she moved here".

"Well, that raises a lot more questions than it answers" remarked Gemma. "I have to say, though, that if it were me, I wouldn't want everyone talking behind my back and cooking up their own interpretations of my story, so I think it's kind of you to protect her – and Verity. It won't be easy, but I'm prepared to reserve judgement and hear what they both have to say when we reconvene for book club."

"Wow I must say – you have been amazing about this" gasped Lucy, breathing a sigh of relief. "I'm not sure I would have been as strong in your shoes, even with all my training".

"Oh I think you would have been" replied Gemma. "Not only that – you deserve a lot of credit for the hard work you are putting in to help resolve all this. What do you say we have a cheeky glass of prosecco to wash down the rest of our cake? It is lunchtime after all – and it's the weekend. What's more, I think we both deserve it!"

"Well, when you put it like that, I can hardly refuse, can I?"

The two friends looked at each other and smiled, then Gemma stood up and headed off in search of a bottle.

✳ ✳ ✳

Later that same day, Arabella stopped her car outside the security gate in front of Emily's farm, got out and rang the bell.

"Hi Emily, it's me" she shouted when Emily answered. "Can I come in for a few minutes? I've got something to tell you".

"Yes of course; come on in" replied Emily. Immediately a buzzer sounded and the security gate slowly began to open. Bella trotted back to her car and drove through the widening gap into the farmyard beyond.

Emily was standing at the back door of the farmhouse.

"Your timing is perfect" she announced "I have just put the kettle on as Mum is here with a batch of her home-made scones, so we can all have afternoon tea. Very lady-like, don't you think?" she finished with a cheeky grin.

Bella followed her into the kitchen where Peggy was at the table, filling a tray of scones with jam and clotted cream.

"Hi Peggy – those look delicious!"

The two women gave each other a brief hug, then Emily set the teapot on the table and the three of them settled down for an impromptu calorie-fest. As she reached for her first scone, Bella decided to get the difficult news out of the way right at the start.

"Look - I'm sorry to be the bearer of bad news, but I just wanted to let you both know in advance of the next book club. After you left book club last time to go round to Gemma's house and speak to Robert – well - Lucy, Alice and I found out from Jane that she did make that cake – and put ground almonds in it, Peggy – as you suggested".

"I thought as much!" snarled Emily, immediately incandescent with rage. "That wicked little cow. I'm going to go round there and beat the crap out of her – she could have killed Gemma!"

"Calm down, Em" said Peggy. "I know you're angry, but we need to refer this one to the Police, rather than acting like vigilantes. What Jane has done constitutes assault, I think, or even attempted murder – we can get her charged and hopefully convicted. That will be much more effective than confronting her ourselves, which would just land us in a whole heap of trouble".

"Can I just ask you both to hold fire for a moment, while I explain a few things?" interrupted Bella hastily. "I think it's worth waiting until after book club before doing anything, and here's why..."

Over several scones and cups of tea, Bella gave Emily and Peggy the same update that Lucy had earlier given to Gemma.

"So we're sure that Gemma's OK?" asked Peggy. "That's my main concern right now."

"Yes – Lucy messaged me earlier to say that Gemma is fine and is willing to wait until book club for the full story" replied Bella. "She was amazed at how brave and understanding Gemma was".

"Well, if Gemma's agreed to wait, then I'll do the same" mumbled Emily grudgingly. "I'm nowhere near as understanding as she is, though, and I'll tell you one thing. If I run into Jane in the pub, or anywhere else, between now and book club, I will not be responsible for my actions! But I promise I won't actively seek her out".

"I doubt you will see her between now and book club" Bella confided. "She is going to be keeping her head down and focusing on her counselling sessions".

"I think that's just as well" concluded Peggy. "In the meantime, I suggest we all have another scone and talk about something else".

\* \* \*

The next Friday night, Aidan headed down the road through the chill darkness to The Mallard, accompanied by a pale and subdued Verity. As the two of them entered the pub he made straight for the bar, whilst Verity joined Rick next to the fireplace, where the two of them stood shivering and grumbling about the cold.

"A pint of Landlord for me please, Toby, and a Becks Blue for Verity" Aidan called over to Toby, who was engrossed in his laptop.

Dave, Melvin and Wesley wandered over to join Rick and Verity for a chat by the fire. After a few minutes, Dave enquired:

"By the way Verity, I have been meaning to ask you – have you seen Jane recently? We were only saying last night that we hadn't seen her for a while, and we were just wondering if she was OK".

"She's not too well at the moment, I'm afraid" replied Verity. "She's got a few health issues" she continued vaguely "but she should be on the mend soon, I hope".

"Well if you see her, could you tell her that we have all been asking after her?" asked Melvin. "We'd like her to know that we miss her in here. We've got used to having her around, you see, so we hope she feels better soon".

"I'll be sure to pass the message on, if I do run into her" Verity promised. "I'm sure she'd love to know that you are thinking of her".

\* \* \*

A few days later, Martine returned home late, exhausted

after a long day at work followed by an intense and challenging counselling session. Wearily she struggled out of her car, hoisted her heavy work bag onto her shoulder and trudged up the pathway to her cottage.

As she reached her doorstep and fumbled in her bag for her keys, she almost tripped over a strange-looking bundle lying on the ground in front of the cottage door. Wrapped up in colourful paper, it was open at one end, from which protruded a small envelope. Martine picked the bundle up, carried it into the hallway and switched on the light.

Once her eyes adjusted to the brightness, Martine tore open the loosely wrapped parcel to reveal a prettily tied bunch of late autumn berries and wild flowers plus two large, deep yellow sunflowers. Astonished, she opened the accompanying envelope and withdrew a small greetings card, which read:

"Sorry your not feeling well. Your friends down The Mallard are missing you and so am I. If you need to talk, ring this number anytime. With best wishes from A Friend".

Puzzled but immensely flattered, Martine carefully arranged the flowers and berries in a vase and placed it in the centre of her kitchen table, before heading to the sink to fill the kettle.

As she switched the kettle on to boil, her phone pinged with a WhatsApp message. As she picked it up, she saw that there were a number of unread messages in the recently created group comprising only those members of the book club who had been at Verity's house after the last meeting.

The first message was from Alice:

"Hi Martine. Just wanted to say that I'm thinking of you. Hope you're OK".

The second message was from Lucy:

"Me too. FYI Gemma knows the truth about 'Nutgate' ;-). She took it very well and has agreed to wait until book club to get the full story from you and V. Hang on in there xx".

The third message was from Bella:

"Peggy and Emily know too, as we agreed. Emily was pretty angry but I'm sure she will come round once she hears what you have to say. In the meantime I would keep out of her way until book club. Stay strong – I'm sure it'll work out ☺".

Verity concluded the exchange by writing:

"Let us know if you need anything – see you soon and hope the rest of the counselling goes well. All the best".

Martine gazed at her screen, a look of incredulity on her face. She was awestruck by the ability of these women to forgive and move on – and suddenly felt eager to emulate them. Before she could change her mind, she tapped her Phone icon, then clicked on the Keypad option – and dialled the mystery number.

\* \* \*

The weather remained damp and miserable for most of November, and book club day was no exception. Alice, who hated the return of the cold weather at this time of year, had turned up the Aga and was gratefully absorbing its warmth as she stirred a huge vat of mulled wine in her cosy kitchen. On the worktop next to the pan was a litre bottle of cooking brandy. Alice unscrewed the cap and poured a hefty slug into the mulled wine, hesitated, then tipped in some more.

"What the hell" she muttered to herself. "I think we're

going to need an extra shot this month!"

She wandered over to the kitchen window and stared out into her garden where, in the fast fading light, two chubby squirrels were happily excavating the remains of the family's Halloween pumpkins. Crossing her fingers behind her back, Alice prayed fervently that this month's book club meeting would not turn out to be a horror show as well. Once again she went over in her mind the plan that she, Bella and Lucy had devised for the meeting and wordlessly entreated the Almighty to help them execute it successfully.

An hour or so later, the book club posse began to arrive. Lorelei, who had the longest journey and had allowed herself plenty of time, was the first to show up. She gratefully accepted a mug of mulled wine from her hostess and remarked:

"I had better make this one last as I am driving – it smells gorgeous. From what I hear, though, I'll probably need a bit of alcohol to get through this meeting – Peggy warned me to have my flak jacket on!"

"I hope it won't be that bad" Alice answered quickly as the doorbell rang.

Jos and Anna, who had walked down together, were huddled on the doorstep with their hoods up against the drizzle, which had just started again after a short respite. Alice ushered them in and quickly dispensed restorative mugs of mulled wine. No sooner had they all settled down in the living room than the bell rang once more and they were joined by Nicky, who had given Irene a lift. After she had greeted everyone Nicky, who was never one to avoid awkward topics of conversation, wasted no time in saying what some of the group had privately been thinking:

"So – do we think Jane will show up tonight? I wouldn't

be surprised if she gave it a miss after last month – given everything that happened".

Alice was saved by the bell from having to answer Nicky's question. Leaving the others to speculate about the night ahead, she opened the door to Peggy and Emily.

"Don't look so worried!" whispered Emily as she hugged her friend in greeting. "I promise I will be calm and re-strained, whatever happens tonight. After all, we don't want to get blood on your lovely soft furnishings, now do we?" She winked at her friend, who smiled back ner-vously.

"I'll be glad when tonight's over" Alice confessed. "In the meantime, let me give you a large quantity of booze!"

Gemma was the next to arrive, apologising profusely for being one of the last, although she had only yards to walk from her own house.

"Don't be silly, you're not late at all." Alice gave her friend a big hug. "Jane isn't here yet, by the way. I know I've asked you before, but are you going to be alright?"

"I'll be fine" Gemma reassured her. "Don't worry about me. Oh – there's the bell. I'll go on into the living room and leave you to it".

"Go via the kitchen and grab yourself a mulled wine" called Alice, heading back towards the door. Taking a deep breath, she opened it and greeted Martine, who was flanked by Lucy and Arabella.

"Evening, ladies. How are you all – you OK, Martine?"

"I'm fine" answered Martine. "A bit anxious of course, but I'll cope".

"Excellent – let me get you all a drink, first of all" offered Alice.

"Just a small one for me, please" urged Martine. "I haven't

really been drinking since – well, since all this kicked off last month".

Alice directed the three women into the kitchen, handed them each a drink and filled a large earthenware jug with mulled wine. Then she looked at them and said quietly:

"Are you all ready?"

The three of them looked gravely at their hostess and nodded.

"Right then – let's do this". Before she could change her mind, Alice opened the door to the living room and the four of them walked in.

The rest of the book club members had been chatting idly, but they immediately fell silent as soon as they saw Jane. Alice directed her and Lucy to a small sofa near the fireplace, whilst Bella settled herself next to Peggy and Emily.

"OK everyone" Alice began. "I know we all normally have a good old gossip at this point but, given what happened at last month's meeting, I think it would be good if you could just listen to Jane for a few minutes while she tells you some things you ought to know. Is that OK? Also, while you're listening, please pass around the jug and top your drinks up – and make a start on the canapés".

The women remained silent and stared expectantly at Jane. The jug started to do the rounds, but the canapés remained untouched.

Perching nervously on the edge of the sofa, Jane pulled a sheaf of handwritten notes from her bag, the paper fluttering in her unsteady hands.

"Thanks everyone for agreeing to listen" she began quietly.

"Well, I guess the first thing you all want to know is – did

I know there were nuts in the cake? The answer to that question is yes".

There was an audible gasp from Jos at this point, whilst the others for whom this was news sat in silent shock.

"In fact, I made the cake and deliberately added a small quantity of ground almonds so that Gemma would not notice them, but would immediately experience a mild attack with some alarming symptoms" Jane continued.

"And why the fuck would you do that? Do tell". Emily's voice was sarcastic and eerily calm, but full of venom and suppressed rage. Peggy put a hand on her daughter's arm to silence her.

"The main thing you should know is that Gemma was not my target – Verity was. I needed to get Verity out of the way so that I could go and tell Aidan some secrets about her that I hoped would destabilise their marriage and turn him against her, along with all of you".

The women collectively turned to look at Verity, puzzled.

"You see, I know Verity – we were at the same school a long time ago" continued Jane. "I have loathed her ever since because I believed that she ruined my life. For so many years I have dreamed about getting my own back on her so when I came across her, quite by chance, in The Partridge last Christmas, I seized the opportunity to make my dream of revenge come true".

Irene could keep silent no longer.

"Sorry, but I don't get it" she said. "V, how come you didn't recognise Jane and suspect that she was up to something?"

Verity looked at Irene and shrugged, blushing slightly.

"Now I'm the first to admit that I'm not the most observant of people, as Aidan is always reminding me" she began. "However, in my defence, Jane has changed out of all recognition. She has lost a ton of weight, transformed her hairstyle and colour completely – and she used to have a strong West Country accent, which she has clearly lost. Also, she's obviously older than when I last saw her. Are you sure that you would recognise a person whom you hadn't seen since she was a teenager? Not only that; she has been using a false name since she has been living here. Her name is not really Jane – it's Martine".

"OK, I get it" snarled Emily. "So – Martine, or whatever your name is – what did our Verity do that was so terrible it justified putting Gemma's life in danger? I'm sure we'd all like to know the answer to that one".

"To answer that properly, Emily, I need to give you a quick life history, so please bear with me. I spent most of my childhood living with my parents in a commune in Somerset; hence the accent which Verity remembers but which I worked so hard to lose, as it brings back some traumatic memories. You see, my folks embraced an alternative lifestyle, which in reality meant that they were grossly negligent and mainly too stoned to remember I existed. Even when a swing I was playing on collapsed and chunks of it got embedded in my leg and face, other members of the commune had to take me to hospital as my Mum and Dad were too out of it to be of any use. I had to have thirty stitches in my leg and I still have the scar to this day, although the scars on my face are fainter and I can cover them with make-up. Anyway, to cut a long story short, I grew up without the loving care that most children take for granted.

I thought that things would improve when we left the commune and moved to Manchester, but instead they just got worse. At my new inner-city school, I was labelled a yokel because of my accent and a weirdo because my parents and I were odd looking and didn't have a TV, which meant that I couldn't join in with all the conversations about favourite programmes. So I was still ignored and uncared for at home but now, on top of that, I was bullied, victimised and beaten up at school. I didn't have a friend in the world, and this miserable existence continued up until the day I met Jason".

Martine pause and swigged some mulled wine from her mug.

"Jason was a few years older than me. He was charming, good-looking and attentive – I couldn't believe that he was interested in me. I fell head over heels in love with him and I was happy and secure for the first time in my life. We were together for over three years and had started planning our wedding, even though I was obviously still very young. I left school, got a job in a hotel and spent most of my spare time at Jason's flat. In fact, I was there on the night when the Police came and took him away. He was arrested and charged with raping a girl a few years younger than me, who was still at school – the same school that I had been to, as it turned out. Then, once the case came to court, I discovered that the alleged victim was Verity, whom I knew slightly. You see, we were both rubbish at hockey and netball so we were forced to join the school gymnastics club instead, which is how I had come across her.

Anyway, it might sound odd, but I wasn't actually very concerned about the rape charge, as I knew that my Jason wouldn't ever do anything like that. I didn't even stay in court to listen to the case for the prosecution, as I didn't want to hear the lies that they were spreading about him. When Verity admitted that she had made up the story about the rape and asked for all the charges to be dropped, I knew that I had been right all along and expected that things would just return to normal. It didn't work out that way, though.

When I went round to Jason's flat after the acquittal, I discovered that he had packed up and left, without even leaving so much as a note. The only love I had ever known in my life was gone, and all because of her. I never saw Verity again either - her parents shipped her off to some posh boarding school in the countryside – but I though of her constantly over the years as I lurched from one dead end job and one disastrous, abusive relationship to another. I vowed that, if I ever set eyes on her again, I would ruin her life like she destroyed mine".

"Is this true, Verity?" asked Anna.

"Yes, pretty much" mumbled Verity, staring at the floor.

"So, when I recognised Verity on the night of your Christmas dinner in The Partridge, I started hatching a plan to take revenge" Martine explained. "Sean, the barman at The Partridge, told me that you were all in the Oak Welby Book Club so I moved to the village, started going into The Mallard and, soon enough, I ran into you, Peggy. I persuaded you to let me join book club so that I could find out more about Verity and devise a way to ruin her life. I quickly found out that she had no kids, so I made her husband my main focus along with you, her friends. I wanted to make you all hate her as much as I did. I was pretty sure that she wouldn't recognise me after all these years as I have changed so much and, sure enough, she didn't".

Jos leaned forwardly and regarded Martine shrewdly.

"I bet you were relieved you didn't have to share a room with Verity at Waterside View" she commented. "She would definitely have recognised you then, wouldn't she?"

"What are you talking about, Jos?" asked Peggy.

"I'm talking about her scar" replied Jos "the one on your

right femur, Martine – from your childhood accident on the swing. Verity would have surely seen it when you were both getting changed for gym club, all those years ago. It's pretty big and distinctive, after all – I certainly couldn't help noticing it when we shared a room that weekend. Even though Verity's no Miss Marple, if you had shared a room with her, there's a good chance that she would have recognised it and put two and two together".

"So that's why you were worried about going away to Waterside View!" exclaimed Alice. "You thought you might have to share a room with Verity! However, once I mentioned that she always shares with Lorelei, you changed your tune pretty quickly and agreed to come along".

"That's right" admitted Martine "mystery solved. Anyway, I managed to remain incognito and spent a lot of time finding out about Aidan. Once I discovered that he was a Police Officer, with a pretty black and white view of what constitutes right and wrong, plus some severe emotional scars from his long and eventful career, I knew I'd be able to cause a lot of damage by telling him all about Verity's lies. However, it proved incredibly difficult to find the right opportunity to speak to him, as the two of them were always together.

I made my first real attempt to speak to Aidan on the day of the wedding but that failed, and shortly afterwards he was sent away – ironically, to Manchester, of all places - so that meant my plans had to be put on hold for a few months. However, I was undeterred and used the time productively to devise a number of alternative plans for wreaking my revenge. The one I eventually got to deploy involved using Gemma's nut allergy to get Verity out of the way, so that I could go round to her house and confront Aidan. For that plan to work, I needed you to be away, Jos, otherwise you might have been able to use your medical training to help Gemma, without her having to go to hospital. I also needed you all to be drinking, except for Verity, so that she was the only person able to drive Gemma to Heatherfield".

Emily could stay silent no longer. As Martine paused to take another drink, she growled:

"And, luckily for you, all the planets were aligned for our October book club. Jos was away looking after Cian and Esme, the rest of us either got lifts or walked to your house – and you were positively pouring prosecco down our necks once we got there. After that, all you had to do was serve a big slice of your lovely chocolate cake, to trigger Gemma's attack, hide her bag with her kit in it, then watch the whole thing unfold. Well I for one don't care what Verity did to you. However bad it was, it didn't justify putting Gemma's life at risk and deceiving all of us".

"Hang on a sec, Em" interrupted Gemma. "Jane, sorry Martine, didn't put my life at risk. She only used a small quantity of nuts and chose almonds, not peanuts, as she knew that they would not trigger anaphylaxis - just some dramatic, but ultimately not very harmful symptoms".

"Wow, that was big of her" retorted Emily sarcastically.

"Gemma, I can't believe that you, of all people, are defending her" remarked Anna. "I don't get it".

"Actually, I completely forgive her" said Gemma. "I can understand that she had a difficult and traumatic childhood and was devastated when Jason, the only person she had ever trusted, betrayed that trust by deserting her".

"I agree" added Lucy quickly. "Martine received no support afterwards so she had no way of recovering and that, compounded by her childhood traumas and subsequent abusive relationships, has left her with some deep-rooted issues. That's why I have put her in touch with a great counselling service and she is finally getting the help she deserves. I for one think that she deserves our support, friendship – and forgiveness".

"A few things are starting to make sense now" observed Lorelei. "Take the August meeting at my house, when Lucy was talking about Narcissistic Personality Disorder and you got pretty upset, Martine. I guess the subject was a bit close to home".

"Oh God – your tattoos, your paintings – even your under-cut pixie – it's all starting to fall into place!" cried Nicky. "You must have been so angry all these years".

"And you were constantly banging on about revenge and sin, during the various book reviews" remarked Irene. "I always thought that was a bit weird".

"Right – and that's why you sang the lyrics of Back to Black with so much feeling!" added Anna. "Not to mention your Mohican and your punk outfit at Gemma's party..."

"Hang on a minute" interrupted Martine, smiling faintly. "There are limits to the conclusions you can draw from this. I'm just into punk, OK? That's what comes from having two hippies as parents – I was bound to rebel and go to the other extreme, musically speaking. Anyway, can I just say one last thing?"

Again the room fell silent as the women braced themselves for another potential revelation.

"I never came to this village to make friends, obviously" Martine began. "Nevertheless, I have encountered more warmth and friendship here, in this crazy little corner of middle England, than anywhere else in my life. I totally understand if some of you can't bear to be friends with me any longer, but I just wanted to say thank you to each of you, in any case. You have all helped me more than you know".

"Well I for one forgive you" said Peggy firmly. "It's obvious to me that you've had a difficult life, but you're working hard to turn it around, and I respect that. As far as I'm concerned, you're still a Titswiper!"

"I agree" said Lorelei. "We're a forgiving bunch around here. You can be like that woman in the book the other month, who had a load of counselling and then finally got her life back on track – and we will be here to support you".

"But what about me?" said Verity quietly from the corner of the room, clutching her mug of fruit punch. "Am I still in the gang? After all, I'm the one who made the false accusation of rape that set this whole thing off".

"Of course you're still in the gang, you silly sod!" cried Emily. "It was all a long time ago and you were very young. Nothing to forgive, in my opinion".

"I totally agree" murmured Martine, and the group stared at her in surprise as she walked across the room, sat down next to Verity and put her arm around her. Smiling at the book club posse, she added:

"The counselling I am having, thanks to Lucy, is helping me to face up to the truth about Jason, the so-called love of my life. He did not rape Verity, that's true – but he did assault her so badly that she still bears some physical scars, although she did get help pretty promptly at that posh school of hers to sort her head out. At the end of the day, we were both victims, but it has taken me until now to accept that. I only wish that Verity had taken her lawyer's advice all those years ago and had Jason charged with sexual assault. It's funny though. I always assumed that my revelations would cause a real rift between Aidan and Verity. Because I had created a picture of her in my head as a pathological liar, it never occurred to me that she would have told Aidan the whole story, before they got married".

Turning to Verity, Martine smiled. "So I was completely wrong-footed by your honesty – and the solid relationship that you have with Aidan".

"Not so solid that he didn't feel the need to check up on me" replied Verity with a wry and slightly wounded smile. Seeing the puzzled faces of the book club posse, Verity explained to them how Aidan had accessed the Court records to ensure that her version of events was in fact true.

"To be honest, finding out that he checked up on me, and didn't trust me to tell the truth, has caused quite a few problems in our house over the last few weeks" finished Verity sadly. "So to some extent your original wish did come true – Jane".

"I'm so sorry" said Martine simply.

"Let it go, V" advised Lucy. "Don't forget that Aidan had his own demons too, back then – the failure of his first marriage, not to mention the traumas of the double murder that he had just wrecked his health to help solve. He was only protecting himself".

"I agree" said Peggy. "I think that we should, as a group, make a collective decision to move on. Martine, you stick with your counselling, do your wonderful painting, keep that funky haircut and stay a Titswiper – even after you leave us to go to France. And as for you, Verity – you go home later and give that husband of yours a big hug. He's a good man".

"Right – now that we have got all that out of the way" laughed Gemma "can we please get on and review the bloody book?"

"Good idea!" cried Alice, inwardly heaving a huge sigh

of relief. "I'll top everyone up – and for goodness' sake, please eat the mountain of food that I have lovingly prepared for you. Just one more question for you though, Martine..."

Everyone stopped what they were doing and turned their attention to Alice and Martine.

"Yes – what is it?" Martine smiled pleasantly at Alice.

"When we were at Waterside View – why did you knock me off the paddleboard? I can't see where that fits into the picture at all".

"That had nothing to do with anything" answered Martine. "I'm afraid that it was an accident – pure and simple. No more water sports for me in future!"

Now that the drama appeared to be over, appetites started to kick in and the women began happily demolishing the plates of canapés that were strategically placed all around Alice's living room.

"These mini quiches are lovely – can someone stop me eating them, please? I've already had five" laughed Lorelei.

"In that case I will save you from yourself by asking you to kick off the book review!" suggested Gemma, never one to miss an opportunity.

"OK, I'm happy to start us off. I actually really enjoyed it and I could definitely empathise with the main character" began Lorelei. "I thought at the time that his life was quite interesting, as he certainly had his ups and downs" she added "but now, having heard Jane's – sorry Martine's – story tonight, his seems quite uneventful by comparison! Even so, it was a pleasant, if not exactly earth-shattering book, in my opinion".

Emily was next. "Well I'm sorry to disagree, but I couldn't empathise with him at all" she retorted in characteristically forthright fashion. "I thought he was a bit of a wimp and, as you all know, I don't do wimps. Overall he was far too meek for my taste, especially when it came to his ex-wife". Turning to Martine, Emily remarked:

"I noticed the contrast with you tonight, Martine, when you were talking earlier. I'll say one thing for you – no-one could describe you as meek, and I can certainly relate to that!"

The two women smiled at each other then turned towards Jos, who had begun her review.

"If we are comparing the protagonist with our Martine, I must say that I did spot some similarities" Jos observed. "For instance, he showed signs of self-loathing, just as you have, Martine, at various different times during the year".

Martine inclined her head in acknowledgement.

"I really hope that your counselling will help you to work through that and learn to like yourself – anyway sorry, I digress. Back to the book" Jos admonished herself. "Like you, Lorelei, I thought it was a pleasant enough read and it ended on a positive and optimistic note, which I liked".

"I agree" said Anna warmly. "The guy has obviously been through a tough time, but the book offers hope for a happier and more fulfilling future. I wish you the same thing, Martine".

The reviews all continued in much the same vein, with each woman commenting briefly but positively on the pleasant, feel-good novel and adding a supportive message for Martine, who seemed to grow in stature and glow with pleasure as she heard each new word of encouragement.

By the time the last book club member had finished speaking, only a few crumbs and token lettuce leaves remained on the canapé plates and the mulled wine was all gone. Undaunted, Alice the bountiful hostess disappeared briefly into the kitchen, emerging just moments later with a couple of chilled bottles of champagne, an alcohol-free bottle of Bees Knees for Verity and a tray full of champagne flutes.

"I thought we would round off this month's book club by drinking a toast to bright futures and new beginnings – for Martine and for us all!" announced their host.

Once their glasses were all suitably charged, the indomitable women of the Oak Welby Book Club stood up, raised their glasses and chorused:

"Bright futures and new beginnings!"

As they sat back down, Peggy remembered a few housekeeping issues that needed to be agreed with the group before they all left.

"Talking of the future" she began "I just need a word about the book club Christmas Dinner next month. As discussed, I have hired a minibus so we don't have to worry about driving or parking. It will pick Nicky up first at around 6.45pm, followed by you, Irene; then it will carry on to the farm and collect Emily, Lorelei and myself – Lol I assume you'll be staying with me? The bus will then stop outside your house, Anna, to pick up everyone else from the village, before heading off to The Partridge. Is that OK with you all – are you happy to gather outside Anna's by seven?"

Everyone nodded in agreement.

"Also, Sigrid at The Partridge has confirmed that she has reserved our usual table in the corner, to minimise any disruption to the other diners – they live in hope, as usual!" laughed Peggy. "One of these days they'll realise that it doesn't make the slightest difference. Anyway, I think that's the Christmas Dinner all sorted, unless anyone has any questions?"

"I'd just like to get everyone's thoughts on next month's book" Gemma answered. "As no-one is going to be hosting a meeting in December, because we're going for dinner instead, how do you think we should decide which book we're going to read?"

Peggy looked across at Martine.

"Well, I don't know about the rest of you, but I think that Martine has provided us with quite enough drama to last us for the rest of the year!" she joked, winking at Martine, whose face had fallen suddenly. "Also, we all have a busy month ahead, what with the Village Hall Christmas Party and all the other festive celebrations – not to mention the dreaded shopping and cooking. I therefore suggest that we have a month off, resume our reading in the New Year and, in the meantime, relax and enjoy our Christmas break".

Peggy's suggestion received the thumbs up from the rest of the group, who then chatted idly about their Christmas plans for a few minutes whilst they finished the last of the champagne. By this time it was getting very late, so as soon as their glasses were empty the women started packing up to leave, thanking Alice for a lovely evening.

As Alice opened the front door for her friends, she saw that the rain had redoubled its efforts compared with the earlier half-hearted drizzle. Water was cascading in rivulets from the roof tiles and huge, fat droplets rebounded on the pathway leading from her house to the road.

"Typical – I forgot my umbrella" muttered Martine, turning up her coat collar and preparing to head off alone, as her walk home took her in a different direction from everyone else.

"Hang on a sec, Martine!" called Verity. "I brought my car

tonight as the weather looked a bit dodgy – I'll give you a lift home, if you like?"

"Are you sure?" Martine replied.

"Of course – what are friends for?" Verity smiled as she nodded her head in the direction of her car, then the two women scuttled off together towards the waiting vehicle.

The rest of the book club members left in small groups, either huddled under umbrellas or shivering damply in their SUVs until only Lucy, Bella and Gemma, who had the shortest distances to walk, remained alongside Alice on the doorstep.

"Well, ladies – or what did Aidan call us – the No.1 Ladies' Detective Agency?" asked Lucy. "What do we think about tonight? Job done?"

"Job well and truly done, in my opinion" replied Bella firmly.

The four women embraced each other warmly in a group hug, oblivious to the raindrops that soaked their hair and faces. Maybe a few tears added to the trickles of water that ran down their cheeks, but they went largely unnoticed and were soon washed away.

* * *

Early on the Friday morning after the book club meeting, Verity shuffled into her study clutching a cup of coffee and wearing her winter 'working from home' uniform comprising a skiing base layer, a tattered fleece and an ancient pair of ripped, faded jeans. The top half of the uniform could hastily be replaced by a white shirt if an unexpected video conference got added to Verity's schedule but the jeans were a permanent fixture, as they could happily remain out of sight of the webcam.

When she opened her inbox Verity was intrigued to see, at the top of a long list of unread items, an email from Jos, Peggy and Irene, entitled 'Open Me First – Work Emails Can Wait!' Verity smiled as she obediently double-clicked, thinking of the team at her firm's headquarters which carefully monitored employees' email traffic.

The tone of Jos's email was unusually assertive.

"Peggy, Lol and I are going to take you out for dinner tonight at the new Thai restaurant in Hanningford. We have checked your availability with Aidan and he says you're free, so no excuses! I'll pick you up at seven and, before you ask, I'm fine to drive. I'm babysitting for Esme on Saturday morning so I will need to have my wits about me – Cian can be quite a handful! You're always driving us about the place so it's time someone else took a turn. See you later – much love xx"

Verity had no time to speculate on the reason for the impromptu girls' night out as, at that very moment, the sender of the next email in her inbox, which really should have been read first, called her mobile. A crisis had occurred overnight, heralding the start of a day's disaster recovery.

"The joys of project management" Verity concluded later, as she finished describing her day to her friends over pre-dinner drinks at their table in the Thai restaurant. "It can get pretty intense sometimes but, as Aidan is so fond of telling me, no-one actually dies on my projects. Not so far, anyway", she added, tapping the wooden table.

"It doesn't mean it's not stressful, though" Peggy replied firmly, passing round the Thai crackers. "And as for Aidan, I'm willing to bet that he does his fair share of paper-shuffling in that office of his! His job isn't all about saving children from the jaws of death, contrary to what he would have us believe!"

"Quite right" laughed Jos. "It's probably a bit like my job – 1% saving lives and 99% runny noses and ingrown toe-nails!"

"Perfect timing" joked Irene "here are our starters! Can we talk about something else while we are eating?"

"Maybe you should tell me why we're here" said Verity gently, smiling over at Lorelei, who had been unusually quiet. "I know that Lol doesn't drive all the way over here for nothing, so soon after a book club meeting. Why don't you tell me what's going on?"

"OK, I'll start". Lorelei put down her knife and fork. "After book club, Peggy and I were having a bit of a debrief on the phone, as we often do. We got talking about how Jane, sorry Martine, and Gemma have both been getting a lot of support from Lucy, and others in the book club, ever since things kicked off in October. That's all well and good, and we're happy that Martine is getting counselling and all that, but we both agreed that you rather seemed to have been forgotten in all of this. I mean, the whole in-cident must have stirred up a lot of unpleasant memories for you.

We also thought that you were incredibly brave, back then, to admit to the lawyers and the judge that you had made a mistake; and that you might be regretting having let that guy Jason off the hook. Anyway, whatever – we just figured you probably needed a few friends to let you know that we're here for you and you haven't been for-gotten, so we gave Jos a call and asked her to come with us, as she's such a good listener. We didn't want to invite everyone – we thought we'd keep it to just the four of us. I hope we did the right thing – oh God Verity I'm sorry – what's wrong?"

Verity's head was bowed and she was trying to wipe her

eyes discreetly with one of the restaurant's paper napkins, completely failing to disguise how tearful she was. Jos, who was sitting next to her, put her arm around her friend's shoulder.

"Will it help to talk?" she suggested gently to Verity, who nodded in response and blew her nose before speaking.

"You know how Martine casually said that I was sent away to a posh boarding school and seemed to assume that they had somehow 'fixed' me?" she began in a bitter tone of voice that her friends her never heard her use before. "Well – she was dead wrong about that. I mean – the school was great and I had loads of professional help, but despite their best efforts they couldn't stop the panic attacks and the self-harming, which continued for years. Even now I occasionally get a panic attack, although I have mostly learned to control them. It usually happens when by chance I hear a Manchester accent that sounds like Jason's, or when I'm walking through a park alone - that kind of thing tends to trigger them off.

Anyway, I tried to carry on as normal, on the surface at least, and I got my 'A' levels just fine, but underneath I was a mess, all through my university years. Afterwards, I got married too young in a bid for security, but the marriage failed as, fundamentally, I couldn't trust any man. The poor bloke never stood a chance.

After my divorce, I managed to build a decent career, but my personal life was still a disaster area – years of failed relationships with total losers. Not dissimilar to Martine, in fact..." Verity observed with a wry smile.

"It wasn't until I finally spent several years on my own that I managed to recover properly" she continued. "Then I met Aidan, and this time the marriage worked as I had done the heavy lifting myself, before we got together. Also he was, well – Aidan. So things have been pretty much fine for quite a few years now; but I have spent a large chunk of my life trying to recover from what that man did to me".

Verity took a large swig of alcohol-free wine before continuing.

"As for Martine, she did bring some of it back, but do you know what? She isn't him – she isn't Jason. Sure she can stir up a few traumatic memories, but that's the extent of her power. She's obviously got a lot of problems, so I'm choosing to feel sorry for her and move on. Aidan's been very supportive, and the fact that you noticed and cared enough to help – well, that means everything".

Verity raised her glass and looked around the table at her friends, her eyes still shining with unshed tears.

"Here's to good friends" she concluded "and to keeping the past right where it belongs".

❊ ❊ ❊

# CHAPTER 12

*December Book Club*

The Partridge was the cosiest place at Christmas time. Golden light spilled from its long, low windows, reflecting off the bonnet of the gleaming white minibus that had just pulled up outside the rustic front door. The driver walked smartly round to the side of the bus, opened the sliding doors, then quickly stepped back as the noisy occupants spilled chaotically out of the vehicle, laughing and jostling each other playfully.

The ladies of the Oak Welby Book Club hurried through the front door of the village inn, eager to escape the bitterly cold December weather. As they pulled off their winter coats and gloves they looked around them, taking in the welcoming Christmas ambience of the main bar. As usual, every inch of exposed wooden beam was twined with holly and twinkling fairy lights and striking, yet tasteful, decorations were suspended artfully from the ancient farm machinery hanging from the ceiling. On the walls, the horses and hounds in the hunting pictures had once again been adorned with a glittering fandangle of tinsel in honour of the festive season.

Not to be outdone by the décor, the book club members were all gussied up for the evening, each woman conforming to the implicit yuletide fashion rule that every garment worn after 5pm during the month of December must be either glittery, shiny, sequinned, plush and velvety, or all of the above. The eyes of every person in the room were fixated upon the women as, resplendent in their finery, their hair sleek and shiny thanks to Nicky's expert ministrations, they made their way towards the bar for the first drink of the evening.

"Come on, you lot – let's get some drinks ordered!" called Emily impatiently. Sean, the barman, quickly set up a tab and began taking orders for this year's bespoke Christmas cocktail – Perdrix de Noël, a mixture of champagne and ginger liqueur. Rhubarb gin and tonic was another popular choice of aperitif along with a simple glass of prosecco, the perennial middle England favourite.

As Martine picked up her usual glass of white wine she smiled over at Sean, enjoying his look of surprise and confusion as recognition dawned on his face.

"Hi Martine – wow, I almost didn't recognise you, old friend! I love the hair – very funky. Are you here with the book club?"

Martine nodded.

"Well, how things have changed for you since last year!" continued Sean. "Instead of waiting on tables, you're the customer now, coming in to enjoy your dinner. Mind you, I bet you miss working here, though" he observed wryly. "Not".

"Actually" replied Martine "it was nice working with you and the team, if a little stressful at times, but I must confess that I don't miss doling out smoked salmon and game terrines to the pissed-up Christmas punters. That I can do without".

"I bet you can" agreed Sean. "Still, it looks as though you

have settled in very well among the good people of Oak Welby. Has it all worked out nicely for you this year?"

Martine took a large gulp of her wine before answering.

"Let's just say that it hasn't all been plain sailing, Sean – but I'm getting there".

Before she could say any more, Martine was interrupted by Nicky.

"Hey Jay-sorry, Martine – come over here!" Nicky yelled, waving a mobile phone in the air. "You've got to have a look at this..."

As Martine and the others clustered around the phone, Nicky replayed a video shot at the Village Hall Christmas Party, which had taken place the previous Saturday. On the stage Mack, Stan and George, wearing glitter wigs and brandishing inflatable guitars, were proudly strutting their stuff to 'Merry Christmas Everybody' by Slade. As the women watched, George skidded on a stray mince pie and nearly fell off the stage whilst Stan nonchalantly swigged, Keith Richards style, from a large whisky bottle.

"We won that bottle of whisky in the raffle and the three of them practically demolished it at our table" explained Peggy, laughing. "There's no way they would have got up on stage otherwise".

"That's epic!" gasped Gemma, breathless with laughter. "Don't forget to share it on the village Facebook page – let's see if we can get it to go viral" she joked.

"If you think that's good, wait until you see this picture" said Lucy, fishing in her bag for her own phone. "Here we go – take a look at this".

Holding out her phone, Lucy displayed a photo of Toby, who was normally a bit bah-humbug about Christmas but who this year had been the proud winner of the 'Best Christmas Accessory' competition at the Village

Hall party. In the picture, Toby's smiling face looked as though it was emerging from a turkey's rear end, so realistic was his 3D Christmas Turkey hat. As they giggled at his happy countenance, framed by turkey wings and drumsticks, the women remarked on how much more cheerful Toby had become since the consortium took over The Mallard.

"It certainly seems as though the shared responsibility suits him" remarked Alice. "I think he rather likes being part of our new team".

"It was such a great night, the Village Hall Christmas Party – I think everyone enjoyed it" reflected Irene. "You missed a good one, Martine – why didn't you come?"

"I was sorry to miss out, but I had a prior engagement, I'm afraid" Martine answered.

"Sounds mysterious" said Bella, looking over at Martine with one eyebrow raised.

Luckily for Martine, she was saved from having to reply as Sigrid appeared and called the group over to their dinner table. All thoughts of her alternative social life were forgotten by everyone as the book club took their seats at the artfully decorated dinner table and immediately began letting off their party poppers, to the delight of the diners at the neighbouring tables.

Dinner was a sumptuous, riotous and predictably alcohol-fuelled affair. The book club feasted on baked camembert, smoked salmon and a full turkey dinner followed by Christmas pudding, mince pies and cheese, all washed down by an endless stream of prosecco, sauvignon blanc, shiraz and port. Crackers were pulled, paper hats were tried on and quickly abandoned, cracker jokes were shared and immediately forgotten.

During dinner Martine was content mainly to listen to

the rapid-fire conversation rather than attempting to get a word in edgeways. After her eventful year, it was enough for her simply to sip her wine, enjoy her food, look around her and reflect upon her good fortune in finding such a forgiving bunch of women - and beginning her recovery in such an unlikely place. She had expected to be keen to say her goodbyes and escape to France but now, with her departure date approaching fast, she silently acknowledged that she was going to find it hard to leave. Still, there were a couple of jobs left to do first, and one had to be accomplished tonight.

Once coffee and liqueurs had been served and the assembled company appeared suitably mellow, Martine took a deep breath, picked up a knife and tapped it repeatedly against her wine glass. Immediately everyone at the table fell silent, along with most of the neighbouring diners. Looking nervously around her, Martine almost faltered, then she plucked up her courage and began to speak:

"I'm not going to talk for very long, you'll be pleased to hear" she began. "After all, I think you all know how grateful I am to each one of you. However, I wanted to find a way to show my appreciation, so I thought about doing a Secret Santa, but I think all of you have had enough of my secrets for one year!" she smiled.

"You can say that again" murmured Peggy discreetly to Lorelei, who was sitting next to her.

"So instead" continued Martine "I decided to do a Saucy Santa by getting each of you a small gift that is just a little bit rude, to bring a smile to your faces at Christmas and say thank you".

Martine reached down to the floor, rooted around in her bag and began handing out a series of small packages. As they opened them, the women shrieked with laughter and waved the gifts at one another as, one by one, the dining tables around them began to empty.

Jos and Anna were amused by their willy-shaped soaps and chocolates, whilst Alice and Irene laughed out loud as they each opened their parcels to reveal a G-string made out of candy sweets. Lucy also received a gift made of candy – a pair of nipple tassels, in honour of her role as the creator of the Titswiping game that they had all enjoyed so much at Waterside View back in May.

Nicky and Verity loved their Kama Sutra playing cards and Emily and Gemma declared that they would both be making good use of their Stressticles – two graphic sets of stress balls. Peggy and Lorelei enjoyed their Swearing Parrot key rings and Bella was particularly pleased with her 'strip mug', which promised to transform the man pictured on the side of the mug from fully clothed to completely naked as a hot drink was poured in.

Once the mayhem of Saucy Santa had died down to an acceptable level, Alice tapped her own glass and once again the group fell silent.

"Martine, I think I speak for all of us when I say that we're a little embarrassed here" she confessed. "We too have bought you a gift to take with you to France, but I'm afraid that it's not as exciting as the presents you have bought us!"

With that, Alice handed Martine a rectangular parcel, tastefully wrapped and tied up with red ribbons. Smiling happily, Martine opened it to reveal a novel called Life Swap.

"Apparently it's a funny, feel-good novel about starting again" explained Alice. "We thought it was kind of appropriate. We have all signed it, to say all the best for the future".

Martine scanned the affectionate good luck messages on

the inside cover of the novel, then looked up at her friends, her eyes shining with tears.

"I'm going to miss you all" she said. "I promise I'll keep in touch".

"You'd better" replied Lucy. "And make sure you keep up with the counselling, too" she urged "the practice I found for you in France comes highly recommended".

"Also, the skiers among us will be expecting regular reports on the snow conditions!" smiled Verity.

At that moment Sigrid walked over to their table with the message that the minibus had just arrived to take them back to Oak Welby.

"As usual, the night is over far too soon" sighed Lorelei. "It has been such a lovely evening".

"It's not over yet!" Emily reminded her aunt. "Who knows what mischief we can get up to on the bus – and I could be persuaded to open a few more bottles of prosecco for us all at the farmhouse when we get back. Come on – let's go!"

Cheered by the prospect of more fizz, the members of the book club pushed back their chairs and were starting to leave the table when Martine suddenly called them back.

"Er – hang on guys. I'm sorry but I'm not going to be joining you on the bus. I'd like to come for drinks at the farmhouse, Emily, but I can't, I'm afraid".

The women all turned to look at Martine, puzzled.

"Why not?" asked Nicky. "Was it something we said?"

"No, of course not!" answered Martine with a smile. "It's just that I am getting a lift with someone – in fact, here he is now!"

The book club posse looked over towards the door of the restaurant as a tall, wiry man, sporting a trendy, spiky hairstyle, stepped tentatively into the room, looking nervously around him. Dressed smartly in a pair of dark blue jeans and a crisply pressed white shirt, he absently fiddled with his inexpertly knotted woollen tie as he searched for the person he had come to collect.

"Bloody hell" gasped Irene "it's Rick!"

Martine got up from her seat, walked over to Rick and stood on tiptoes to give him a peck on the cheek, before taking his arm and leading him over to the table where the members of the book club sat open-mouthed. Nicky was the first among them to recover the power of speech.

"So Rick" she began with a smile "it looks like that new haircut was a worthwhile investment! How did the two of you manage to keep your romance a secret all this time?"

"Oh no; it's only a fairly recent thing" Martine corrected her. "Obviously we had been friendly for a while, after meeting in The Mallard, but when I was in a bad way after the October book club, Rick sent me some flowers and we talked on the phone – then it kind of went from there…"

"Well, it looks as though someone is definitely starting a new life!" declared Arabella. "I have still got half an inch of prosecco in my glass so I would like to propose a toast – to Martine and Rick!"

"Martine and Rick!" everyone chorused.

"I can't get used to the name Martine – I still keep calling her Jane" confessed Rick. "Anyway, thanks everyone – come on love, let's go". With that, he put his arm around Martine and guided her towards the front door of The Partridge. Behind them, the rest of the book club giggled and shushed each other, trying in vain to be discreet while they put on their coats and headed outside to board the minibus.

As soon as the couple were out of earshot, Nicky whispered theatrically:

"Well he can say what he likes, but I still believe that Rick did not change his image for nothing. I reckon he had a crush on her, right from the very beginning!"

Irene put a hand on Nicky's arm to silence her as she spotted Martine running back across the car park towards them. As Martine reached the group, she grabbed Verity's hand and pushed a large envelope into it.

"What's this?" enquired Verity, her voice full of trepidation. Despite their reconciliation, she didn't think that she was up to reading a long and heartfelt letter from Martine.

"Don't look so worried!" exclaimed Martine. "I heard on the grapevine that the skiers among you would appreciate mates' rates at the resort I'm going to be working in, so I have arranged a package of discounts for you on ski passes, accommodation and ski hire. Maybe I'll see you on the slopes next season, but in the meantime – have a very Merry Christmas!"

Martine gave Verity a quick peck on the cheek, then turned and hurried back across the car park to where Rick was waiting in his car. As the women watched, the rather battered vehicle accelerated away and quickly vanished into the cold, dark December night.

\* \* \*

# EPILOGUE

Bella finished setting up her laptop on the large table in her airy, open-plan kitchen. As she waited for the others to arrive, she checked its connection to the big monitor positioned carefully in the centre of the table, then set the volume level on the laptop to maximum.

Satisfied that the technology was primed and ready to go, Bella poured herself another cup of coffee, wandered over to the patio doors and looked out onto her monochrome winter garden. Here and there a few brave and jaunty snowdrops had emerged triumphantly from the thin crust of snow that covered the lawn and flowerbeds, but otherwise there were few signs of plant life. On the bird feeder a cheery-looking robin swung energetically to and fro as he wrestled a few hard-won fragments of peanut through the wire mesh, whilst a crafty pigeon waited below to mine sweep the crumbs.

At that moment the doorbell rang. Bella heard George hurry to answer it, then retreat to his study as Anna, Alice, Gemma and Verity walked into the kitchen.

"Impressive set-up!" remarked Gemma, giving her friend a hug. "That big screen will really come in handy".

"We use it regularly to FaceTime the girls" answered

Bella. "It means that we can talk to them quite easily and they can see us both – plus the dogs, of course! In fact, if the dogs could just learn how to click on the FaceTime icon, George and I would be largely superfluous, I sometimes think. Now, let me get you all a coffee and a bacon roll".

A few minutes later Peggy, Lorelei and Emily arrived, closely followed by Irene and Nicky. The women all gratefully tucked into the bacon rolls, the perfect antidote to a snowy Saturday morning when winter was stubbornly refusing to loosen its grip.

"Can we do this every Saturday, please?" asked Nicky. "Or maybe just the coffee and bacon roll bit" she added hurriedly. "Ooh hang on, my phone just beeped…"

"Mine too" said Peggy. "It's a WhatsApp message from Jos. She says she can't make it as her sister isn't very well, so she has to pop over and check she's OK. She says to send Jane her love" Peggy finished with a smile. "Do you think we'll ever completely stop calling her Jane?"

"Probably not. Right, come on everyone – time to take a seat!" called Bella, pointing towards the group of chairs arranged in front of the laptop and monitor.

No sooner were they all settled in place, gazing expectantly at the screen, than the doorbell rang yet again. A flustered Lucy hurried in, pink-faced from the cold and apologetic.

"Sorry I'm late, everyone!" she gasped.

"No worries" Bella reassured her "we haven't started yet, so you've got time to catch your breath and grab a coffee".

"Thanks, I'll do that" breathed Lucy. "It's all Edward's fault that I'm late" she explained as she filled her mug from the coffee pot and added milk. "He's so excited as he just had a letter in the post from our preferred candidate, accepting the job of Manager at The Mallard! He insisted on reading it out to me, which is why I was delayed".

Everyone in the group, particularly those who were part of the Mallard consortium, turned away from the screen to look at Lucy with interest. Alice was the first to comment.

"Well, Sandy will be pleased!" she remarked. "He was so impressed with the guy at interview".

"So was Kit" added Anna "he was just worried that he was a bit over-qualified, so might be unlikely to accept the job if it were offered to him. He will be relieved".

"I was sorry to miss the chance to take part in the recruitment process" said Verity "but I just couldn't get back home during the week, what with my assignment in Bristol being at such a critical stage".

"It was a shame that none of us could make the interview" agreed Lucy "I would have preferred us not to have an all-male interview panel".

"Too right" quipped Verity "we can pretty much guarantee that our new Manager won't be anything to look at – our husbands won't want the competition! Ah well; you can't have everything, I guess".

"On a rather more professional note" said Alice, smiling at her friend "his CV was very impressive – all that hospitality work overseas and on cruise liners. I'm sure he'll bring some great experience to our little local pub!"

"Not only that; it also means that Toby can start his new life" Anna reminded them. "I get the distinct impression that he's ready to move on".

The book club's speculation about Toby's relationship with Bridget, his mystery business partner, had proved to be correct. The two of them were now officially a couple and Toby was planning to move in to Bridget's imposing manor house on the north Norfolk coast as soon as he could be released from his daily duties at The Mallard. However, he and Bridget would both remain part of the Mallard consortium and would be visiting the village frequently to attend the various meetings and check on progress in the pub. Toby would also be doing some freelance design work from home, with occasional business trips to London.

"I don't think he'll have to worry much about money, though" speculated Emily. "I hear she's absolutely loaded, so Toby will be able to put his feet up a bit!"

Everyone agreed that they were looking forward to meeting the new Manager of the Mallard and were happy for Toby, who had not been very lucky in love over the years and deserved a shot at a new life.

"Talking of new lives – here she is at last!" cried Bella as the FaceTime ringtone blared out from the laptop and Martine's name and face appeared on the screen.

"Hi, Martine!" cried Bella, as the rest of the women waved at the screen and shouted out their various greetings. "How's life in France?"

"Hello everyone – I'm so excited to see you all!" laughed Martine. "The job is going really well. My French is improving – although most of the customers in the hotel are English, so I don't always get as much chance as I would like to practise. I have also starting learning to ski – in fact, I did my first blue run yesterday - and I'm enjoying it, despite a few bumps and bruises!"

"How is Rick adapting to life in a ski resort?" asked Nicky.

"Oh he's doing really well!" answered Martine. "He's building himself a pretty impressive portfolio career – doing airport transfers for a few of the chalets and maintenance work in our hotel as well. In fact, he's just heading out now to pick up a group of snowboarders from Geneva Airport – and he's learning to snowboard himself, by the way, in his limited spare time. Rick – come and say hi to the book club girls before you go!"

Rick's face appeared on screen. "Hello ladies" he smiled.

"How are you doing, Rick?" enquired Verity.

"Alright, mate. You can't get a decent pint of real ale out here, but otherwise it's all good. Gotta go – see you soon". With that, Rick disappeared from view.

"A man of few words, as always!" laughed Nicky.

"That's right, but he does love it out here – we both do" said Martine. "In fact, we have decided to stay for the summer season – there's plenty of work to be had, looking after the mountain bikers. Also, we've bought an old camper van and we're planning to drive down to the south of France for a holiday in between seasons".

"Well it sounds as though you have got it all worked out!" remarked Irene. "Good for you".

"It is turning out well – and the counselling is going fine, Lucy, before you ask! I am missing you all, though, and I hope some of you will be able to drop by and say hello during your skiing holidays" said Martine a trifle wistfully.

"Aidan and I will, definitely" Verity reassured her. "We have booked a week in a chalet just over the border in Switzerland, so we'll be able to pop across and see you on at least one day. We can do a few blue runs together! I'll be in touch separately to work out the details".

"Bill and I will be in the area as well, with the rest of the family" added Nicky "so we'll also be in touch and we'll arrange to meet up".

"That's great, I'm so pleased" said Martine. "Now tell me;

what's the latest gossip from Oak Welby?"

"Hot off the press", said Lucy "we have hired a new Manager for The Mallard, who will be starting in a week or so, and Toby is off to embark on a life of luxury on the north Norfolk Coast with Bridget – remember we always thought there was something going on there?"

"Once again, your instincts were proved correct!" observed Martine with a cheeky smile. "What a bunch of super-sleuths you are. Anything else to report?"

"Well, Burns Night was a suitably drunken affair – as it is every year!" laughed Peggy. "And that's about it as far as gossip is concerned. The whole cycle of village life is beginning afresh – and we're hoping for a slightly quieter year this year" she joked.

"Well with me out of the picture, maybe you'll get your wish". Martine smiled at the screen, then her expression changed abruptly to one of shock.

"Sorry everyone – I just noticed the time on my laptop – I didn't realise that it was so late! I must head off and get ready for my lunchtime shift. I'll send you a date and time for another FaceTime chat – and I'll forward you a video Rick took of me skiing! That should give you all a laugh!"

The women signed off FaceTime in a flurry of goodbyes, friendly waves and hastily blown kisses. Then, as Bella refilled the coffee pot and brought out a plate of biscuits, they settled in for a debrief.

"Well, it's good to know that she's finally making a life for herself" concluded Peggy some time later. "I for one am mightily relieved. Definitely a case of All's Well That Ends Well".

The rest of the book club nodded their agreement.

\* \* \*

A few weeks later, Verity and Aidan had just returned from their skiing holiday and were spending a dismal, rain-soaked Sunday morning catching up on e mail and working their way through an enormous pile of washing. When Verity's phone pinged with a WhatsApp message from Lucy, it provided a welcome excuse to take a break.

"Lucy just messaged me!" shouted Verity up the stairs to her husband, who was in the bedroom sorting the next batch of laundry. "She was asking how we enjoyed our skiing trip and whether we were free for Club Sunday later on. I guess she wants to check how Martine is doing".

Club Sunday was the name given by regulars of The Mallard to the extended Sunday lunchtime drinking session that attracted the same eager participants every week, subject to availability. Several members of the book club, including Lucy, Verity and their husbands, were Club Sunday devotees.

Predictably, Aidan did not take much persuading to leave the laundry behind. For Verity's husband, a skiing trip was not complete until he had regaled his long-suffering drinking buddies in the village with tales of his antics, both on and off-piste.

"I'll be right there – just let me stick this lot in the washing machine" he yelled. "I want to get down there a bit earlier than usual so that I can check out the new Manager and hopefully have a chat with him before the bar gets too crowded".

Not long afterwards Verity and Aidan, keen to escape the driving rain, scuttled across the pub car park and pushed open the door of The Mallard. Aidan walked into the bar ahead of his wife, eager for his first pint of real ale in over a week. Pulling down the hood of his waterproof jacket, he turned to Verity who was standing behind him, removing her sodden bobble hat.

"Becks Blue, love? Or do you want me to see if our new Manager has got any other varieties of alcohol-free beer in stock? Stranger things have happened…"

Aidan fell silent as he noticed that his wife had suddenly turned deathly pale and was staring in mute terror at the man standing behind the bar.

"What is it, darling? What's wrong?" Aidan gently placed his hand on his wife's arm, which was trembling violently.

"It's him" she gasped.

Aidan followed Verity's gaze towards the bar where a tall, craggily handsome middle-aged man with dark hair was staring back at him, a taunting smile on his face. Instantly, Aidan understood who the man was. Quickly her turned to comfort his wife, but Verity broke free from his grasp and ran from the pub, tears streaming down her face.

❊ ❊ ❊

Later that week, Martine and Rick were lucky enough to have the same night off, a rare occurrence since their arrival in France. At Rick's suggestion, they had headed down to one of the local après-ski bars to take advantage of Happy Hour and listen to a live band. Afterwards, they planned to round off the evening by sharing a fondue at the restaurant next door.

Beaming proudly, Rick plonked two Dirty Martinis down in front of Martine and poured himself a beer from a large jug meant for sharing. "Two for one cocktails – and these jugs of beer are quite reasonable, too. Not as cheap as a pint in The Mallard, mind you, but still - not bad for a holiday resort. Cheers - here's to 'Date Night'!" Smiling, he made quotation marks with his fingers.

"Cheers". Martine smiled back, downing half of her first Dirty Martini in one gulp. "Wow - I needed that! It feels like ages since we had a night off. Thanks for planning it all - drinks, music and dinner. It'll be good to relax for a change".

The two of them settled down on their bar stools, clutching their drinks, and traded anecdotes about their favourite gigs as they watched the band setting up in the corner of the bar. Then, just as the musicians started their sound checks, Martine felt her mobile phone vibrate in her pocket. Pulling it out, she quickly glanced at the screen and then at Rick who was watching the band, oblivious.

"I'm going to take this on the terrace, Rick!" yelled Martine over the sound of the lead guitarist tuning up. Jumping down from her stool, she called back over her shoulder at her boyfriend as she headed for the door. "Can you get some more drinks in, while Happy Hour is still on?"

"Hello? Sorry, bear with me – I'm just going outside..." Martine shouted into her phone as she hurried away. Once on the terrace, she glanced furtively around her before resuming her conversation.

"Hi there" she began. "Sorry about all that racket . I've got a night off so I'm just enjoying a bit of après-ski – without the ski bit".

"And I'm sorry for interrupting" the caller replied. "You with Rick?"

"Yep".

"How's it going?"

"Oh, we're having fun" Martine answered. "He's a nice guy; we're enjoying each others' company and that's enough for me. I've never been a great believer in all that 'love of my life' crap, as you know. Not since I grew up, anyway.

And what about you?" she asked, deftly changing the subject. "Have they sacked you yet?"

"Not quite" the man answered. "I was expecting them to get rid of me pretty quickly, of course, but once they realised what they had done it created rather an awkward situation for their little investor group and, as you know, there's nothing a bunch of nice, polite English people hate more than an awkward situation".

"You're dead right there" laughed Martine.

"Anyway, while they have been deciding what to do, I have already put our little plan into action".

"Excellent" Martine purred. "I'm so glad I managed to track you down, and that you agreed to help".

"It was the least I could do" the man responded. "I figured I owed you one. I shouldn't have split on you all those years ago without telling you where I was going – it was wrong of me. But I reckon we're quits now. I'm going to hand my notice in tomorrow and move on pretty sharpish".

"Yeah – you've got previous for that" said Martine drily.

"Touché – but seriously; I've managed to avoid her husband for now, but my luck won't hold out much longer. Besides, as I said, my work here is done. It didn't take too much effort, to be honest. I won't go into detail; suffice to say that your mate Verity will be having a few more panic attacks from now on".

"That's great news. We were just so lucky that she was still working away in Bristol during the week so couldn't attend your interview. Quick question though" asked Martine "does anyone in the village suspect that I got you to apply for the job?"

"Not a chance" said Jason firmly. "They all think it's just

an unfortunate coincidence. To them, you're still a poor, mixed up woman who is trying to put her life back together. Don't worry – you can still keep in touch with the book club. I'm sure some of the ladies will let slip before long how Verity seems to be having a bit of a hard time…"

"Wonderful" Martine said. "You're a legend. We should keep each others' numbers, but I don't think we need to stay in touch. It sounds like it's job done. Thanks for your help, Jason".

"No worries, Martine. I agree there's no need to keep in touch. Goodbye – and have a nice life".

Martine ended the call and stared reflectively at her screen for a moment. Then she shoved her phone back in her pocket and shivered, suddenly noticing how cold it was outside. Time to go in. Squaring her shoulders and clearing her conscience, she turned and marched defiantly back towards the warm, cosy bar.

**THE END**

Printed in Great Britain
by Amazon